Dear Elliot,
Thank you for your kind
and supportive words. Your
encouragement has been
consequential, and I am
grateful.   With affection,
                  Rich

FIRE IN THE YEAR
OF FOUR EMPERORS

HADRIANI
Deva
Eboracum
Lindum
BRITANNIA
Corinium
Londinium
Venta Belgarum
Gesoriacum
Heruli
Angli
Saxones
Varini
Rugii
Frisii
Chauci
Langobardi
Semnones
Cherusci
Chamavi
Burgund
Noviomagus
Castra Vetera
Sugambri
Colonia Agrippina
GERMANIA INFERIOR
Tencteri
Chatti
Suebi
Naharvali
Bonna
Bagacum
Rotomagus
BELGICA
Durocortorum
Augusta Treverorum
Mogontiacum
Lutetia
Hermunduri
Marcomanni
Divodurum
Argentorate
GERMANIA SUPERIOR
Caesarodunum
Naristi
GALLIA
RAETIA
Augusta Vindelicorum
Vindobona
Carnuntum
Vesontio
Augusta Rauricorum
Avaricum
Augustodunum
Augustoritum
Iuvavum
Brigetio
Aventicum
Curia
NORICUM
AQUITANIA
Lugdunum
Octodurus
Virunum
Poetovio
Emona
PANNONIA SUPERIOR
PANNONIA INFERIOR
Mediolanum
Verona
Aquileia
Patavium
NARBONENSIS
ALPES
G.
C.
M.
Siscia
Placentia
Tarsatica
Tolosa
Nemausus
Aquae Sextiae
Ebrodunum
Genua
Bononia
Ravenna
Narbo
Massilia
Cemenelum
Pisae
Florentia
DALMATIA
MARE ADRIATICUM
Asculum
Salona
Barcino
G. - GRAIAE
C. - COTTIAE
M.- MARITIMAE
CORSICA
Aleria
Spoletum
ITALIA
Narona
ROMA
Ostia
ET
Turris
Capua
Beneventum
Dyrrachi
Neapolis
SARDINIA
Brundisium
MARE
Tarentum
Caralis
TYRRHENUM
M A R E
Panormus
Rhegium
Saldae
Hippo Regius
Utica
SICILIA
IONI
Sitifis
Cirta
Carthago
Agrigentum
Syracusae
Thagaste

Rick Deragon

FIRE IN THE YEAR OF FOUR EMPERORS

de Ventadorn Press

Published by
de Ventadorn Press
51 Lynn Drive
Napa, California 94558

Cover Design: Grzegorz Laszczyk
Cover Painting: Rick Deragon
Map: Andrei N. – Wikimedia Commons user: Andrein

Library of Congress Control Number: 2016921134
ISBN: 978-0-9984105-0-0

For Karen Nagano

CONTENTS

ONE

Outside a Gate of Rome, 69 AD

Rokus watched expressionless as the nail plunged through the man's wrist. A legionnaire hammered, nail biting into wood, spatters of blood shooting up with each blow. The man pulled and jerked, his contortions in time with the falling hammerhead as he strained against the ropes that cinched his forearms and legs. He wailed against the pain and lurched, even though he was hopelessly pinned to the transom of his crucifix.

The morning breeze swept the man's screams away leaving the solitary criminal to writhe alone. His executioners moved with the deliberation their sorry duty required. One legionnaire, annoyed with the man, or perhaps with his assignment, raised the butt of his whip and smacked him across his torn face in an attempt to silence him, but to no effect. Looking over his shoulder at the praetor, who scowled at him, the legionnaire tucked his whip behind his belt and knelt to help his comrades. Valerius, the praetor, rolled the scroll he had been reading, slipped it into the pocket of his toga and turned to Rokus.

The other men in the entourage flanking Rokus were aediles; one of them nudged him in the back, but he resisted. Rokus observed the Roman efficiency: four soldiers now hoisted the transom up and bolted it into the notch on the post. They untied the condemned man's legs and roped them to straddle the post; in seconds, one legionnaire held the man's feet while another drove nails through them into the sides of the post, fixing the man vertically for the final bleeding and asphyxiation.

"That could be you, Gaius Julius Civilis," one of the aediles declared.

Rokus turned to examine the aedile's face, a soft visage floating over tunic and toga, two scornful eyes meeting his. Rokus wondered what it was that drives a man to lose compassion for another.

"Could be, but isn't," Rokus muttered.

They all turned back when the man wailed. Rokus tightened his muscles, and the aedile pushed his back again. They watched the crucified man stand on the spikes running through his feet, his arms carrying his weight as the nails tore bigger holes. Each wound—at wrists and below ankles—had swollen; purple rings of new and coagulated blood as well as the torn tissue across his shoulders, back, wrists and feet stood out in marked contrast to the rest of his skin.

A crowd of onlookers loitered at the edge of the clearing and gawked at the scene of the condemned man, with Rokus' entourage and the other officials watching his execution. They were not relatives or friends but vultures, bloodthirsty citizens circling the spectacle for the thrill of it. This grove of posts mounted in the Latin earth arrayed before them like trees stripped of everything, leaves supplanted by the horror lingering in the air—this acre stained with lifeblood was host to this man whose history remained unknown but whose future was clear. They reveled in this, found succor in this place of execution. Each of them standing there in their short greasy tunics and tattered sandals rejoiced in the condemned man's fate, if for no other reason than to make their own seem a little better. Their daily afflictions would be temporarily relieved as after-images of the condemned man assuaged them.

"Wait." Rokus turned back to look at the city.

"Civilis, you have to catch the riverboat," Valerius insisted, pulling out the scroll again and nudging Rokus' elbow.

"Go hang yourself," Rokus replied as he scanned the city—the bleached arch of the Esquiline Gate, the new wall growing from it north and south, the red tile rooftops of apartments, the warren of streets. Thrusting columns and soaring arches of grand structures lorded over piazzas. He could not help but admire the signature of power everywhere; in every magnificent edifice were centuries of engineering, political debate, military adventure and international commerce.

To the west, the Palatine Hill burst with verdant gardens full of lush flowers from Narbonensis, Hispania, Numidia, Phrygia and beyond. He imagined the feasts being served to the wealthy Romans there, meats and delicacies like flamingo tongue carried on trays by slaves who wore their new Roman clothes with unexpressed resentment. Rokus could hear more than he saw—a city of voices tested and tortured. Contempt replaced his admiration.

Power, submission, slavery—that was the Roman way.

His conflict burdened him. There was Gaius Julius Civilis, the Roman citizen, who recognized the greatness in the marble structures to gods and men, the concrete works of civic comforts that guided water and traffic long distances, and the monuments to pleasure and hygiene—the circuses, amphitheaters and cavernous baths, marvels of civic order, steam and water flow; he pictured the faces of Roman scholars, philosophers, engineers, statesmen and soldiers working together for the body politic, and these things humbled him: the march, the constancy, the impregnable machine.

But there was also Rokus, the tribesman, prince of Betuwe, son of King Uulfnoth, commander of the Batavian Auxiliary, fourth generation royalty who drew vitality from their marshland. Thick rivers bordered the Batavian flatlands, and he and his people absorbed them into their veins so that land and water were one. The sky he had known since infancy, with its dazzling stars and brilliant reflections from cumulus clouds, setting suns, and sea storms cascading across the Batavian plain, filled his heart. Though they had migrated from far away and settled there in days scarcely remembered, they had adapted to the sodden land and waterways to become fabled swimmers, adept ice skaters, and horsemen who husbanded prized animals on the turf of that limited land. His people were an ineffable component of the place. These folk melded with land, sea and air to form a singular force. Rokus and Julius Civilis, two identities inside one conflicted man, felt both the pull of the marble Empire and the flow of the great River Rhenus, the geometry of the conqueror and the midnight calls of spirits across the barbarian darkness.

The streets of Rome teemed with people and a steady stream of them flowed out of the Esquiline Gate and passed along the road. Most were merchants with carts, housewives going riverside to do laundry with baskets perched on top of their heads or shoulders, or travelers spreading to the compass. But some were those that joined the vultures at the grove of death—for life was a series of opportunities and this execution proffered cathartic witness to another's suffering.

"Let's move on, Civilis." Valerius nudged him in the back.

Rokus jerked his arm away.

"We have to get you to your command in Germania," Valerius persisted. "There is a riverboat waiting for you on the north Tiber shore."

"A boat to Germania?"

"You go to Ostia, take a ship to Arelate, then up the river to Lugdunum, and from there, overland to Helvetia. The escort will take you up the River Rhenus to Castra Vetera."

"Such privileged treatment. Seems like just yesterday I was in a cell counting my days."

"You can count your blessings now, Civilis. Galba means to make things right. He won't be another Nero. He knows you have always been true to the Empire."

"Galba's an old fool." Rokus' words bit the autumn air.

"You're free, Civilis. Be grateful."

"What about my brother? If I am innocent, then so was he. What did he do to earn the sword?"

"Unfortunate. It's Nero's nature; such a hasty assassin."

TWO
On the Tiber River to Ostia

They arrived at the river. The praetor and his aediles guided Rokus past the construction of a stone bridge. Towers of massive posts and crossbeams surrounded an army of men, blocks of stone and piles of rubble were everywhere, and bins of concrete mixture worked by slaves with long paddles and water-filled amphorae were positioned along the structure. Slaves rolled barrows to the foundation, and engineers hoisted blocks in place. Masons worked in rows along a scaffold, trowels flashing in the sun. Rokus paused to assess the grand scale of the bridge— another sign of Roman might— and walked with other pedestrians to the wooden bridge just beyond.

The tribunes surrounded Rokus as they crossed the wooden bridge, and the irony of being surrounded while being set free soured him.

"Let me see that from over here." He stopped at the rail to study the pilings disappearing into the Tiber, the wooden forms and braces, and the huge baffle soon to divert the river. The masons were placing stones, and he observed their arrangement of hoists and fat ropes and massive forms of block and tackle hanging from double lintels.

"Civilis, I fear we are late. Please," Valerius pressed.

Rokus moved along but kept to the rail. They came to the riverboat roped to the quay. The tribune handed the pilot the scroll and he nodded slowly as he read it. He looked up.

"This way," the man said before he led them over the gunwale and down a plank to the deck. He turned to them, gesturing to a bench amidships.

Just as Rokus boarded, a terrible clatter of hooves and screams exploded from the river. Ten horsemen in Praetorian dress had plowed into the crowd and burst onto the wooden bridge, tossing people to the sides or trampling them. A flurry of arms and legs and tunics seemed to hold the horsemen in suspension as they crossed, hooves tattooing the bridge furiously.

Everyone turned to the commotion.

Valerius disembarked and entered the road along the river.

"What is the meaning of this?" he shouted to the lead horseman, who pranced in place waiting for his fellows.

Amid the shrieks of outrage and fear, the Praetorian horseman shouted back to the tribune, "Emperor has discharged the Guard! We're going home."

The horseman, now joined by the nine others, struck the air with his fist, and then pointed down the road with the blade of his hand. Several horses blew and snorted approval, reared, clattered impatient hooves, and the cloud of armed men galloped away.

"That's the end of something and the beginning of something else," Rokus declared.

Valerius nodded.

Another fury thundered from the bridge, and another squadron of Batavian horsemen crossed. More followed them in their thunder and more still until the bridge shook precariously. Even more of their cavalry followed, but finding the bridge full, plunged into the river and crossed, clinging deftly to the sides of their mounts. Fretful women ran upstream for safety, sweeping up their baskets of clothes and errant children who craned back at the Guard in their white and red uniforms, silver helmets radiant in the sun.

With a single motion, the Guardsmen swung to horseback as they left the turgid water. One cavalier paced his horse back and forth on the north side of the river as the cavalry completed the crossing. Then he reared his mount in a show for the bystanders, front hooves reaching skyward, and his legs squeezed the animal to plunge forward in a gallop.

"Renhard!" Rokus shouted.

The horseman pulled back and his horse's rear hooves dug into the road in a flurry of dust. He whipped the horse around, returning to where Rokus and the praetor stood.

He studied the praetor, his long bleached toga with its red stripe announcing rank, and the other man clad in a plain tunic. The horse blew hard, impatient to run, and pranced in place until the rider pulled the reins again. The horse's ears lay back, and the beast filled a grand circle with its might. Rokus and Valerius stepped back.

"Rokus?" the guardsman shouted. "Is that Prince Rokus of Betuwe? Yes? It is. The prince. We thought you were dead."

The rider reached down and Rokus reached up and they embraced with outstretched arms.

"What is this, Renhard?" Rokus asked

"Galba has replaced us. No payment, just our discharge. The men are not happy, Rokus." Renhard shouted over the din of horsemen and civilian protests.

"You're going home, then?"

"Straightaway."

"I am, too.

"Riding?"

"Not now. Let's meet at the solstice feast in Betuwe."

"See you then, my prince and friend."

The guardsman sank his heels into the horse's sides and launched down the road. Valerius and Rokus watched the hooves of Renhard's horse and the whirling dust, and then Valerius turned to the riverboat.

"Let's go, Civilis."

They sat on the bench amidships. The pilot caught the ropes tossed by the deckhand, who jumped on, took a position aft, and wielded a single long oar mounted there. He began a rhythmic back-and-forth cut of the blade in the water so that silently the barge moved as if its wooden mind had decided on Ostia. The pilot took the tiller and began to sing to himself.

Rokus watched the praetor's hands fuss with his toga, arranging its folds again and again. The praetor stared at the shore, but

Rokus knew the man saw nothing, his eyes fixed on some inner turmoil.

Rokus imagined the seeds of Roman discontent taking root. Galba, governor of Hispania, receives the nomination for Emperor from the noble, idealistic Vindex, governor of Gallia. Looming before Nero then is a united Gallia and Hispania, their armies, and the discontent of the Romans. Driven by the prospect of defeat and humiliation, Nero commits suicide, but not before he has ordered Vindex killed. Without the support of Vindex, the governor of Hispania curtails his ambitions, but then the Praetorian Guard expresses support for him. Flattered and inspired, Galba again declares his acceptance of the nomination and comes to Rome with a large army—an army with a history of unspectacular campaigns full of cowardice and brutality and fecklessness in spite of their superior numbers.

The new Praetorian Guard would likely come from these soldiers.

If the Guard is the Emperor's protector, it must be bound by warriors' honor; if the Guard is comprised of lesser men, then Galba will certainly die by their hands unless he is willing to buy their allegiance. Rokus could feel the coming strife in the air. Valerius twitched and Rokus realized their minds worked the same terrain.

"What kind of Guard can Galba assemble around him?" Rokus asked.

"Galba will use some of his men from Hispania, I'm sure, and men recommended by generals and senators, no doubt. In any case, the new Guard will do his bidding.

"For a price."

"Protection for sale."

"But Renhard said payments had stopped."

"Galba is notorious for tight purse strings."

"He's a liar. He promised them."

"Be careful, Civilis."

"There will be chaos."

"Agreed. May the gods watch over us when a lesser Guard takes their place."

The riverboat floated easily with the mild current. The pilot continued singing while the deckhand leaned and pulled at his oar, and the craft responded in small jerks starboard and port, the bow cutting through the water with gentle hisses and lapping sounds that merged with the pilot's tune.

Rokus sensed the change. It wasn't the discharge of the Praetorian Guard, his Batavian kin, but his own embrace of the day. He hadn't noticed the sun and clear air and the autumn breeze wafting up from the sea. He had been preoccupied with the crucifixion and his simmering revenge, Renhard's announcement, and the images of the feast of solstice on Betuwe. Now, the pilot's tune soared overhead with migrating birds, and the Tuscan hills seemed to float by, their autumnal yellow-orange shoulders holding stands of trees in their clefts and the leeward slopes. Along the embankment a road ran, plied by farmers' carts and travelers and merchants, their uniform tunics forming a pleasing rhythm of natural whites flecking the green-black backdrop of cypress trees.

By late afternoon the barge had turned off the main river and down a canal that sliced through a region of stores and houses, workshops and repair docks. From beyond the rooftops rose a din, fused sounds of commands and guttural responses of workers, calls and warnings, and the clanking of cranes and pulleys hoisting thousands of pounds of goods from deck to dock. Everyone in the barge perceived the great amalgam of industry vibrating with the energies of a seaport town of an empire, a vortex of destinations and destinies—a knot of infinite strands that stretched from Lusitania to Judea, Carthage to Britannia. The passengers all sat up in anticipation.

Floating along the canal, Rokus smelled the sea and rotting dross around docks and pilings. He watched the sky change to a hazy blue and followed a flock of seagulls that strafed and hovered with avian entitlement. The deckhand called at the birds and swung his arm reproachfully, but they ignored him. As the barge progressed down the canal, the workshops became bigger and stood closer together, taverns and bars were interspersed, and crowds of craftsmen and seamen and indeterminate races of men, tunics smeared with fish oil and the grease of decks and holds, showed the class of their labors. Occasionally, a squad of soldiers, grasping their scabbards, pushed through the crowds. Clots of prostitutes stood in doorways and at corners, pushing up their breasts and sticking out their tongues like strange tropical animals.

The barge bumped the dock at the end of a long waterfront that was lined with stone walls curving round like great arms embracing the sea traders anchored everywhere. The waterfront bustled with thousands of people dedicated to loading and unloading, carting and dealing wares, and servicing the tired sailors with wine, bread, and women with blonde-tinted hair.

❦

Rokus surveyed the harbor, which was dominated by an endless forest of masts and booms as jibs and rudder-oars thrust from the water or swayed with the tide. These naval trees and branches extended as far as he could see, and a jungle of ropes, taut and drooping, connected every element of this merchant marine like a fantastic web.

Valerius commanded the men of the entourage to gather the baggage and to follow him and the newly pardoned man to the larger dock farther down the way.

"Civilis, I am passing you on to another escort. Gaius Marius Camillus will accompany you all the way to your home in Betuwe," he said.

"Just let me go. I will go straight to the Rhenus and into Germania."

"As a courtesy, we are ensuring your safe passage with an escort," the praetor insisted.

"You do not want this good citizen and soldier to stir up trouble."

"We want you safe. The Rhenus region is on fire of late."

"Good praetor," Rokus mocked.

The sky turned gray with a series of breezes that came in from the far sea bringing the first hints of winter. Valerius adjusted his toga, while Rokus took his haversack from an aedile and pulled out a cloak which he threw over his shoulders. The breeze rose again and now gusted through the harbor in fits. Rokus stood waiting in front of Valerius. He spied Valerius' dagger among the toga folds and considered grabbing it and slashing his way off the dock but chastised himself for considering the rash maneuver worthy of some young buck intent on heroic death. His two-year sequester had eroded his patience and judgment. No, he realized, he must sail on with these men and replenish himself with his ruminations, take long walks, ponder his command, and vitalize his love of Veleda.

He and the red-haired beauty had once known each other in the realm beyond words, and she had taken him to her in defiance of her tribal loyalties and all virginal expectations. After a frenzy of love with him, she had read prophetic messages in the forest shadow language, divining past and future in the jagged and swaying trees and fingers of limbs, and she listened, head and neck outstretched toward the dark green wall, and drew secrets from the rustling. She interpreted tongues of flame in the night hearth, or she incised the belly of calf or pig or lamb, guts disgorging, to study the viscera, reading into the blood stew messages from the goddess earth or god of the sky dome of stars above the Bructeri lands. With hands dripping red, she hoisted an organ or crosscut of steaming meat and chanted the Bructeri call for the spirits.

Veleda, he realized, knew him better than did any other person, man or woman, father or mother, brother or son, warrior or statesman. She combed his hair with her fingers and worked his broad shoulders. She kissed his neck and coursed a fingertip along his cheekbone and beard. She studied his green eyes and, caressing him, said, "I see flashes of fire and restlessness but also peace." He heard these words again as the aediles led him away, and he knew the promises she made to wait for him in Germania seemed optimistic, for life in her frontier tower along the River Lupia was fragile.

The new wind buffeted his hair, tunic and cloak. Valerius studied him as they walked along the quay; and Rokus knew the praetor had seen his scar exposed in the drafts, his long hair fluttering off the line of raised skin that formed a fast arc across his side skull, a remnant of the battle, pitched and horrible, when Renhard vanquished the long-sword-wielding Briton about to finish Rokus with a swipe. The eyes of praetor and free prisoner met, and then the praetor discovered the scar's continuation at the base of Rokus' neck and looked puzzled or impressed, imagining the desperate battle with the man that cleaved this message.

"I see your memento there." Valerius nodded at Rokus' head.

"Britannia, years ago. That horseman, the one I called Renhard, saved my life on that day; and I saved his on the next."

They arrived at a wharf lined with vessels, some sleek, others squat, their masts thrusting skyward and poised for journey. Rokus wondered which boat was his—one of the those that might fly the sea surface like a thing of beauty or one that carried tons of cargo and punched through the sea gracelessly as if making way by accident. Valerius paused, looked up and down the wharf, then continued down to the end where a sleek vessel was roped to four stanchions. Against one of them leaned an officer.

"Marius Camillus," Valerius called across the dock traced with men carrying loads on their backs and in their arms.

The praetor wended through the menagerie of dockworkers, carts and cranes and stood face-to-face with Gaius Marius Camillus, a former centurion now in the direct service of the Senate.

"Hail, sir," Marius said.

Rokus stopped short, for he recognized this Marius Camillus, and until he remembered why and where, he stayed back. As the aediles formed a semi-circle around Marius, and one of them produced another scroll for the man to read, Rokus travelled to Britannia, Gallia and Germania to place the man. Rokus ran through the ranks of legionnaires and auxiliary tribesmen aligned next to the man. Down rows of men and lanes of tents, through lines of mounted squadrons, over the hills and valleys of fields where battles had raged and around the feasts and games that followed victories, he ran and recalled. Finally, in western Britannia he remembered him leaning against a tree stump at the edge of a wood while legions assaulted a hill fortress nearby. The Silurian tribe of Britons repelled missile and man as the Romans were failing for the fourth day. On that morning, sun dappling through knotted branches and leaf clusters, this Roman soldier sat out of his mind next to a Briton mutilated beyond recognition. Dents and brutal scrapings marked the helmet perched crookedly on the Roman's head. Crimson streams flowed down from the recesses, across cheek and jaw, and soaked his tunic shoulders. At his feet lay a gross mistake of a human, its arm-things twisted like a carcass ravaged by starving wolves; the lacerated trunk, with its ripped leather loincloth pulled obscenely up to expose shiny entrails, consisted of more gashes and slashes than skin. He—it—was entirely shades of red, dried to deep red-brown or glistening as blood coagulated in its hour-old cascade.

Rokus saw the big Briton spread in death and the victorious legionnaire clinging to something like life. The soldier talked haltingly under his breath, whispering threats to the dead man, as well as apologies; he relived the contest in sputtered words as Rokus removed his smashed helmet and wiped his forehead and neck. The legionnaire grunted with each remembered thrust, spat triumphant oaths, and whimpered sympathetic benedictions. While the man straddled the line of consciousness, Rokus had dressed wounds as best he could while other Batavi beat a path toward the mounds and ditches and pointed stockades that were littered with legionnaires' bodies and those of Silurian warriors who'd jumped the walls to defend their ground.

Rokus stood in the afternoon breeze as it swirled around the harbor, remembering the broad shoulders and square jaw and thick forearms of that strong man. He'd recovered at the infirmary in Camulodunum and joined the Batavi for the remainder of the campaign and its aftermath, as most of his own cohort had been cut down. As soon as the generals had reformed the cohort with fresh reinforcements from Gallia, they'd promoted this man

and, leaving him in the dirt, led them to the countryside where more Romans flanked them, held them fast, and then, disregarding Claudius Paulus' demand for explanation, ran Paulus through. Rokus saw vividly how this man had gripped his sword and thrust with intention. Moreover, he had rotated the blade to ensure Paulus' painful demise.

Rokus tightened his muscles as heat surged through his arms and legs; his heart beat faster.

"Rokus, let me get these men settled in, then we can talk. It's been . . . what? Fifteen years?"

"I reckon twenty."

Marius shook his head and directed the soldiers to follow him to the cabin. As they climbed below deck, the last soldier looked back, his eyes fixing on Rokus as Rokus returned his gaze. In that moment their histories converged, knotted in conflicting notions and full of revenge. The soldier froze, as if he, too, revisited the past and weighed his complicity and safety in this venture. Then he turned and disappeared below. Rokus resolved to watch rather than act, for he wished to set the stage for his revenge with a clear exit and escape.

Marius emerged from the cabin, talked with the captain of the ship, and then approached Rokus who lifted his bag of clothes and sundries to the ship, crossed the gunwale, and stood regarding the placement of things on board.

"Rokus, will the Furies shout, 'What did you do to merit such a full escort?'"

THREE
On the Tyrrhenian Sea

The Zephyrus cast long shadows over swells and deepened the sea's color, and as the sun disappeared below the horizon, the expanse appeared in red-orange bands and then changed to purple shapes, and, finally as twilight fell, the ship rose and fell over black waves that came from the night void. Splashes and jolts against the hull brought the soldiery to the foredeck to peer into the darkness.

The next morning the soldiers, to a man, could not find the balance in their legs. They stumbled in drunken lurches, failing to reconcile with the sea so that the pitch and yaw of beam and rail disoriented them, their stomachs constricting like fists as their balance departed, and they leaned over the side to disgorge bile into that dawning light. They continued like that through the day until, wasted from the inside, they flopped down onto the deck, shadows of men.

Rokus perched himself on a bench near the steering oars to watch the sea the next day. He, like all Batavi, had salt and fresh water running through his veins so that land and sea were a seamless world; he never knew seasickness. The ship rose and fell, and the muffled clanking of the amphorae stored below filtered up. Rokus pictured the two thousand clay containers of barley, oats, olive oil, and wine to exchange for several thousand filled with millet, almonds and walnuts, and farmers' savories from Gaul.

Ruminating, he saw his brother's death once again: the sword and its owner's grasp of its hilt, the strength, the single-mindedness. With his arms seized by legionnaires, Rokus had struggled in vain to stop the blade. It tore through his brother's chest, right of center, and a deep rouge soused his tunic. As Paulus collapsed, he looked at Rokus with the surety of a brother's love, and then the affectionate gaze became abstract, as if he saw a dream place appear, unexpected, familiar and welcome.

Rokus pictured the soldier's mighty wrist and the glistening hilt and the blade withdrawn with his brother's blood tinting it and saw his killer's tattoos. Many soldiers incorporated the designs of the vanquished, for it was not as barbaric as a necklace of ears or fingers; this appropriation had been the fashion in Gallia ten years before, until the prefect there had forbidden the practice for men born citizens of Rome.

"You'd never know these are calm waters from the looks of that bunch." Marius interrupted his brooding, but he may as well have not spoken as Rokus did not hear him. He thought again of his brother falling, and he memorized the Celtic tattoos, that line of blue-black dots ringing the wrist three times and crossing a strong, sword-wielding arm. He wanted to call his brother's Batavian name, Habo. He wanted his brother to answer.

"The sea doesn't agree with those men," Marius tried again.

Rokus eyed him and then watched the legionnaires, wan and dour, clinging to the sides. The soldier Rokus had noticed seemed in the best condition and had struggled to his feet and stayed there; his spewing had ceased, but he was still clearly unwell.

"Captain says several more days. Do you think they can last?" Marius said with a chuckle.

"I'd rather look at clouds." Rokus turned to the horizon.

Marius stood. "I'll talk to you later, commander." He circumnavigated the deck, chatting with the captain and individual deckhands at work mending sails and fixing the hinge of the hatch. He talked with the legionnaires who, following his advice, stepped carefully through the cabin door and vanished below.

Rokus' thoughts returned to the ship. As Marius stood talking to the captain again, Rokus saw not only vestiges of the soldier from Britannia, but also someone aware of his abilities and the glory of his rank.

He stood and walked the deck toward him. "I've been distracted, friend."

"This is a new life for you, Rokus. Your confinement is in the past; your command awaits you."

"There is confinement still."

"These are turbulent times."

Rokus and Marius stood together at the rail, scanning the swells that lifted the ship with a gentle rhythm. A cluster of clouds floated on the horizon, and above them haze drifted up to a tumbling vapor, white and gray in its rolling changes. They stood there a long time studying the white chopping wake before a gust of cold air buffeted them. Rokus shivered, suddenly reminded of the inconstant nature of things. As Marius pulled his cloak tighter and shifted his weight against the wind, he turned to look into Rokus' eyes.

"Wind is picking up." Rokus sniffed the air.

"So we get to Arelate sooner."

As the two men stood there in friendly satisfaction, the watchman's bell resounded.

Rokus and Marius spun round as the watchman, studying the distance, leaned out of his basket. The captain gestured to his sailors, waving one hand to the man at the top of the rigging, the other to the man mending cloth. The mender jumped to and ran to the foredeck, while other sailors positioned themselves near mast, jib, and lines.

"What is it?" the captain shouted.

"Ship portside, forty minutes out," the man in the rigging called down, cupping his hands around his mouth.

"Look hard, sailor, we need details," demanded the captain.

Rokus and Marius joined the captain at the helm. They strained to see the ship in the haze. Gradually, it took shape, a black ship with black sail blades filled with west wind, cutting toward them. Rokus read its wake and its angle, and he felt the Zephyrus was the target for their arrow.

"Are there extra swords?" Rokus looked into the captain's face, then across the decks fore and aft.

"Sailor," the captain called into the rigging. "Tell me her design and what flag she flies. What is her business? Are they freebooters?"

"A Liburnian, oars working fast," the sailor shouted down.

"Good. And her markings?" The captain's voice was terse.

"All-over black, save the emblem. A Gorgon in gold."

"What can you tell of her crew?"

"Gathering amidships, sir."

"Armed or friendly?"

"Can't tell, sir."

The captain dashed to a cabinet at the stern and swung open the thick door. He wheeled out a cart with swords and javelins strapped to it. "All men to arms," he called. "First mate, stay the course; we will be ready when they show their intention."

Rokus pulled a legionnaire's gladius and four javelins from the collection. Marius ran to the cabin below deck.

"Twenty minutes. Bearing down!" shouted the watchman clinging to the basket.

The captain handed javelins and swords to six sailors filing by. As he watched them take positions along the portside, his expression darkened, for he observed, as Rokus did, that the sailors were more comfortable with ropes and rigging than with weapons and that dread hunched their backs and weighted their feet.

Not a prize group of warriors, Rokus thought.

"Pull her starboard; let's outrun them," the captain commanded.

The black ship cut the sea behind them and gained as the Zephyrus flew full sail, plowing through swells, and as the amphorae rattled, they all felt her sluggishness. Rokus stood on the poop deck gripping the helm of his sword, getting the feel of its contours and heft.

"Captain, are there shields?" Rokus secured the gladius under his belt and hefted a javelin.

The captain took the rudder and instructed the first mate to fetch the shields behind the door. The first mate ran to the cabinet and then disappeared before reappearing, pulling a cart with ten scuta lying in a rack. He relieved the captain, who brought a scutum to Rokus.

The black ship was a sleek thing, but that was all, for its color was determined by factors of neglect as much as paint. Grease and sea-dripping taint covered it, and Rokus smelled a stench of decay from something that was once living wafting ahead of the black ship like a demon's heralding breath. Its mainsail flew full of wind but was tattered, and the vessel's rigging hung to the mainmast by frayed lines. The rows of stained and rotting oars dug into the water without precision. The mascot, a crudely stitched Medusa's head glaring amid writhing serpent-hair, loomed from the mainsail above a chaotic litter of broken chests, armor, crates, rope and spools. The gunwales were worn and broken as if great beams had fallen on them, and the prow was a splintered Gorgon, rendered ghostly by sea decay.

Along the black ship's shattered rails surged a destitute crew of killers. Some heads were shaved, others ratted, drooping tufts bobbed as they danced jigs celebrating the hunt. They leered obscenely out of scar-slashed faces covered with a scum of salt and dried blood, and their naked chests shone with blotches that glistened off starving muscles and tendons. Pointed teeth and slithering tongues and grunts of anticipation shot up from their numbers as they gaped. They wore loincloths like some primitive tribe or pantaloons from Phoenicia, half-tunics from Carthage, and skirts made from the flayed tattooed skin of vanquished souls. As they pulled alongside, their stench corrupted the air and was so devastating in its festering cloud that the Zephyrus sailors flinched.

The rowers stood their oars, mismatched and unevenly spaced, creating a kind of partition that screened the black deeds on board. Several pirates wielded coils of rope with tri-hooks that they began to swing in circles over their heads.

Then Rokus saw the black ship's ornaments mounted like idols on the gunwales: a series of decapitated heads gazed out with empty eyes. Some appeared on the verge of speaking; some mouthed unspoken terror, their unheard screams smeared across their chins and mutilated cheeks. Others were older residents on the gunwales, desiccated lumps turned black with hollows where the gulls had fed. A blackened stain ran the entire perimeter, these heads having drained and sopped the wood forever.

The ships now bobbed athwart. Rokus reacted to the demented jeering across the railings, their theater of perversions rocking with the sea, their instruments a macabre assortment of blades and points, spikes and hooks, clubs and daggers, ropes and chains.

Well before the ships touched, he threw his first javelin. The goons gawked at the missile, as if Rokus had sent them a shaft strung with sweetmeats. Then it found its mark, renting one face just below an eye and splashing through with the mud of his brains. He jumped back upon impact and then stood for a second as the protrusion from his face and knowledge of his death joined as one revelation. His companions jumped around him like idiots at feeding time while Rokus threw three more javelins into their midst, all of them skewering in a gallery of writhing and howling.

The captain, first mate and four sailors stood aft, armed and poised, waiting for the surge of the forty crazed pirates to break over their rails. Rokus sidestepped a hook as it slammed and bit into the Zephyrus' gunwale. He chopped its rope cleanly with his sword, and the ships parted. But five more hooks descended and bit into wood fore and aft, their taut lines groaning, and then the ships touched again and the swarm jumped onto the Zephyrus in a din of howls from some prehistoric era when beasts and men were the same.

The captain swiped from behind his shield, the arc of his blade missing but thwarting the onslaught with its intention. The first mate stood his ground and parried with one pirate while others charged past. The other five sailors ran in retreat, overwhelmed by fear and the cruel mayhem unfolding. After stumbling back and tripping, the sailors turned to meet a horde of blades, and Rokus lost them in the ensuing tangle of arms and legs, poles and swords.

A pirate jumped in front of him, and Rokus cleaved the man under the arm. Another threatened, and Rokus jabbed his blade between the man's ribs. Holding up his shield, Rokus readied himself just as several crashes of bronze and iron blades fell. The shield deflected the barrage and allowed him to thrust again, rapidly, gouging several raiders.

He spun around searching for Marius but witnessed instead the gruesome spoil of two of the deckhands, lacerated beyond acquaintance, devoid of all features save stumps that might have once been legs or arms.

Swinging both arms furiously, his short sword kept the creatures at bay, and his thrusts found homes in stomachs and ribs. But the beating on his shield and his swordplay sapped his strength—it had been two years since he'd last waged battle. He staggered, glancing back for Marius and the legionnaires. The captain and first mate were back-to-back securing the quarterdeck, but the pirates swarmed amidships and appeared ready to flank them. Rokus dashed into their midst, cut three down, and joined the captain and first mate. Beyond several slumped forms, two of the Zephyrus sailors held their own with valiant, desperate cuts and swings.

"Men, here!" Rokus shouted.

The men scrambled over to them.

His command was terse. "Stand at this rail and face them; you, stand next to him. Stay low, thrust rather than swipe, stay in formation. Be patient, conserve your strength." Pirates roamed the deck, kicking in doors, prying hatches. Some attacked, but many others scavenged, ripping into the ship's compartments and holds. Rokus' phalanx held its formation, the two Zephyrus men maintaining their positions next to the captain and first mate. Attackers continued their invasion fore and aft, screaming with perverse joy.

One heavily tattooed attacker raised his arms in triumph and yelled wildly as he faced the new formation of defenders. His face, deformed by an old gash that pulled his mouth in a grin, turned to Rokus. He pointed his sword and grunted. All the invaders swarmed back to the quarterdeck behind him, faced Rokus, the captain, first mate and two sailors against the rail, and began to chant, waving their assorted weapons overhead, and closing in.

Rokus felt the weight of their numbers and thrust and slashed in reaction. This point had been reached; unless Marius and the others appeared, Rokus and the Zephyrus crew would be cut down. And if Rokus was going to fall, he was going to slash and strike as many as he could on the way.

As if summoned by this fleeting thought, Marius and the six legionnaires burst through the cabin door, ran to the cart holding the shields, donned them, and then lined up abreast. Marius shouted commands and the men responded, no trace of their seasickness, and focused on the pirates across the deck.

The rabble was bent on gorging themselves on the sailors' demise. They yelled their death chorus and pummeled Rokus and crew. One or two flinched and buckled with a stab or slash from the phalanx, but the shrieks for death increased, and their bloodthirsty eyes glared at their prize.

"Advance!" Marius commanded.

The legionnaires, side-by-side, crossed the deck amidships, turned as one, and bore down on the pirates. Grim Roman faces targeted the invaders, who now faced the intrusion. Roman shields formed a wall, and with deadly rhythm, short swords shot out from behind in lethal thrusts that found muscle and bone six men at a time.

The force of the legionnaires' wall of shields pushed the raiders back. During the distraction, Rokus, the captain and first mate all found targets of flesh as they wielded blades with effect.

The horde pushed back against the legionnaires, but now their chant faltered, replaced by animal growls that shook the rigging. Rokus killed one assaulting pirate with a thrust through his stomach, and Marius jumped in with a mighty swing that severed another's head.

The legionnaires pressed, and the pirates fell together to face them. But there was nothing they could do, so solid was the wall of scuta, so determined was the advance. One by one, the raiders were cut down or pushed over the rail. These creatures that had so caroused across the deck of the Zephyrus retreated, and by the time they realized their collective defeat, they were being swept like jetsam into the sea.

The one with the shaven head stood his ground with four remaining raiders. They glanced back at their ship, abandoned now by the motley forms thrashing about in the sliver of sea between ships. He howled another bestial aria, and his men brandished their swords, cleavers and clubs, and surged into the teeth of Marius and the legionnaires' barbed wall. In short order, the four minions had been impaled and sliced and tumbled to the red-slippery deck, their groans the denouement to the death chant they had mouthed thirty minutes before.

Rokus dropped his weary arms, and the men of his phalanx followed. The legionnaires emerged from their shell of shields and looked at the last marauder standing defiant, his sick grin ringed with spittle. Before this scene of victory could establish itself, an arm thrust from the legionnaires' ranks to drive home his gladius deep into the man's chest.

The legionnaire held the man up and expressed contempt for him, lingering in position, turning his blade inside. Blood bubbled at the hilt and flowed freely down the man's stomach, legs, and feet. He looked past them all at some single point only he perceived. Rokus clenched his own sword tightly; the legionnaire's face showed too much pleasure and satisfaction. But Rokus' eyes were drawn to how the he gripped his weapon and the Celtic dots on his wrist and sweaty arm.

Rokus' memory served him; this was his brother's killer. With a hobnailed boot, the legionnaire kicked the now lifeless man in the chest to extract the sword and then pushed him overboard with the rest. Rokus thought to charge the soldier and cut him down but held back; that was the young buck again reacting, not the veteran with a plan.

The legionnaire glared at Rokus, and Rokus weighed the soldier's defiance and contempt—or challenge.

I will meet him soon in some arena we make for ourselves, thought Rokus, nodding to the man once, an acknowledgement of the battle deed witnessed, a promise that they would tangle.

"Right," the captain said, sitting on the gunwale bench. "Let's rest a minute and then go inspect their craft before we offer them all to Pluto."

Rokus sat with him, and together they surveyed the carnage and listened to the grunts and groans emanating from the bloodied contortions strewn across the deck.

Marius roamed the deck with the tattooed legionnaire dispatching surviving marauders. Soon, the breeze swept across a silent ship as the sailors and legionnaires dressed their cuts and slashed skin. Marius commanded the legionnaires to clear the deck, and they began the gruesome undertaking, flopping bodies overboard. The captain ordered the sailors to clean weapons and return them to the cabinet and prepare sails. He turned to Rokus. "I'm curious. Will you come with me?"

"Yes."

Marius watched them climb aboard the pirate vessel. "Finish this," he told the tattooed legionnaire, "and get these men to swab the deck."

"I'll join you," he called to the captain and Rokus.

All manner of depravity surrounded them on the black ship. As they stepped over the disarray, the mounted heads watched with vacant eyes and shadowed cavities. Heaped on the foredeck, a pile of corpses—women and children—rotted under a cloud of flies. Some bodies were bloated into weird bladders with limbs; others had blackened and stiffened into a congress of victims, pathetic in their twisted remains.

The men turned away.

"What is this place?" the captain implored.

"The part of us we bury with our joys." Rokus stared at the carnage in front of them, trying to imagine each corpse a living human being.

"Let us leave this place," Marius said.

"Wait. The captain's lair will reveal much." Rokus stepped over a broken chest and headed for a door beneath the poop deck.

"I'm not sure I want to know after all," the captain said.

They entered the captain's cabin, dark and stinking, and covered their mouths. Ransacked cabin drawers hung open like maws, cabinet doors were torn from hinges, and stools, benches and tables lay scattered and broken amid tattered scrolls and maps. Lording over the mess, in the solitary beam of sunlight, sat a bejeweled carcass of a man glaring out with one eye; the other had an ornate hilt of a dagger protruding from the socket reddish-brown with dried blood. His hair was short, and parting it was a gash through the skull. His gaping mouth was filled with a severed hand, a bizarre mutation of purpose, and resting on the table before him were his arms, sartorial with their Cilician raiment. His remaining hand was posed holding a long dagger and sat disembodied like an island off the cape of his wrist. He leaned back in his chair as if waiting.

The captain went to him, reached over, and grasped the several gold chains of medallions and pendants and jewels dangling like obscene reminders of pillage; he jerked them free. "This is for my lost seamen; the least this excrement can pay me."

"These madmen held nothing dear, even their leader." Marius spoke with disgust lacing his words.

"He commanded a westward course—they wanted to go east." Rokus raised a brow sardonically.

The captain pulled his dagger out and, picking up the island hand, sawed until he could pull off the ornate ring with its massive bauble that might be precious. "And this is to repair my ship."

"I have to get out of here." Marius began to retch.

"Good idea," Rokus agreed.

Marius strode to the cabin door, kicked it open, and left. Rokus and the captain followed him across the wreckage, and then the three stood on the Zephyrus looking back.

The captain called for an amphora of pitch, and when it was delivered to him, he opened the lid, and he, Rokus and Marius smelled the rich pine vapors. The captain called for his brazier, and when that was delivered, he plunged a stick into the pitch, twirled it deeply and then held the resinous blob over the charcoal; it smoldered and ignited, and he tossed the torch thus made onto the deck of the Medusa and commanded the sailors to break the amphora over the torch there. They did as commanded and soon jumped back aboard the Zephyrus, leaving a growing conflagration behind. The captain and Marius brought their swords down on the ropes connected to the tri-hooks, and they all felt the new freedom as it severed. The crackling flames took over, chasing each other across the deck and running up the mast to consume the black sail and its odious face. The forsaken vessel drifted away, a black silhouette blackening more as the tongues of fire ascended.

FOUR

In Arelate, Gallia Narbonensis, an Inland Port
on the River Rhodanus

Rokus studied the ships moored to buoys, anchored, or berthed along the riverfront and the small boats full of cargo being rowed by brown men up and down the docking district. Cranes hoisted broad pallets filled with amphorae, arranging small cities of them along the docks. Big carts rolled on solid wooden wheels, their loads of crates and amphorae covered with nets and thick rope. Beyond the forest of masts were the shops, taverns, markets, and warehouses running with men and squads of legionnaires standing watch, the ever-present guardians of the Pax Romana.

Reclining on his bench near the steering oars, Rokus soaked up the Mediterranean sun. A salty breeze passed over him, and gulls fluttered and called. A melody floated through his mind, a plaintive line of notes full of memory—Batavian festivals and entertainments under a summer night sky. But it was more; the pulse of the melody reminded him of the northern tribes in general, the Bructeri, the Cherusci, the Cananefates, the Chatti, the Marsi, including the mesh of their dialects, their beautiful faces, strong children, vigorous men, capable women. He remembered their villages scattered through forest and meadow, along rivers and gentle ridges, intimate workings of people hunting, sowing, reaping and loving, and he wondered how it was that sounds could communicate the heart of a people.

And now this sound in his head, a dancing tune from some distant time in Betuwe—firelight animating faces as young couples jigged in clearings, snuggled and swore oaths of devotion—penetrated his being and spawned happiness he'd not felt in two years. It was his music; Romans sang and danced like dainty flowers and the Batavi and the northern tribes created music that was the voice of wild nature, the heartbeat of earth and themselves and the rhythm of days, and it was essential to their experience. Just as the Batavi produced warriors, they revealed their connection to the lands by producing musicians—magicians, really—as well. He was grateful that music was central to all the festivals and that the solstice celebration approached. That meant there would be much music and celebration.

As the Zephyrus crew put the ship in trim while waiting for their berth, the music in his head grew louder. It was a pleasant sensation: pulsing gently, a single line of melody, like voices in the distance, dancing over the beats. The captain signaled to a messenger in a dinghy; the first mate opened the hatch covers and the legionnaires stood at the rails like tourists. Rokus embraced the sun, smelled the balmy air, and smiled. Marius saw Rokus and joined him.

"All right there?" he asked.

Rokus looked at the bandage around his thigh and the wrap on his forearm.

"Never better."

"Hope Arelate isn't as exciting as the journey here."

"Not that type of excitement."

Marius stood and strolled to the rail, scanning the riverfront. "Seems like a little diversion is in order, don't you agree, Rokus?"

"A decent meal first?"

"And then we pay homage to Bacchus."

"And those six men?"

"I'll give them the night off. They've earned it."

After the crew roped the Zephyrus to a dock near the end of the riverfront, the men stood together.

"Marius, thank you for saving our skins back there." The captain pointed to the horizon.

"Sorry we took so long. Had to cure the men of the seasickness."

"How did you do that?"

"Military's secret elixir."

"And Gaius Julius Civilis, thank you for everything. You truly saved us from those monsters."

"You're welcome, captain. They were monsters." Rokus put his hand on the captain's shoulder.

"So, Marius, the river barges are at the opposite end of the harbor. Contact the wharf magistrate to confirm your place. We made good time."

"I'll find the place and the man, sir."

"But now, we want a good hot meal." Rokus patted his stomach.

"Join us, captain?" Marius asked.

"I can't. Business here. But I'll tell you of a place."

"Do."

"Maximus. Three blocks in from the river. Great cooking there. And Maximus is a good host who serves the best wine from the Rhodanus valley."

"That's the place we want, then." Rokus nodded.

After checking in with the quartermaster at the fort, Rokus and Marius walked the track to the town. The harbor and buildings were aglow in the twilight, and there was movement everywhere. As they walked the streets into the heart of the town, Rokus heard the music again, a faint rhythm with a soaring melody from an instrument he couldn't identify. It summoned him and gave him dialogue with elements both human and animal, present and past, earthen and sky-borne. Its completeness, in that moment, was something like joy.

They entered the tavern as a burst of laughter filled the air. Lamps lined the walls. Their illumination defined groups of men at tables; most were sailors, others wore togas of the merchant class, some had the look of low-ranking officials. In the corner, two hardened characters sat at empty plates and two empty pitchers of wine; their red faces showed they were soldiers on leave getting drunk. Several women stood in the corners observing the evening crowd; their bleached hair and rouged faces were wraithlike masks in the shadow. Two other women—pretty and squarely built, one older than the other—worked tables. Rokus reckoned they were Maximus' wife and daughter. The proprietor himself worked behind a counter, flitting from fire pit to stove, calling out dishes to be served while haranguing the men at a nearby table. Their choking laughter erupted.

"Jolly," Marius observed.

"Basil, marjoram, garlic and butter."

Rokus raised his eyebrows as Marius looked at him with surprise before working his way through the crowd to a long table with bench seats. Two places were empty at the end and they sat.

The daughter came to them.

"We have stew. Bread and this," she said, holding up a jug.

"What's that?" Marius gestured to the jug.

"Wine what's come from hills far and near," she said.

Rokus lifted his head and flared his nostrils. "I smell the vegetables, and grain, and something—a meat not bovine."

She put the jug between them. "Sorry, out of pitchers."

"Boar," Rokus said.

"Is it boar, girl?" Marius was laughing now.

"'Tis," she said grinning, a gap showing where a tooth had been.

"Rokus, you've a nose on you." Marius filled two clay cups from the jug and raised his cup. "Made with grapes what come from hills far and near."

Marius watched the girl's hips sway as she moved away to the next table, smirked at Rokus, and sighed. "Here's to a safer journey upriver and across mountains."

Rokus lifted his cup, touched brims. "To a good life." He drank deeply, ending with a smack of lips, and then refilled their cups.

"Rokus, I have heard your command has separated from their legion and awaits your return."

"I wonder how that sits with the legate."

"Probably doesn't miss them too much right now since he is likely watching Rome."

Marius poured more wine, and they drank, and the process repeated whenever the daughter brought more. Rokus sat over his cleared plate, pushing a crust of bread through the juices. The tavern hummed with conversation and Marius watched him as he spoke.

"We have fought together often, Marius. We have seen each other pushed to the limit. I would always want a warrior such as you by my side." Rokus ate the crust and chewed slowly, watching the veteran.

"I remember well those fields of battle in Britannia," Marius said.

"I trust you, Marius, and wish to confide in you."

"Your words are safe with me, Rokus."

"Betuwe is my place, and the Batavi are my people. Good people, with good hearts, Marius. We are a great tribe, we produce great warriors, but we are more.

"The Roman army relies on the Batavi."

"Yes."

Rokus looked away. He scanned the heavy rafters and plaster coving of the room, then allowed the faintest smile to form before he paused.

"It is mostly flat, between the Rhenus and Vahalis, but there is great variety even in the flatness. As a boy I wandered along streams and the stands of trees along their banks, and as the land would rise, you could see for an eternity. And there is no sky quite like that of Betuwe. The vastness is noble, and the streaks of clouds, like mountains floating overhead, and rainstorms rolling in from the sea, are events by themselves. The gods dance together then."

"Seems like I'm there, Rokus."

"The sky. Nowhere as magnificent. Not in Britannia, not in Hispania, not in Gallia, not in Tuscany. In Betuwe the sky is boundless in silver splendor and enters the land, and the flatness everywhere absorbs the sky. Everywhere, blue, green and brown, and endless shades of gray, because every cloud overhead has earthen colors below, the turf, the muddy banks, the furrows of the fields, the rivers and streams."

Marius leaned forward, red-faced.

"It all amounts to an endless sky and an endless earth. And the Batavi is nourished by it, wherever they pitch their tents."

Marius poured wine into their cups.

"And it is a land of contradiction. It is vast, yet the earth and sky make you feel right there." Rokus pressed his thumb on the table. "It's peaceful."

"And yet produces the most fearsome of warriors."

"A land of contradiction."

"Swear to the gods, Rokus, you sound like a poet."

"I've had much time to think about it. And wine," he said, chuckling

They sat back, sated. Marius gave the daughter a palm full of coins, and she beamed. They walked through the tavern's great room full of contentment and smells and the headiness of wine from the Rhodanus valley. In the street it was twilight, men passing as shadowy forms, women lurking in doorways. A pride of feral cats scrambled away from them at a corner, and they could hear the dock sounds three blocks away—barked commands, laughter, signal bells, groan of rigging.

Rokus noted the quality of darkness, weighted with moisture and the potency of trouble befalling street and alley. He listened, and though he heard nothing amiss, he felt it, like birds taking flight before an ambush.

"Something is wrong."

"What's that?"

Three of the legionnaires from the Zephyrus appeared from a darkened side street. Two held each other up, the third groped a woman who slapped his hand. They stopped and stumbled attempting to go around Marius and Rokus, and then recognized them. The soldier with the woman, feeling her breasts and nuzzling her neck, gave a drunken salute and pulled her down the street into the descending night. The other two presented themselves, swaying.

"Good evening, sir," one slurred.

"Evening, brother of Claudius Paulus," the other declared.

Rokus clenched his fist as the urge to hit him boiled inside. The tranquil plain of Betuwe vanished and a thunderhead loomed.

He felt the loss of his brother and the souring of his dinner. He breathed deeply.

"You were the one who executed my brother," Rokus stated.

"Orders, Julius Civilis."

"I should slay you."

"Nero condemned him; I had the detail. That's what I know." The soldier planted his hands on his hips.

"But I will wait for the time when you are not drunk so that you can watch my sword run through you, just like you watched yours go into my brother."

Marius grabbed the man's tunic. "Soldier, report to me first thing in the morning. And for now, disappear or I will get you for insubordination."

"I quit your command an hour ago."

"You're a drunken fool. Rokus, I've got to take this man in. Got to cut our night short."

The soldier, defiant with the power of wine and a lifetime of killing, pillaging and rape, pushed the officer. Marius stepped back, drew his sword, glared at the man.

"You've no command over me," the soldier slurred.

Marius smiled, shook his head and then sheathed his sword. Just as the weight of the iron settled in the scabbard, Marius pivoted in one fluid motion, as if rehearsed, and drove his forearm into the man's neck, and as the man staggered back choking, Marius swung a punch into the man's jaw. His head snapped, and he crumbled to the street. Marius regarded the twisted figure on

the flagstones and addressed the other soldier who had been observing from his stupor.

"Go get lover boy down the street, and get this man back to
the barracks. Now."

Very soon the drunks struggled with the unconscious form
between them, grunting and staggering down the street. Rokus
and Marius followed them until they reached the outskirts and
the track toward the fort's gate.

"You should go with them. I want to walk." Rokus pointed
down the street.

"The man is a fool. Too bad he's such a good soldier."

"I will kill him in any case."

❁

During the next two days of waiting for their barge, Rokus explored the countryside, cutting through tall dried grasses, jumping over the meandering streams that fed the river, observing
the ways of watershed and tides. He followed muddy banks and
rested under trees. He crossed the plain and, surveying the vis-
ta, embraced the dance of sky and earth. He watched the massive clouds slide westward, sometimes like ships listing in rolling
seas, sometimes bullied by the Mistral. And always he was a part
of the organism as the round shadows flew over the terrain and
him, blinking sunlight, and the immensity of air and land held
him. And in this flow of celestial and earthbound events he saw

himself as a point in the marshy plain, a freed prisoner of politics, a commander returning to his warriors, a displaced prince seeking to lead his people, a man wishing to lose himself in the wavy red mane of the beautiful woman.

The land, thus conjured, stretched to the horizon and summoned memories of his people and the tumult that was rising all around. He recalled the uncanny serenity before a battle, as if the earth and all creatures held breath in a collective hush before fury broke land and body wide open. That pause served as a reflection where earth might see a tranquil place before the mayhem, where men might see themselves whole before rage and fear blinded them of all reason.

He thought of Renhard and the discharge of the Praetorian Guard and what that might mean. Galba, a tired old man, had taken an imprudent path dismissing them, one the Senate surely understood; he had ordered old and forgotten debts paid while courting allies with enhancements, and then truncated funding for projects he didn't like. It would get worse, because men do not like to be controlled by the withholding or bestowing of money.

Without the influence of the Batavian Guard, Rome would become a battleground for private armies. Who had the strongest army? Some senator? Perhaps a governor with his own resources? There were so many pretenders; where would it end?

Coursing through the meadow, he stepped broadly, pushing grasses aside and making headway with the thwack and crunch of his stride. He came to the track along the river, pulled the burrs from his tunic and the hair on his legs and the straps of his leather boots, and continued back to Arelate.

A soldier appeared in the distance; his helmet and hauberk shone brightly, and his red cloak flashed in the breeze. He swaggered, an army of one. The man was squarely built, upright, fit. He looked like the best kind of soldier the Roman legions produced, and in his physique Rokus saw the years of victories across Britannia and Germania but also Belgica, Lugdunensis, Aquitannia, Tarraconensis, Raetia, Noricum and Dalmatia. He had seen this kind of man; he had served side-by-side with him in these places and admired how each soldier fought, dug earthworks and built walls and bridges, and always adapted to mountain and beach, meadow and hill, river and stream—broad and precipitous terrain—with the single-mindedness of a professional.

The legionnaire approached wearing parade dress—polished metal, oiled leathers, bright cloak and tunic. The man seemed misplaced in this regalia on the river track, his parade event having been scheduled elsewhere. But as the soldier drew nearer, his arm crossed to draw his sword, and his free hand pushed the cloak back off his arms. They stood face-to-face, the Celtic tattoos dotting the man's wrists and forearms in clear view. "Greetings, old man."

"Soldier."

"I've been following you."

"You won't kill any rabbits with that thing."

"I knew I would find you out here."

"You had best put that back and return to town."

"I've come to finish what I started."

Rokus widened his stance. A familiar chill climbed his back and enveloped his shoulders and neck; it always did moments before combat. It was a healthy fear, full of awareness of details like the attitude of adversary and terrain, the advantages of weather and the direction of sunlight. He sidestepped to his left to put the sun at his back.

"I've come to finish what I started," the soldier repeated.

"And what is that, soldier?"

Rokus inched closer, and the soldier instinctively backed away. His feet left the dirt track, and he now stood amid clusters of supple greens and flowers, chicory, jasmine, mallow. He brandished his sword and sneered.

"Nero ordered your brother dead and told us to use discretion with you. My commander decided to spare you, and I regret he did."

"What is it you have against me, soldier?"

"You're a treasonous old man."

"Don't be an ignorant ass."

"My commander allowed himself to be intimidated by you, and he let you live against Nero's wishes. But an old man will not intimidate me." The legionnaire unclasped his cloak.

"I'll walk back with you and hear the details of your case." Rokus pointed down the path.

"Step no closer."

"You have a sense of duty." Rokus steadied his voice.

"You were condemned." The legionnaire sneered.

"Served my time, and was freed."

"I will carry out the orders my commander was afraid to act on." The legionnaire pushed his cloak off his shoulders and brandished his sword.

Rokus looked around for a pole or stick but saw nothing that would do. He decided to engage immediately, partly because the man was addled with hatred, partly for lack of options, partly for the surprise. He faced the legionnaire squarely, arms suspended, and sprang forward.

With his weight shifted to his back leg, the soldier thrust, straight and true, at Rokus' chest. The blade glistened, cutting the air, but passed under his arm because of his catlike shift to the side. He gripped the legionnaire's arm but let go for lack of leverage. The soldier recoiled into striking position again, and Rokus stood, knees bent, arms taut, ready.

Another thrust shot forth, and again Rokus slipped to the side and locked his arms around the weapon-wielding limb. But this time he pulled the man around and tripped him as he passed. They fell among irises, nettles, and glasswort, slipping in the juices and slime of the riverside.

The soldier struggled underneath him, and both seized arms and wrung to squeeze life out. They rolled into a snarl of rosemary, now on their sides; they were set to overpower each other with strength of arm and torque of body. Rokus felt the man's greater youth; his muscles were iron bands holding Rokus in place. They fought rolling in their exertions, each man pinning the other in turn. Tumbling into the reeds nearby, the muddy river water soaked their tunics. The soldier pressed Rokus into the mud, but Rokus jerked his forearms, breaking the man's grasp, and rolled free. The soldier jumped to his feet, looking surprised at the challenge before him, and adjusted his hauberk which had been pushed askew. Rokus stood poised and panting. Glancing around, the soldier then bolted for the sword nestled in a patch of chicory.

Now they were face-to-face again, circling, judging, waiting. The soldier licked his lips nervously while Rokus repositioned himself with the sun at his back. He studied the soldier's belt buckle, the body's central and weighted place, and gauged his own movements based on that indicator of direction. While the soldier feigned countless assaults with his head or shoulders or arms, Rokus remain composed as he read the soldier's waist buckle. Soon they had shifted positions, and Rokus stepped on the cloak. He slowly picked it up without taking his eyes off the man. Wrapping it around his forearm, he walked into the man to prompt the attack that he might control to his advantage.

Responding to the bait, the soldier thrust again, and again Rokus sprang away, throwing the cloak like a net as he did. In a blur he pounced and cinched the cloth around the arm and sword, pulling the man forward and again tripping him as he passed. Rokus fell on him, smashing a forearm into the man's face, and after quickly winding back, crashed down with another blow, this time to the man's temple. Rokus looked around for the sword but couldn't find it. The soldier kicked him off, and Rokus rolled to his feet, ready once again.

They circled, chests heaving, surprised at the even match. Wary of Rokus' quickness and strength, the soldier bought time by circling, glancing to the ground in search of the sword. As he shuffled sideways, his feet stepped on it, and he froze, then stooped for it, and prepared to bring the dual to a bloody end.

As he picked it up, Rokus evaluated his scant time, then pounced on the renegade with cunning and a heightened sense of revenge. They tumbled into the grasses, rolled, punched, strangled and heaved until they came to the starting place, a mash of grasses that knew not the dance of death in its midst. The legionnaire straddled Rokus and bore down on him, hands on his neck, and throttled like a demon. Rokus gripped the man's wrists and, seizing and pushing, attempted to free himself. With an explosion of muscle power, Rokus thrust the man off him for a second and groped the grasses all around for a prod.

The legionnaire was back on him, and again, Rokus redoubled his strength, now grasping one rather than two wrists.

Then he merged with a frame of mind he well knew from days in the fields of battle. In all his experiences of frenzied combat—men become demented creatures with such high stakes—he had always found a temperate place inside himself so that while swords slashed and men groped, stabbed, or beat carelessly answering to the fever of the berserk, he remained the center of a spiral, seeing details and events left and right, front and back, in his opponents' mind and his own. That was why he still lived; he had the ability to assume a place of extraordinary calm.

Summoning his greatest strength, Rokus forced the man's left hand from his neck, but still the man pressed down as their hands traveled across Rokus' jaw and cheek.

The soldier found the eye and clenched. Rokus felt the sharp pain that shot from his eye to his feet, corrupting his strength in a flash. And then he found the warrior's clarity to perceive and weigh actions simultaneously. While the soldier worked the eye socket—Rokus could tell the man sensed the advantage and knew himself the sensitivity of that organ—he gripped the man's wrists anew, then listened to the music as it revisited. There was drumming and on top of that a rhythmic play of strings, and over this a flute or pipes sent a dancing melody. There was the throb, and he knew it was the pulse of the Batavi, the rhythms of their days in his vision, and he listened.

Glasswort and irises lay smeared all around, and he smelled the rosemary that their feet had torn. From the center of his spiral, he took bearings, placing the struggle at an angle to the riverbank and all the plants that served as the scene of this history, and he remembered the moment's struggle when the sword was dashed to the ground, and it had been in a knot of glasswort, now the cushion for his head, and so the sword must be just beyond it; why the soldier hadn't seen it he didn't know, but rejoiced as it must be scuffled under the brush.

But pain intervened. The soldier had adjusted his great fingers and now worked the eye socket with the thumb while his other hand throttled Rokus' neck. Lightning flashes shot through his head, and in between the painful eruptions he heard the music again, sweet and full of sensual rhythms, and he located the pain and distanced himself from it, so that he would better hear the sounds.

Rokus let go of the man's wrists, just as he felt the smear of his own eye blood under the claw in a slippery quagmire. The lilting melody bounced on the drumming pulse, and there was a strange joy overcoming him. Rokus reached beyond his head, plunging his hand into the wort, and there it was, the metal hilt at his fingertips. He seized it.

The soldier released his grip on the neck, and the mangled eye socket was now his prize; he directed all his attention to its disintegration using both hands to inflict their damage. And so directed was the attack on Rokus' eye that the man didn't see his own sword flash in the sun over his head and plunge straight down behind his clavicle to pass through his left lung and enter his heart.

There was no joy in this triumph as Rokus walked back to town. Revenge was fleeting, as the corpse lay slumped in the reeds. The swatch of the soldier's cloak that he used to daub his eye was soaked, and the sweet rhythms of the music had turned staccato, and the pain made his head feel overlarge. The soldier was dead, his brother avenged, yet, two deaths had changed nothing. As the buildings of Arelate sparkled, and as the ships and small boats serviced the riverfront, all buffeted by autumn wind, he knew that Marius' legionnaire was the Roman army and he, Rokus, was the northern tribes, and the killing of one meant the man's replacement with many. The victory march he now made to town was only a commencement.

FIVE
On the River Rhodanus

"I couldn't save it," the surgeon said, wiping his hands.

Marius nodded and walked with the Greek to the door.

"He's sleeping deeply because I've given him a tincture of papaver somniferum. He must have been in great pain, but he isn't now, I assure you."

"Thank you," Marius said.

The Greek left the barracks. Clouds wet with rain amassed in the east, projecting a gray and ominous cast over the town. Marius watched soldiers move about the central square of the fort, a horseman arrive, and the tanner cart skins to the armory. Pensive, he returned to the cot where Rokus lay, head wrapped in white cloth, breathing deeply, his battered frame still strong under the blankets. Marius shook his head as if to ward off some inevitable revelation and then sat on the bedside stool. "He was a fine specimen of a soldier, Rokus, and you are the fighting prince of the Batavi. What do I put in my report? What is going on?"

Marius waited for three more days before he was obliged to board the barge that would journey upriver to Ernaginum.

During that time, he checked on Rokus regularly. Rokus, sunk into the cot's roping, looked defiant.

"Losing an eye was a small price to pay for avenging my brother's death," he said.

Marius didn't answer but rearranged his gear again.

"When do we leave?" Rokus asked.

"They load cargo all day today; we leave in the morning."

"It is time to be with my people. We must have unity to succeed," Rokus said.

Marius ordered the five remaining men to carry Rokus to the riverfront on a brace of planks. Still dreamy and subdued under the medication, Rokus gazed with one eye at the people and streets as they wended through the town.

Slaves carried pallets to pavers who placed stones, tapping them into place while overseers yelled, cracked whips threateningly; other workers climbed on scaffolds against new walls, troweling plaster from bins to the raw surfaces while below merchants barked deals and wagoners delivered goods and bargemen tugged on ropes along the waterfront.

He knew he could walk, but his head throbbed and he was much aware of the void in the eye socket, his arbitrary balance, his uncertain state. Resigned to pain, he leaned back, temporarily diminished.

They boarded a sleek barge that was seventy-five feet long and filled with amphorae and crates, a long house, and numerous benches and chairs along the sides. It sat low in the water. Wrapping round a massive spool fixed to the foredeck was a braid of thick rope that ran from it to drape overboard and dip into the water, climb the embankment and run to a harness set where eighty horses stood in pairs. Tails flicked at flies and hooves stamped, and heads shook traces; some horses braced on three legs in fatigue or boredom.

The soldiers carried Rokus toward the long house while deck-hands swarmed around, tightening ropes around cargo, disappearing through the hold, securing lines to the barges in train, and untying from the dock. The captain welcomed passengers and showed them their berths in the long house.

"Wait," Rokus said, leaning on an elbow.

He lifted his bandage off his right eye and scanned the barges, seven tied in a line, and the horses tied along the bank. This enormity struck him, and the prospect of this train being pulled upstream filled him with anticipation.

"Let me stay here awhile."

Marius nodded to the soldiers, who set the pallet on the deck. A loud bell sounded five times, then three, and once again; whips cracked over the horses' heads, and the animals, leaning upriver against their harnesses, pulled all lines taut. Soon the barge floated twenty feet offshore, and its bulk, attenuated by the train of barges behind it, moved with somber grace. Drovers barked elemental sounds for the horses—yips and huts and gits—urging them on. Rokus studied the column of barges, the bright colors of passengers' garments, the sums of cargo overflowing from the storage holds, the great team of horses whose leaders sometimes disappeared around bends in the river, so long were their ranks.

By noon the horses had pulled the train of barges several miles upriver. Marius had helped Rokus to his berth, where he slept, or maybe it was something else, because the tincture's effect was rife with dreams that melded disparate things, and the dreams were full of feverish desires, fears, bizarre juxtapositions of childhood and warrior's life, people he'd loved and people he'd killed.

At sunset they tied up at Ernaginum. Rokus stood on deck with Marius. They watched the drovers and slaves take the horses to stables and pens nearby where the animals buried noses in bins of grain and drank from troughs fed by an aqueduct from the foothills.

Rokus took a seat on deck to watch the wash of fiery orange saturate the bottoms of western clouds. Along the riverbank torches and lanterns began to flicker, and shadowy shapes of men moved in the twilight like desultory ghosts. The air already grew heavy with dew, and he could smell the upturned dirt and hacked grasses of harvest waft over the land and water. Among all the sounds he heard the gurgle and splash of currents and eddies work the spaces between his barge and the next.

Unwrapping the bandage from his head, he recoiled at the blast of cold air that pierced the wound of his eye. His head began a throbbing reaction to the night air, and he closed his good eye in reflex to protect himself. When he reached up to caress the damage below his brow, his fingertips discovered the hollow there. The skin around the socket and even the scabby flap of lid only hurt a little. But what was truly painful was the void below it all, a point of horrendous discomfort that seemed to jab into his brain.

He thought to get more tincture from Marius, because it brought relief, even though that came with the torrent of strange dreams.

Marius appeared on the dock with several men in togas. He stood respectfully still, almost at attention, while they gestured emphatically. Soon Marius nodded, gave a quick salute, and boarded the barge.

"Have they brought you dinner, Rokus?" he asked.

"I'm not hungry."

"I'll get them to bring you something; you haven't eaten in three days."

"What did those prefects have to say?"

Marius turned away from Rokus as if to avoid divulging something or maybe to find the prefects' words encoded in the people along the embankment. He stood frozen in thought and then sat next to him.

"Prince Rokus, the prefects have received messengers today bearing news from Rome. Our Emperor has begun collecting debts owed from senators, magistrates and even generals. Everyone. He wishes to end Rome's money woes by these measures as well as begin to practice thrift in all government policies and plans. Galba is retrieving awards given by Nero while handing out his own to his favorites. Not only are senators outraged, but so is the army. You already know the Guard was discharged without the extra pay promised them, but now the army has been stiffed. Galba won't pay, or, as he says, 'submit to bribing an army that should be loyal by summary oath.'"

"So, senators are losing privileges and power. They feel they are entitled to pluck the ripe fruit off the empire tree." Rokus tugged at his beard.

"Yes, and more. The games have been cancelled indefinitely, so the plebs are beside themselves, rioting in the streets, calling for the spectacles that they love. The city is furious with Galba. And this is spreading." Marius raised his voice, shook his head.

"If Galba can't keep the throne, someone will take it. Who, then?"

"The prefects report that one of Galba's trusted supporters, Otho, the governor of Lusitania, has amassed his own force." Marius crossed to the gunwale and looked downriver.

"Is he marching?" Rokus asked.

"No one knows."

"Help me up," Rokus offered an arm. Marius returned to Rokus' side. Together they shuffled to the rail of the barge.

While Marius stood staring away, Rokus leaned over the side.

"What about the troops in the north? Where does their allegiance lie?" the Batavian said.

"The prefects said they expect to hear something from Germania soon. Perhaps they know in Avenio already. We will be there tomorrow evening."

"It's predictable. The soldiers have contempt for the soft senators in Rome; they have more respect for a leader who knows and appreciates them. One of their own. I see civil war."

"I'm afraid I do, too."

Marius shook his head then walked to the long house and took a lantern from a hook on a post. He brought it to Rokus' face to inspect the wounded eye. Frowning, he assessed the eye's condition and murmured under his breath. Rokus pulled his head away.

"I will get the surgeon from the fort. Just to clean it," Marius said.

"No. I will go to him—need to get off this boat, walk."

"You sure?"

They walked along the river and into the town, which was already empty of citizens. They passed a roving guard who saluted Marius, and when they crunched down the cinder track to the fort, several more soldiers met them, saluted, and turned to let them pass. In the ever-consuming twilight, the fort's walls and gate loomed; they passed the guards and crossed the open square. Marius knocked on the surgeon's door.

Inside, the surgeon cleaned the wound, slathered Rokus' eye socket with ointment and wrapped it with a new bandage. Rokus carried a bottle of the tincture as they left.

When they boarded the barge, Rokus went directly to the great house.

"Yes, that's it, rest that injury. You'll feel better soon. Oh, here," Marius offered, reaching into his pocket, "The surgeon gave this for you." He held out a black cloth square with rounded corners, sewn to long leather strings. "To make you beautiful."

At his berth, Rokus sat, touching the remains of his face. The jolts emanated from deep in his head, and this made him dizzy, as if the act of thinking severed something essential, leaving him bereft of focus. He popped the cork from the bottle of tincture, smelled its aroma of earth and flower and sourness like bad wine, then put it to his lips and drank one deep gulp.

Only after he fell charmed into a tinctured slumber, did she appear to him in a veil of tears. She glistened. Candlelight danced in her hair in sparkles of orange and maroon, pink and gold. The thick waves of her hair gushed from the top of her head, spilling to her shoulders, cascading over her back and breast like an endless sea of sunsets. Her pale skin radiated warmth, and when Rokus kissed her tears dry, he found his pleasure in her sensational heat. They were without words; her tears expressed both her joy at his arrival and the sorrow of wasted days, and his beating heart, pulsing with resolve, expressed his euphoria at this union in its final making.

He climbed up the spiral stairs that clung to the limestone walls of her tower. Birds sang, their fluttering melodies drifting in through narrow openings spaced every ten feet. From her terrace, he saw the green band meandering through the forest as it flowed toward the River Rhenus. There was a fire pit and an altar against the terrace wall, and flames crackled under some charred thing on a skewer; the altar evinced a sacrifice, for ornate sticks and bejeweled globes surrounded a puddle of blood.

Inside he found her waiting. She stood with her back to a brazier, so he could only discern her shape; her voluptuousness surmounted by the red mane, wild as wind. He unclasped his cloak, unbuckled his belt, and put his scabbard and sword and cloak on a chair. He unstrapped his Roman boots and pushed them underneath. Then he surged across the carpets as if he knew her love already and his senses followed instinct. She was a flower laced with herbs, a blossom rich with complexity. She embraced him, burying her face in his chest, reaching round and squeezing him.

"I knew you would come. My sight told me we have already met," she said.

"Yes, Veleda," Rokus answered before kissing her neck and ear.

They stood embracing, and through bodies so entwined ran familiar and exultant energies; now they were bound, woven together in a combination of selves.

"Rokus. Let me just say your name. Rokus. Roh-koos. This is a long time coming."

"But it seems inevitable, doesn't it?" His hand caressed her hair.

"Thank the spirits," she offered her lips in a kiss, "that we have good messengers."

"That I do in Ansgar, and I am grateful for his help. Here I am." He kissed her neck, then her ear again.

"But you are also a poet who seduces with words."

"I am a warrior prince with poor training in words."

"But you have a best boy that loves you, is devoted to you—who understands beyond his years. I heard young Ansgar's voice, but I heard your poems." She pulled back and touched his lips with a fingertip.

"Now you may have both my poetry and my voice." He wrapped his arms around her in an embrace.

"Sending messengers back and forth across our lands—what a cumbersome way."

"We both had our commitments."

"I am grateful you sent your Ansgar." Veleda leaned back and studied Rokus' face.

"When the Batavian auxiliary marched by here heading home, I couldn't believe my eyes. I had heard about you, but to see you there in your garden..." Rokus said.

"My sacrifice that morning augured a visit from someone, but I thought it was the Bructeri king coming to learn of his fortune in battle against the Langobardi."

"It was the first time I had ever had the experience of knowing someone before actually meeting them. I saw you with your retinue on the river road, and I knew this must be the great Veleda, the oracle of the River Rhenus, the treasure of Germania. I tried to imagine your company. I heard your voice, the song of your laughter; I smelled the honey of you. I imagined your touch, your skin, the magic of your hair. After setting up our camp that night, I retired, full of the wondrous vision of you—the images of someone I had not even met—and I wrote to you. 'Ansgar,' I said after summoning him, 'memorize this and go to the lady in the tower, get an audience with her, and then recite what you have committed to your memory here tonight. Then catch up with us, for we'll have moved north to do business with Brinno and the Cananefates.' So I read what I had written, and the boy repeated; I read several times more, and he repeated it until he had it memorized."

"Ansgar was charming. Your poem was beautiful." Veleda moved the back of her fingers across his face.

They climbed under the blankets as the brazier sizzled and spat pungent resin.

"What is that smell?" Rokus asked.

"Frankincense," she said, kissing him.

"I like it," he said, moaning and tracing his finger down her spine. She kissed him at his collarbone, and he pulled them together.

When the barge pushed off the embankment, it jostled him. The thin line of sleep dividing his memories of Veleda and the train of barges grew thin and then disappeared altogether, and he woke. Rokus pushed up on an elbow, but the weight of his tinctured head was too much to hold and he flopped back down. His head throbbed with rhythmic shots of pain that consumed not only the socket, but also his face and the underlying tissue of his long scar. Scanning the tiny cabin for redress or decoy distraction, he became aware of late afternoon, a million floating particles in a cross column of light that inched along the floor. He had slept all day—maybe two, he thought. He hoped not three.

When he heard the music he struggled to his elbow again, listening to a bow slide over strings in sawing rhymes. Emanating from the deck was a man's singing in a dialect from far off Lugdunensis. As the verses repeated, imagery about a shepherd boy and girl, Rokus recognized the accent and placed it in Lutetia—a northern song.

The melody circled his palpitating head, soothing it with its whispers, and the light was not as hurtful to his good eye. Gradually, the rhythm mesmerized him, and he wandered into a forest place, pleasing in its darkness, and he closed his eye as the shepherd boy and girl vanished behind trees.

Walking into that darkness, he listened to the bowed melody keeping time for him; his feet and heart moved along, dreamy and careless. The voice sang a tale of woe and how the boy and girl were torn apart by the villagers who did not understand their innocent love. The melody strained with tragedy. Rokus rolled over and dreamed on, leaving the shepherds, their flock, and all the meadows and trees of their world.

Presently, he stood on the terrace of Veleda's tower again, enveloped in mist—from the river, from unseen clouds, from his adulterated dream—through which the flame on her altar flickered. It drew him on, and, bowing before it, he saw his garnet amulet dangling from its leather strand, shining in flecks of brilliance through the darkness. He smiled, remembering his gift to her, and entered her chamber.

"Veleda," he said, "I come to you unseen by the guards, and I want you again."

"Rokus, I want you, too."

They undressed as before and climbed onto her bed of piled coverings, embracing each other with unspoken oaths, kissing long and lightly, tinged by the scents of their bodies and the frankincense she'd lit before his arrival.

"This is destiny, for I saw this when I was a girl," Veleda said, circling her fingertips across his shoulder blades.

Rokus sighed. "You saw me?"

"I saw a man who was kind and strong, with a scar there," she said fingering the hair on the side of his head.

"Then let us fulfill this destiny of ours. Would you move to the Batuwe with me?" Rokus asked.

"Move from here?" she said with surprise.

Rokus swept the air over their heads with his outstretched arm. "This providence cannot remain in a chamber at the top of a stone tower on a little river. We must give it room. Space for a house, for children—a barn for our horses."

"Know, Rokus, that I interpret the omens for my people and then tell my tales to the other tribes. And I will protect them all. I reveal cataclysms yet to unfold and comfort them with assurances. My sight has many purposes. They are my people and I am theirs. I will stay in this tower."

"A prophetess can see from any location," he said.

"Yes," she said, kissing him, "but Bructeri believe from the legends that their seer is a single voice in a tower, a solitary force facing the darkness alone for them. This tower was erected on a sacred site where the ancestors witnessed the marriage of wind and land, and from that hallowed tryst came a one-horned beast—part-horse, part-goat, part-lion—that joined with fire right here where we lie. And from that union sprang a race of women, anointed by the spirits. That creature is the symbol of the

Bructeri, and I am the daughter in a line of these daughters with the sight. I will stay here in this tower."

Rokus kissed her neck and shoulder and then traced her chin. "Then I will offer up a lamb in your altar pit—walk on my tiptoes when I climb the stairs."

"The legends describe it, and that is what the people understand. And that is what I desire."

"Let us talk later," he said.

When the candle had burned down to its base and sizzled, and the chamber had grown dark, Rokus got up. He stood over the chair feeling for his clothes.

"Rokus, you must be very careful," she spoke from the bed. "The sacrifice I made this morning augurs danger for you."

"I know danger, Veleda."

"It is a feeling, as constant and sure as the earth below us. Listen. Can you not hear it? I can hear it."

"I hear the guards changing below. I hear the wind outside your windows."

"The crowned one far to the south has spoken. He has decreed that you and your brother must be put to the sword."

"Nero? Why would he care about Claudius Paulus and me?"

"You underestimate yourself, Rokus. Prince Rokus. You have power and effect. What you say matters, and the Emperor listens. Beware the Emperor's men."

Rokus emerged from the forest of dreams accompanied by the bowed melody and singing voice woven into the night. Veleda stood watching him with her hands outstretched, and her tears again flowed down her cheeks as she reconciled her solitary fate.

The barge rocked gently, and the lilting voice and crying strings came to rest just over his head. And there was laughter, and people applauded.

SIX

In the Town of Lugdunum

The days that followed were healing days. As the barge train plied upriver behind the glorious pairs of horses extending far down the riverside track, Rokus studied the terrain and noted the elevations scattered with oaks and pines and the willows along cuts in the land where water gushed during storms. He realized he saw every variation martially, as redoubt or obstacle, and caught himself building walls for defense at every rise and surmounting every escarpment.

"Be a good traveler, won't you," he told himself, "and let the commander rest until he is needed."

He watched merchants and shore men rush to the train of barges when they landed in Avenio and Acumum, and he studied the drovers and slaves as they managed the horses, taking them to feed, inspecting hooves, grooming them; he was pleased when he saw that they did this well. Further upstream, he delighted in the flower market of Valentia Julia, where a plaza at the waterfront was filled with tables and booths bursting with color. Floral aromas floated over the scene, and the inhabitants worked with efficiency and joy that conveyed a long-term peace and more, the presumption of peace.

As at the previous stops, men acted as if war was an alien force that would not enter their city, and Rokus realized that such conditions promoted steady profit in lives and material.

The grid of streets radiated from the different waterfronts as the towns imposed themselves in unique ways. Shops, houses, temples, theaters, assembly halls, baths, bridges and roads settled onto the land's contours, and the great Roman way of commerce filled street and square with productivity and proceeds. And always there were the garrisons. Soldiers stood everywhere, so that Pax Romana was a living thing, enforced by capable men who followed orders, and these orders arrived in the provinces from the capital, issued and acted upon by men who rarely compromised. The hierarchy of Roman power was a flow of commands and promotions, and men were propelled upward by the quality and cruelty of their commands downward.

Rokus pondered these things on long walks whenever the barge train stopped to unload goods and passengers and take on regional wares and produce to be sold in other parts of the Empire. Two ideas always bore down on him as he strolled: the system that was Rome, and languishing Betuwe. These two places transfixed him—Rome, because the Empire was a colossus of organized military and economic might; and Betuwe, because the delta swampland sustained his people and their animals, and they gave away portions of their good future. The sky spirit loved his land, washed it and his people, and they, having grown strong by it, rode and fought with unparalleled ability. But the Batavi were adjuncts, almost supplicants, because of the arrangement with Rome. Rome drained his people with her bargaining, for what once seemed like a privilege had turned into a burden—more than half of all Batavian men and boys of fighting age reported by agreement to the Roman authority in Germania to fight alongside the legions. In exchange, Rome did not tax the Batavi as she did the Bructeri, the Cananefates, the Frisians, the Helvetians, and all the tribes north and west of the alpine ring surrounding Latium. With neither surplus crops nor crafts, the Batavi traded what they had: warriors.

But the arrangement angered him. With the export of men and boys, the Batavi would always be weak, while the legions stayed strong. And without the men to shape the land and husband the horses and cattle, sheep and swine, the Batavi would be a diminished people, sitting on soggy land that never changed.

The Batavi might have more farms; they might grow settlements surrounded by handsome walls. Their homes might be warm and dry and solid against the winter. The Batavi might create goods to trade and sell, might journey to other trade towns to vend their pottery, bolts of wool, textiles, and leather goods. The Batavi, spread out between the rivers, might send representatives to a big hall where he, Rokus, would hear these voices from the country so that he would know the temper of his nation and lead his people.

Such ideas flourished above the treetops, conveyed in the fabulous cumulus clouds that he was certain came from his North.

And like the clouds roiling overhead, Rome herself was in a state of flux. As the senate wrestled with Galba's edicts to return grants and compensations, and as the pretenders gathered forces and the different armies vouchsafed their allegiances, he floated north to a rendezvous he had yet to design.

The great line of paired horses drew them to Lugdunum on a day when the wind was a wintry mantel. Rokus sat on the deck wrapped in his cloak, promising himself to get some Batavian breeches first chance. He realized he'd grown soft while in prison, and he realized, too, that when he was younger he would have used the cold day to fortify himself against the elements. But now, he wanted the warmth of breeches. He tucked himself under his cloak, watching the town gain detail and size, and soon men along the river prepared for their arrival. He adjusted the patch over his eye, tightened its strands. Wagons and carts and horses dotted the area, while at the plaza groups of slaves stood waiting for the cargo bin hatches to be thrown open and the great planks to be set across, deck to shore.

The barge train floated twenty feet from the embankment while drovers and slaves led the horses into the waterside plaza. The men went to work releasing the horses' harnesses while other men lashed the barges to great stanchions placed intermittently, and still others gathered straps and reins to store in a big cart.

Rokus pulled his cloak about his neck and leaned back with some relief, as it was the first day since his duel in Arelate that he had not been wracked with throbbing pain. Instead, the empty socket ached sporadically, and every time he scanned the scene in front of him, his single vision reminded him of his loss.

"Rokus, I have your things," Marius said, and Rokus nodded.

They stood ready to disembark. The five remaining legionnaires lined up behind them. Rokus felt their eyes on his back—points of anger and fear and confusion. As the barge touched the quay, men dropped the gangplank to the dock, and they all entered the plaza. From the other barges emerged passengers in colorful array, and crewmen, tending to ship-to-shore tasks, moved with tired expertise. Hawkers and venders roamed the plaza accosting travelers with their pitches and wares.

Marius stood squarely with the brass box secure under his arm. He lined up his men at attention, commanding their young new leader, named Val, to take them to the garrison quartermaster and secure beds for the night. He, Marius, would secure horses from the cavalry. After assembling food and equipment, they would pack horses and depart for Augusta Raurica.

Rokus circled the plaza taking a path that purposefully bisected throngs of passengers and sellers. The mélange excited him because now he saw non-Roman faces dominant. The crowd may have been subjects of the Empire, but they were still Gauls or Belgae or German from the test of long nose, high cheekbone, tall limb, and fair skin. He reveled in the diversity of colors and clothing—there was no norm; tunic and trouser, skirt and breeches, wool and fur walked side-by-side, while coif of rings or long braids, beard or smooth chin marked station and territory. It was a glorious amalgam, and he drew inspiration from it.

Soldiers stood at each end of the waterfront spectacle; even these veterans reveled in the good cheer of the diverse folk and the enthusiasm brought by a barge train bearing new people, gifts and stores.

He drifted through these masses facing the autumn sun, its thin glow washing everything and everybody with silvery haze and penetrating his patched eye with its healing heat.

His stomach tightened with hunger; it had been days since he'd eaten. Wafts of scented meat came to him and he turned to their source. At the edge of the plaza stood a vendor's booth, a fire pit surrounded by shelves and a counter. On a spit licked by flames was a chunk of meat that dripped juice into sizzling coals. He smelled rosemary and thyme.

"What do you have there, friend?" He spoke in Latin.

The vendor scratched his beard, poked at the meat with a long knife, then spit on the ground. "Horse."

Rokus tipped his head and moved on. At a window of a shop down the way, he found pieces of chicken on long skewers, brushed frequently by a man who dipped back into a bowl of wine and spices. Rokus dug coins from his waist purse, a stipend from Marius, and devoured his chicken while sitting on a wall watching the crowd. He returned for a second serving, and then walked the perimeter again, stopping only at a wine merchant's where he drank a ladleful. He spied a fruit cart and headed for it, but Marius interrupted his line across the plaza.

"Let us talk, Rokus," he said.

They returned to the wine merchant, this time entering the shop and taking seats. Marius ordered a pitcher of watered wine, and they drank it from clay cups.

"The horses are ready, and the supplies are almost assembled. Just a few more things to do, so we will depart for the mountain pass the day after tomorrow," Marius said

"This is good. Why so troubled, Marius?" Rokus leaned toward him.

Marius emptied his cup and began rotating it nervously. "That legionnaire was the best one I have ever seen. His death troubles me. I have to make a report—and I've lost a great soldier.

"Tell your group of senators the truth. The man tried to kill me, so I killed him." Rokus planted his cup abruptly.

"Rokus, it makes me look bad, losing a man like that."

"You cannot control a man's fanaticism. He targeted me, and he paid the price."

"But you threatened him that night in Arelate. I heard you."

"We had a history of bad blood, is all." Rokus turned away.

"But?" Marius looked at the dregs in his cup

"But he thought to follow through with Nero's orders to execute me. Why? Two years after the fact. A big man with a small mind. I had to kill him."

"But I've lost a good soldier, and the man I've been charged to protect has been mutilated." Marius touched his arm.

"Marius, don't trouble yourself with my eye. I saw plenty with it already. I have one left to use for the rest of my life."

"Making light of it, sir."

"Don't worry about it. Just don't report it. The senators want to hear good news. Why upset them with the truth?" Rokus looked back at the wine pitcher, then at his cup.

Marius sat back, adjusted his scabbard, and exhaled. "It's made the men jumpy. They don't know what to think—about you, about me."

"Tell them not to think. They're soldiers; they're not supposed to think like that."

"I could replace them, I suppose."

"If you trust them, keep them."

"They are good soldiers."

"Then keep them."

Marius lowered his head. He massaged his fingers into his hair as if to soothe his troubled mind. Then he sat up and filled his lungs. He poured wine and ordered more. Rokus watched as he wrestled with his thoughts. The journey to Germania would be dangerous if the men were not trustworthy; to release them would announce the conflict and likely implicate Rokus in the death of a valued legionnaire—not the best situation for a newly freed prisoner.

"Everything will work out, won't it?" he said.

"The legionnaire I killed was not balanced. He didn't kill, he murdered; and it was not right, different from being a profession-al soldier. He had no perspective on his job as a legionnaire and his ability to kill. He liked it. No good soldier likes killing that way. You and Rome are better off without him."

Marius rubbed his chin, examined an old scar across the back of his hand. Rokus allowed several minutes to pass, then struck the tabletop.

"So what was in the brass box?" he asked.

Marius paused, and then blurted, "A small fortune, a debt paid."

"Yes?"

"Senate business."

"Dirty business." Rokus said decisively.

"Business." Marius poured, smiled, nodded. He drank fully, and then slammed the cup down. "I've picked a fine horse for you, Prince Rokus."

"I'm looking forward to it."

"Let's go by the stables to look at the lot. They are all fine horses."

As they crossed the town, strains of music drifted on the breeze. When they reached the outskirts, the wind-borne melodies swirled overhead, and Rokus sensed a homecoming. These were tribal strains full of familiar turns, arcing lines and notes that filled the air with noble purpose. A deep drum sounded like a pulse from earth, and in between the terrestrial beats were syncopated taps on skins that created a rolling surge across the clearing.

"Listen," he said.

"I hear it. Let's follow these folks." Marius pointed to a cart piled high with furs and then waved to several fair young women walking next to it. A tall bearded man in leathers pulled the cart, and they joined a troupe of similar characters arranged in a big circle up a hill. Rokus and Marius followed them.

A fire crackled through a pyramid of twigs, sticks and logs, and sparks shot up and spiraled in rhythm to the music. On the edge of the circle stood musicians gyrating to their creation.

The music was a crescendo tale that grew in complexity and volume as more people arrived. A welcoming march, the tune wove a bowed line from a set of strings through flute notes strung together with harmony and grace. These tightened as the drummers beat skins in rhythm, and chimes from exotica joined small bells played by a girl in white fur. These ornaments clung to the bowed and blown melodies that resembled soaring voices but were not, because the singers had not yet begun.

Rokus' blood raced in time as he entered the field of music that seemed to come from the ancient days when such sounds were given to magic, and his folk discovered the community of vibrations that give form to love and fear and the increments in between.

He picked up his pace leaving Marius behind. Soon, he stood at the edge of the circle to watch and celebrate the rediscovery of tribal mysteries as four concentric rings of dancers began prancing in opposite directions, and the musicians increased their fervor. The inner ring circled to the left, the next ring to the right, the next to the left, and so the outer ring to the right. Friends watching the festive march began clapping in time, and only one dancer's rotation passed before all onlookers were beholden to the force and joined the clapping. Now the entire clearing along the road into Lugdunum was alight with cheer and music, even as the flames had risen through the logs to spit and crackle into the merging twilight.

Rokus looked for Marius, that he might share this with him; the Roman, he thought, should enter this tribal conglomeration and partake of the indescribable event that summoned, like invocations, the energies of nature and the unknown. Marius followed Rokus' waving arm and stood with eyes wide as the dancers sprang in their directions and the music's volume increased. The clapping sped until a collective beat of palms rose over them and fused with the melodies that trilled and sawed with greater volition. And presently a singer emerged, a woman with wild hair blown by the winds of four directions, who sang a song with words expressing in tribal dialect what everyone attending felt: that revelry was its own acknowledgement of being.

Marius swayed and clapped, as all swayed and clapped. Rokus closed his eyes to the spectacle around him; in his mind's eye whirled remembrances of Batavi celebrations when earth and sky met in bonfires across the marshland between the great rivers. Marius began to hum along and he had an ear for it—and voice—and with his baritone he approximated the weaving melodies, as he clapped in unison and danced in place.

When Rokus opened his eyes, Marius had been transformed from the centurion escort to someone possessed. His arms moved like birds' wings, and his weight passed from foot to foot. His head rolled on his shoulders, and from deep down in his throat awakened some nonsense words that he sang into the flying melodies afire. A woman dancer, all streamers of pelts and waving arms, saw Marius in his revel and pulled him into the circle. He twirled three times with her, then she flung him onward where he fell in prancing step with the others rotating left.

Rokus studied how the layers of the soldier molted all around the dancing circle, and as Marius gamboled on, he grew lighter and more rhythmic and burst into laughter.

The contradiction amused Rokus: wielding sword then and dancing with joy now, scheming survival plans once and surrendering to abandon again. He clapped in time to help lift the proceedings yet higher, and the musicians played on ever more expressively, and the dancers bounded with glee.

A bearded tribesman joined the singer. He wore a rough tunic over breeches and leather boots of the northern tribes. He extracted a phrase from her song, repeating it to the crowd in rhythm to the minstrels. The people responded, laughing and singing together the ornate phrase. The fire soared as the voices ascended, the hands clapped to the concussive drums, and the clearing was transported to some nameless, placeless site of tribal hegemony; and the non-Romans there felt it in their blood, this brotherhood, this pact with the earth and sky, and all participants burst with rapture.

Rokus joined, remembering steps from his youth. Soon, the clearing throbbed with dancers in concentric rings, feet thumping earth, hands waving like signals to the spirits, heads bobbing, and voices resounding.

Marius glanced about looking self-conscious—a flash of doubt that he could experience mystical convictions. Rokus, in mid-spin, saw this and waved, and Marius, seemingly reassured, danced onward to the right while Rokus danced to the left. Because of the shared sense of purpose among this November tribe, hands clasped hands, arms embraced, and kisses landed on cheeks and mouths for no other reason than joy in the moment. This new sensation tipped Marius, Rokus thought, and he had to fight the disbelief, so etched in his being was the dominator's state of mind.

A blonde woman joined Marius in step and they held hands. A brunette woman took Rokus' hands and they twirled together, and Rokus wrapped his arms around her waist, and she leaned into him and they kissed. The dance was full of such pairings and displays, and all sensed the merging of factions over disappearing boundaries. As this occurred, the musicians played to it, if not inspired it, and the mass raised the mystical revelation of the evening still more.

Rokus reveled in the sensations and the woman's close company. They kissed again and again, dancing in their own orbit while the concentric rings frolicked across the clearing as a singular force. During one kiss, Rokus looked over her shoulder and spied a squad of legionnaires approaching. On duty, they marched four abreast several rows deep; their leader struck a grave aspect three paces ahead of them. Rokus' pulse raced as a familiar disquiet supplanted pleasure.

Shortly, they had surrounded the musicians, and the commander barked an order to the player of a string instrument, who, dumbfounded, lowered his arms. The piper continued to play and the drummers drummed, and this the Romans could not abide; one soldier swiped at the musician's bow. It soared into the trees nearby, and as he turned to track its trajectory, the soldier hit him hard on the shoulders and the musician fell.

The music faltered and the crowd of celebrants acquiesced to the military might, except for the bearded man who had led the tribal chant. He confronted the legionnaire in charge but he was ignored. The legionnaire turned away and swiped the air with a whip handle as if to cleanse the clearing. The singer stepped closer to him and then raised his hands in entreaty. With that, the soldier responded as if accosted, launching a beating across the man's shoulders and torso, back and head, driving him down as a farmer beats stakes into the ground. Gradually at first, then with a groundswell of awareness, the crowd understood, and traces of fear and outrage appeared across their faces. Some withdrew into the night shadows along the clearing's edge, others joined as a force near the bonfire. Their long hair and beards, furs and leathers looked like a pack of animals in the flickering light— slinking gestures, flashing eyes, bared teeth.

After another barked command, pairs of legionnaires pushed into the revelers and, using their spears as plows and baffles, channeled people to the road and down its darkening way. Any tribesman who protested or pushed back was struck mercilessly, and then taken to four soldiers whose placement formed makeshift corners of a pen. Eventually, the insurrectionists—that was how their crime would appear on reports—would march at spear point back to the garrison to meet their fate.

The other tribal folk slapped the rumps of horses and ponies, urging carts and wagons to depart.

While the soldiers followed orders, their leader found Marius and the blonde woman observing the destruction of the ritual dance. Rokus, suspicious of legionnaires and unsure of his status as a freed prisoner, waited in the shadows with the other woman as he adjusted his eyepatch and strained to see. The leader, his face red with intolerance, faced Marius and recited what he knew: that Marius had been consorting with the barbarians thereby tainting Roman honor while rendering undignified the legionnaire's bearing. Having not recognized the decorated veteran and senate agent, the brash officer lashed out, full of self-importance.

"I fought Britons when you were at your mother's teat," Marius said, stepping forward with clenched fists.

The officer ignored Marius and berated him about dignity and the Roman way and the place for barbarians and illegal Druid worshipping and necessary consequences. Incredulous, Marius studied the officer; Rokus could tell that Marius held back a natural instinct to strike sense into the man, electing instead to ride this through peacefully. On orders, two legionnaires seized Marius' arms, jerked him away from his companion, and led him down the road back to Lugdunum.

"I'll be back!" he called to Rokus.

Other legionnaires pulled the fire apart, scattering logs and kicking dirt on coals. They snapped leather straps toward the wagons, which rolled off the clearing for the road. The officer strode around demanding the crowd to return to the forest, to respect Roman law, to reject barbarian ways. His diatribe fueled itself as he shouted, and soon he cited Julius Caesar's sequence of victories over the Gauls and the establishment of civilization along the Rhodanus and beyond and for these events they should all be grateful.

Rokus suppressed his hatred of this frothy mouth spouting into the once-magic twilight and walked with a group down the road away from the town, finding simple pleasure in the men and women who joked about the little officer sounding off.

SEVEN

In the Forest Outside Lugdunum

"I am pleased the little man has the night watch." Rokus threw his cloak over his shoulders.

"Yes, sir. When the general told him who I was, he did indeed lose some stature." Marius laughed and turned the cloth over as he continued to polish his boots.

"The livery has that horse ready for me. Thought I would ride into the country. Like to join me?" Rokus cinched his belt and picked up his cloak.

"Not now, Rokus. Too many things to prepare; we leave in the morning."

"See you at the evening meal."

Rokus rode the roan mare north along the river road, and then turned east. A double track entered the forest that stretched miles toward the foothills and mountains; in the timberland, a society of winter birds ranged among the bare trunks and branches, and a trio of wolves darted into the brush. The moist gray sky heralded winter.

His roan had been an easy walker along the river, with a smooth gait and dignified air. Now she grew skittish. Her ears twitched as crows alighted, and she snorted when the breeze passed; she raised her head at the scent of badger and marmot and stopped cold when a wolf darted past. As she walked into the wood, she balked at times, but Rokus soothed her with strokes and assurances, clicking sounds and compliments. After forty minutes in, they moved as one.

When another wolf showed itself, then dashed away over rocks and fallen trunks, Rokus drew his sword in preparation. Knowing the territorial nature of the wolf, he weighed the benefits of retreat. But the roan held her head high and stepped sure-footedly forward.

The forest was settling into its dormant phase, fallen leaves swirling in great drifts at the base of trees, and slumping limbs hanging in cold repose. The sky shone dully like a blade neglected, and the cold air absorbed the forest sounds so that it was beyond quiet.

Rokus sheathed his sword, sat straight, and stretched his limbs to let the autumn air permeate him. His imprisonment had kept this from him, as had the sea voyage, as had the river journey. Now, the forest was his, and the tremors of his tribal nature ran through him. The roan felt this, and she picked up her pace and sallied forth at a trot.

Presently she cantered. Rokus loosened the reins and let her go; he trusted her. Together they carried on down the double track as it coursed ever deeper into the woods, undulating over terrain and hugging the contours of hills that came in greater frequency as they sailed eastward and upward.

Then she skidded to a stop, shaking her head. Her ears dropped back and her nostrils flared. He squeezed with his heels, but she stamped and moved sideways, snorting and flashing her eyes.

Rokus slid off the saddle and faced the bend in the track, two ruts cutting through the dense wood, dark with the low metallic light of the season. Something huge had pushed through part of the forest up ahead, as brush and bracken were smashed flat, all stout tree trunks were scarred with recent slashes, and every low hanging pine skirt had been mangled. The serenity created by the population of trees with their verdant canopy, the outcroppings and thick carpet of ferns, terminated at the turn.

As he inched closer, the roan pulled back, until he tied her to a limb and continued afoot. He read signs of horrific intrusion everywhere; nothing was as it should have been. Around the turn in the track he saw a jumbled landscape obliterating the tranquility of a road meandering through a forest.

His mind reached into its recesses for some past experience with similar traits to which he might connect all this but only saw the furor of battle when warriors are held fast in the orgy of killing. At such times, men wield weapons without conscience, striking lest they be struck, maiming lest they be maimed, advancing lest they be crushed. And from the battle memories his mind fixed to extra-military affairs, when, the fever of killing high, soldiers launched into settlements, wreaking havoc among the peasantry, the nameless wives and children without weapons clutching each other in corners of huts and along the fences as swords rained down. These frenzied men continued their annihilations, plunging swords and lopping limbs with demented gratification. Some, inflamed, opened their breeches or hitched their tunics and, after dismembering children, raped the women and girls before butchering them. It wasn't a battle scene Rokus spied ahead—it was the mayhem driven by the killing fever.

As he approached, shapes and silhouettes became clearer. Hundreds of branches had been cut and strewn and drenched with tawny mud throughout the glade—but then Rokus came upon a context for the massive cutting. Resting on the crushed remains of the forest floor were wagon wheels, limbers and shafts, horses' legs, and, frozen in throes, their barrels and necks in freak tableaux. At his feet lay the head of the brunette he had kissed so exquisitely just days before, her eyes wider now, her neck bejeweled with a line of clotted blood. He glanced around without finding the rest of her body and then scanned the glade of destruction. There had been no hacking of trees but a slaughter, and the array of cuttings before him was the remains of the dead—and the dead were the troupe of dancers he and Marius had joined.

"Gods!" Rokus blurted.

He stepped into the maelstrom of death where the bodies of men and women lay defiled. The farther into the heaps he moved, the more mutilation he encountered, especially hands. It was as if the legionnaires, or Roman command, wanted to prevent the crafting of any useful thing by these people who danced to the sky spirits in November.

Toward the back of this gruesome place, he came upon the musicians in a final performance for the age. Perched along a fallen trunk, the nine men held their own heads in their laps with the splintered remnants of their instruments jammed into the open stumps of their necks.

There was bloody pleasure farther still, because beyond the musicians lay twenty women's bodies without heads. Their tattered skirts were flounced up, and awful stains covered their pelvises and legs.

Standing at the edge, the weight of it all bore down on him. He sat on a rock near these vanquished souls who implored the sky with rigid arms or lay protecting their absent faces from the onslaught. One hand still attached to its arm caught his eye; shining on a finger was a silver ring with a great stone containing the green of the forest and the blood of that day. He had seen one other like it before, at the seaport of Ravenna. The merchant told him it was from India, a land beyond Judea, beyond Baghdad and Persia, beyond even the empire of the Great Alexander. He held the cold hand and worked the ring off the finger, promising the woman who owned it, promising the troupe—promising himself—that the ring and its Mars stone or bloodstone would serve as a memory and a challenge. He would not forget the Roman way, and he would make his own peace with them through rebellion and the founding of a separate nation for tribes.

He looked back at such a senseless act against happy innocents, and it turned his stomach. He turned in the direction of Lugdunum. Squaring his shoulders and flexing his muscles, he wailed, "No!" in a drawn out, grief-stricken howl that reverberated down the dark forest track.

As he picked his way back to the roan, he studied the surprise and horror on faces and twisted poses. Some figures, already bloated and gone to slow decay, raised arms invoking some rescuing goddess, still others glared at unseen blades or the faces of the attacking legionnaires. Then there were others who rested with eyes half open to the commencement of their next journey.

Rokus stared at the harvest of slaughter, sixty bodies and eight horses. He imagined the officer who had disrupted the autumn dance reporting back to the commandant with a false account of ringleaders and rebels, conspiracy.

Considering the generals and proconsuls ranking above him and the senators watching him from Rome—and cache of power gained from quick action—the commandant followed the troupe into the forest. He knew word would spread, instilling fear in the tribes of Gallia Celtica, Belgica, and Aquitania.

But Rokus was not from Gallia.

EIGHT

On the Mountain Roads East of Lugdunum

Men and horses rumbled northeast on the Rhodanus River road at dawn, with a loud clopping and clattering of hooves that sent Rokus' blood racing. Finally, there would be movement over land and not the listless passage that marked so much of the river and sea. Seven riders and three packhorses traveled ahead of a cloud of dust that flurried up and drifted over the river.

"Two days at most," called Marius excitedly. "First stop: Milestone Ten!" Like Rokus, he was a man of action thwarted by the slow barge train.

"It will be great for you to be home, no?" he called to Rokus over the din.

"Long time coming," Rokus called back.

After an hour they passed the double track that veered off the river road and led to the place of slaughter. Rokus imagined the tribes descending upon the site for the rites of burial. They would have known what had happened; their soothsayers would have delivered the news, informed themselves by the black ravens of the forest, messengers of the spirits. He heard the weeping and grief—the vows for revenge, the utter fatalism tormenting the

elders—and saw the long assembly of bodies and the cleans-
ings and more weeping and the pyre's flames filling the eternal
branches with smoke.

"They killed them all," he called to Marius.

"What's that?" Marius asked.

"I said Junius Lepidus Crassus had them all killed. That troupe.
The dancers. Down there." Rokus pointed to the track.

Marius nodded. They rode quietly listening to the easy clomp-
ing of hooves and groan of leather.

"Local tribes will protest that," Marius said, looking straight
down the track.

"Protest?"

"The tribes will rise up."

"Marius, it's a war," Rokus said.

"Hope not."

"How can there not be a war?"

"Rome is too big."

"Tribal hearts are big."

They let their misgivings drop by the roadside; the Roman
tactic of crushing dissent was familiar and consistent and repug-
nant; words simply ornamented their disdain.

Looking up the road, they saw a rider, a Roman horseman, approaching at a gallop, lashing the flanks of his beast mercilessly.
He came like thunder, and before long he pulled up in a flurry of
dust, flying commands and snorting. Agitated and wild-eyed, his
horse pranced in place as the rider pulled the scarf off his mouth
to address them.

"How much farther to Lugdunum?" he called.

"Almost there," Marius replied. "What is your business?"

The rider saluted when he saw the quality of Marius' hauberk, the marks of rank on his tunic and cloak, his plume.

"I bring a message to General Crassus of Lugdunum. Galba has appointed Vitellius commander of the northern legions."

"Vitellius, the proconsul of Africa?" Marius frowned.

"The same."

"Carry on, soldier," he said.

The messenger saluted and then whipped his horse, which bolted down the road. Rokus and Marius watched them disappear around a bend.

"A politician, not a soldier?" Marius surmised.

"An outsider coming to lead the hardened troops of the north—looks like trouble for both Galba and Germania."

"If there is war, I doubt Galba's Spanish legions will be enough for him," Marius said slowly.

"Not against the northern legions. They are the best. That is, if this Vitellius can control them."

Rokus and Marius led the mounted legionnaires and the packhorses far away from Lugdunum and into the eastern reaches of Lugdunensis. Having overheard the messenger, the legionnaires rode with sober faces, as if the crux of their training was about to be tried. Marius, too, had duty etched on his face, while Rokus gave in to random images, feelings, senses: the smell of Veleda's hair; the marshy expanse of Batavia; the wizened face of Erenbrecht, his counselor from days long past; and that of Fretherik, the Batavian sage who examined events as if they were a multi-faceted crystal and made accurate predictions of events to come. Such times, he thought, demanded all these people, and he was glad they filled his thoughts and hoped he would see them.

After another hour, the road bent to the east and began to climb; two hours later they stopped to eat and water the horses. They chose a meadow bordered by a stream at one end and a grove at the other. They sat under the trees and pulled at strips of dried beef and hard bread and drank watered wine.

"Rokus?" Marius began. "It has been your auxiliary service all these years. Any family?"

"My tribesmen are my family."

"Any woman?" Marius studied his face.

Rokus drank from his cup, then turned to Marius and smiled. Marius offered his cup as a sign of confidence, and theirs clinked with tacit understanding.

"And you?" Rokus asked.

"I left for the legions when I was very young. Lied about my age. Haven't been back. Not much to return to. I became a soldier, remain so, and will die as one."

Marius pulled at the dried meat and chewed while gazing across the meadow. He finished his cup and exhaled, "Better go."

The seven riders and their packhorses climbed up the alpine road to a plateau that led to Milestone Ten. Once, they sat their horses to rest for twenty minutes and then continued across the plain, a low mountain vale filled with trees and streams. On the other side near the base of a climbing road, they found the crossroads and campsite, with fire pits and clearings for tents and gear. The horses snorted their relief, stamping the ground and waiting for the water trough. Their sides were patches of sweat and lather under saddles and pack straps, and they steamed in the mountain air.

Marius directed the men to divide the tasks—to start a fire and try their hand at game from the woods, to relieve the pack-horses of their burdens, to water and fetter the horses. There would be no tents tonight.

Rokus volunteered to tend to the horses, which freed the last two legionnaires to join the hunting party. The soldiers grabbed their bows and full quivers and ran on stiff legs after the others; they disappeared into the maze of trees. Rokus hummed a low tune with no words, stroking the animals' flanks and telling each one how distinctly beautiful it was—"never has there been such a silken coat, nowhere in Lugdunensis is there such proud bearing, has any horse in the Empire such muscles, such a sleek coat, a mane and tail such as these are gifts from the gods."

Shortly, the packs sat on the ground, and the horses grazed in the meadow, their coats brushed to shine, their manes and tails combed and free of debris, their fetters in place. Loved and cared for, they chomped the green grasses along a little stream cutting through. Their tails swung at flies, and two of them nuzzled.

Rokus sat at the edge of the field watching them loll, as Marius welcomed back the legionnaires. They carried several dead birds and a badger, impaled. The soldiers gloated and then went back into the forest to clean the kills and prepare them for the fire.

Rokus studied his new ring, blood spots flecking the green of spring growth, the welter of significance in its luster. He turned the jewel over and over in his fingers. The evening breezes rattled through the branches, and then he realized he was at the heart of something, the green stone activated by flecks of red, vegetation, blood.

He joined the feast around the fire, watching the legionnaires slice off meat from the spit. Marius poured a cup of wine for Rokus and gave him a metal plate and spooned him several spelt fry cakes. Rokus cut two slices of meat and then joined Marius on the opposite side of the clearing from the legionnaires.

Inhaling deeply, Rokus sat and ate quickly.

"Now I remember your touch with horses," Marius said.

"They deserve it—they've worked hard today." Rokus watched them across the meadow.

Marius drank deeply, smacked his lips. "Rokus, when you get to your auxiliary, will you back Vitellius?"

"I don't know Vitellius."

"Rome is unstable. Seems like the armies control the way."

"That's Rome's business, not mine."

"Galba will try to get the new Guard's support and please the senators. He's considered an outsider."

"Been outsiders before." Rokus picked up a stick and scratched the ground with it.

"If he doesn't have Rome, he cannot survive."

"My allegiance to Rome has been shaken." Rokus drew two ovals in the dirt, then a slash separating them. "But I will meet with my auxiliary before I declare anything. I wish to act with them, not separate from them."

"Here's to our good journey, then," Marius said, raising his cup.

"With the protection of the forest spirits," Rokus offered.

They drank. Rokus paused, drank again, and then drank deeply. "What is this?" he said.

"Wine from the Rhodanus valley, without water. Great harvest two years ago, merchant told me."

At dawn, they decamped and moved north. The track climbed sharply. The easy gait used across river road and forest track now slowed as the horses placed hooves carefully on the natural steps worn into the mountain. Trees became entirely evergreen, and only stout birds such as crows flew over their heads. They reached a crest and entered a long alpine valley. Rokus noted how they were ripe for ambush as the meadow narrowed and the trees thickened with shadows as they closed in on the road.

But the riders passed without incident. They climbed out of the valley, rode up the switchback track, and then followed the ridgeline above the next valley. Rokus adjusted his seat in the saddle repeatedly, becoming uneasy, vigilant. Some impending danger haunted him, and his hand went to his hilt, and he sought an escape route at every turn.

The sun crossed the sky, and they stopped at a ford at the bottom of the valley. As the legionnaires walked the horses to a pasture and Marius unpacked, Rokus wrestled with his uneasiness. He scanned the trees, the meadow, the slopes, the ridges. He saw nothing but sensed everything. There would be an attack, he knew it.

Then, the snap of twig, the snuff of horse. He drew his sword.

"Marius," he whispered.

Marius saw the drawn sword and drew his own. Rokus crept to a place behind a rock from which he studied the direction of the sounds. Among the web of shadow forms, he saw the shapes of two men. Tribal, they wore fur cloaks and fur hats—great things that trailed strings of feathers and bones. Rokus fixed on them, waiting for telltale signs.

Presently, Marius crouched with him at his side. "What do you think?" he whispered.

"Germans." Rokus covered his mouth.

"Many?"

"I see two."

Marius reached down and picked up a short thick branch for a club.

"No, let's wait for the legionnaires to return and then draw them out."

They sat on their haunches for minutes until the soldiers walked back to the site, leaving horses hobbled in the meadow. Marius motioned for them to prepare for an attack, and each one fixed his shield on his arm and drew his sword and put on his helmet.

Rokus stood to reveal himself to the men in shadows. With arms out, sword in one hand, dagger in the other, he stepped closer to the trees, staring at the men while gathering all movement into his peripheral vision. Taut, he was ready to spring in any direction as he stood motionless at the edge of the clearing.

One of the men stood up looking like a bear in his long fur cloak. He raised his spear. Rokus flexed his knees and brought all senses to high alert.

"It is Prince Rokus. By the gods, it's our prince!" cried one bounding out of the thicket with open arms.

"Prince Rokus," called the second shape, who came forward stealthily. "Prince Rokus it is."

Rokus stood agog, lowering his sword as he watched the second man emerge. There they were, two warriors in fur finery with talismans dangling and charms sewn in patterns. One, tall and slender, wore his beard and hair long; the second was shorthaired, short and round. His ruddy cheeks doubled the width of his face with his smiling, and his little eyes disappeared in flesh. The tall man was an essay in hunting—for beast, fowl or man—with straps securing knives, darts, sling, and sword; with hat and cloak well fit; and with his bow, sleek and oiled, held like a precious thing.

His smile barely cut through his solemnity. "Thonkrik. Bentet," Rokus called.

They stood face-to-face. Rokus relaxed with this unlikely rendezvous, while the hunters leaned on their spears, pleased that their suspicions held true. "You've been following us."

"For two valleys and three ridges," Thonkrik, the tall one, said.

"We weren't sure it was our prince, so we waited to confirm before we dealt with this Roman squad."

"Why aren't you with your auxiliary?" Rokus asked.

"Men, let us have some wine to warm us and sit to rest our bones," Marius said, leading them to the packs before he turned to a legionnaire. "Start a fire."

They took places on rocks and logs to form a kind of circle, and Marius, having freed a wine bag from its store, passed it around.

"Where's your outfit?" Rokus asked. "And what are you doing here?

Thonkrik and Bentet glanced at each other.

Thonkrik stood and paced the length of the clearing and took off his hat. "We come from Massilia, where we were stationed with the Batavian auxiliary. Just decided to go home."

"Oh, Rokus, things have changed since you left." Bentet took a long draught from the wine bag before he cackled with joviality. "It's no fun anymore."

"The senators of Massilia have drawn off many troops for their maneuvering back in Rome. We Batavi have had to work extra detail without extra pay. Long hours, stupid chores. You know how we are with such things, Rokus."

"And you know how we are with stingy pay," Bentet said, gulping again.

Thonkrik took the wine bag from him. "A city like Massilia has slaves and freedmen to do the work. They don't need Batavian warriors digging trenches for waterways or foundations for their temples, much less guarding the parapets and roads, daily, nightly. Where are the legions?"

"And that Tullus, the general, went on a tear enforcing his orders," said Bentet.

"Rokus, we are fighters, we are horsemen, we are hunters—not common laborers," Thonkrik added.

"Then Tullus started his examples." Bentet shrugged and twisted his torso.

Rokus searched their faces before he glanced at Marius whose brow furrowed as he listened.

Bentet jumped to his feet. Though stocky, he nimbly played the legionnaire whipping someone. Then he switched places and became the victim. Rokus and Marius and the legionnaires watched this mimicry closely, a thick, round man in fur swinging at the air and then receiving the blows in mock pain. Finally, having whipped the air brutally, Bentet lifted up his sleeve to reveal mangled skin in rows of rope-like scar tissue; though healed, the arm had a strange pink cast to it, as if it were scalded.

"Example!" he cried.

"They did this to you, Bentet?" Marius asked.

"Tullus made examples often, for any slight, real or in his imagination. And if you were to see Bentet's back, you would curse the man," Thonkrik added.

Bentet took the wine from Thonkrik, squeezed the leather bladder, and drank. As he held it out, tattooed patterns of dots and dashes circled his wrists and moved up his arm until the skin became knotted in folds, torn and healed in the shiny ridges.

"All the men hate this state of things; they grumble about it, we acted, is all. We have no issue with the legionnaires." Thonkrik looked directly at the soldiers. "We just think the general and his underlings are drunk on power. So, we travelled due north along the base of the mountains."

"Riding some nice Roman horses we borrowed," Bentet said.

"We were entering the good hunting grounds to the west of the great mountains, when we saw you. Thought at first you were the party sent to bring us in. Then I thought I recognized you."

"But it was your eye that threw us," Bentet said. "We weren't sure it was you. And we didn't wish to engage any legionnaires since we'd cut out. What happened to that eye?"

"A fight to the death to avenge Habo's murder." Rokus touched the patch.

"Habo?" Marius said.

"My brother, Habo, or Claudius Paulus to Romans."

"And you won." Thonkrik placed his hand on Rokus' shoulder.

"Poor Habo." Bentet slouched on a rock shaking his head.

"He is avenged," Thonkrik declared.

"Is there other news from Rome?" Rokus raised his voice.

Thonkrik sat down next to Bentet. He took the wine and handed it to Marius, who drank and handed it to the row of legionnaires.

"What I've heard is enough to send me home—not counting what Tullus did to Bentet and the others." Thonkrik sat up and drew the story in the air. "The Emperor has outraged everybody in Rome, it seems. Has sentenced senators and equites to death without trial, cause or not. Restricted all official appointments to short periods, cancelled tenures; cancelled all Nero's awards, taken back the money that Nero gave away; while he himself heaps riches on friends and awards high places to some of Nero's vilest assistants. Stripped the palace of valuables to sell them in the marketplace. But, word has it he's set off the army by breaking his promise for payments for their support while he was in Spain. And, more, he has reduced pay for the Praetorian Guard and all troops stationed in Latium." Thonkrik took the wine bag from the last legionnaire and drank deeply. "The senate, they say, is so unhappy that its members are looking among themselves for a replacement and sending word throughout the Empire that Galba's days are numbered."

Thonkrik looked left and right as if conspiring, lowering his head and voice.

"I've even heard that senators are forming their own militias, little armies to help tip the scales in their direction when words lose their effect."

"I'm glad we are here, and not in Rome," Marius said.

The legionnaires leaned into each other talking about their fellow soldiers in Rome, and the variables of their next assignments. Rokus stood and rested his hand on, first, Bentet's shoulder, then Thonkrik's.

"You've been through much, friends."

"So, what brings you here in Helvetia?" Thonkrik looked up at Rokus.

"Heading north," Bentet observed. "Are you going home?"

"We shall all travel together," Rokus said, looking back at Marius, who nodded. "These soldiers are escorting me to Betuwe, ensuring my safety."

"Delivering Prince Rokus to his auxiliary," Marius added.

"Protecting a respected commander from his enemies." Bentet nodded.

"Enemies of Rome." Thonkrik stood to look directly at Rokus as he gripped the hilt of his sword.

"All enemies," Marius asserted.

They led their horses back to the track running through the valley. A long narrow cleft among wooded mountains, the valley snaked along several miles, and then ended in a sheer face with no apparent egress.

To a man, they pulled their cloaks up tight around their necks and settled into their saddles with arms tight to their torsos. Rokus thought of the Batavian breeches again.

The sky turned and Rokus smelled the heavy air, and when the wind blustered, he saw the first snowflakes flutter down. Soon, snowfall was heavy, and horse and man lowered their heads against it.

They forged onward toward the valley's end trusting Roman engineering for a way out, for the track they followed was well used and well-maintained, with milestones, and populated with stone bridges; there had to be some ingeniously designed road leading out.

Snow gathered around trees and rocks in wisps and alighted on their eyelashes. The legionnaires lowered their helmet visors for protection from this element, while Bentet reached into his saddlebag to extract another fur cap, which he handed to Rokus. Rokus studied it: it had just been made, having no fixed shape, and new stitching inside. He thanked Bentet, who bowed.

The road turned and dropped into a swale full of rocks and a thread of water already icing over. Marius led them through the maze of pebbles and boulders, the horses snorting protest in clouds of steam, shaking their reins for attention. Each man sank his heels into his horse's sides to confirm their intention to continue; each horse blew disapproval.

As they crested the rise from the rocky channel, a deep music overcame Rokus. Full of sonorous rumbling, it spiraled up from his chest and then merged with a string of pulsating notes drawn from his memory: notes, heard at festivals in Betuwe, created by bows pushed and pulled across a set of strings, flowing into the world as spectral breath. He knew these signals—they had saved his life innumerable times.

He sat up in his saddle, pushing his new hat back, pricking his ears to the snowfall. The riders gained flat ground again, and a stronger wind came across them, and in its rush came unnatural sounds. The party made headway toward the rocky face, now imposing, full of jagged ledges and precipitous formations. They were oblivious to Rokus' vigilance and any rustling beyond, concerned only to find the mysterious pass out of the gorge.

Rokus scanned the trees and rocks alongside the track and listened for information in the wind. Then he saw the horns. Far ahead of them a shape passed from behind a rock to behind a tree. Sequani, he thought, knowing their headdresses with bull's horns or antlers. He pulled back on his reins, slowed, and waited for the first legionnaire to pass alongside. Without taking his eye from the spot, he asked the legionnaire for his bow and arrows. The young soldier consented, reaching across with the bow and his quiver of arrows, following Rokus' gaze down the track. Rokus slung the quiver across his shoulder and then hefted the bow—polished silky, crafted from yew. He caught one end around his ankle and then pulled its opposite end back, pulling the string around the notch. With the bow thus strung, he loaded an arrow and held the assembly at his side.

Presently they arrived at the place he'd seen on the left, a boulder and tree; although there was no one there, he smelled someone. In the breeze came wafts of scat, sweat and offal. Looking left and right, he put himself in the place of an ambusher and so decided the high ground on the right was the best place from which to attack. In a thicket surmounting a knoll there, he located the horns. And as the snowflakes fell at an angle, some came to rest on this Sequanian's own arrow protruding from the tangle of winter branches.

In one quick movement, Rokus turned, raised his bow, drew the string far back, lined the arrow up to a point between the horns, and released. The Sequanian's arrow shivered into a tree trunk high over Marius' head, and the Sequanian stood, emerged thrashing from the thicket, and loomed over the entourage. He gaped, as if words to describe something important eluded him. As the men whipped out their swords in reaction, they watched him, and only when he stumbled forward did they see Rokus' arrow planted in the man's forehead.

NINE

On a Beautiful Road Called Cruelty

From the far reaches down the gorge behind them came the echoing screams of more Sequani. Their piercing cries filled the end of the gorge and rose in such volume that the riders felt the awful imbalance of numbers. Marius kicked his horse, and the others followed suit, lashing left and right and urging their horses to gallop. Rokus, in the back with the last legionnaire and the packhorses, heard the music again and heeled his horse as he looked back.

Men charged them. Riding a menagerie of ponies and draft horses or running furiously afoot, they came as a flood of humanity out of the ravine and filled the road with their turbulence. Some wore headdresses that bore the buck antlers of power and luck; some, like Rokus himself, wore fur caps that trailed strings of talismans, bones, charms and such, while others flew at them with long braids of hair and braided beards framing crazed eyes and shrieking mouths.

They wielded disparate weaponry, a mass of points and blades that bristled like some grotesque beast from their mythology. Then the front row in of them stopped, threw their weight on their back legs, and hurled spears that arced toward Rokus and the legionnaire.

A horrific bellow told Rokus one of the horses had been speared. Turning, he saw the legionnaire roll off of his rearing mount, the end of a spear jutting out of its side, a spew of blood gushing the flank. Rokus' roan spun round, clattering and bucking as she discovered her dying comrade. Rokus consoled her with obdurate control, squeezing her back to the exit path, patting her neck and calling out reassurances. Although the legionnaire had lost his helmet and shield, he had found his feet just as another cloud of spears and slung stones landed around them. Rokus reached down, and the soldier seized the offered arm, and the two of them pulled until they rode the roan paired.

Another roar ensued, and now arrows were shivering into trees and shattering off boulders. At Rokus' command, the horse bolted toward their entourage. The Sequani horses screamed behind them and emitted the fetor of primitive folk; Rokus knew he and the soldier had lost valuable momentum down the track. He worked the roan's sides to pick up speed, and she summoned her strength, reaching forelegs, springing back legs; trees flew by as blurs. He leaned with her, and the soldier, arms wrapped around Rokus' waist, leaned with him. Rokus still heard extra galloping hooves and then the vengeful cry in some Celto-Germanic dialect.

The legionnaire's grip loosened. Rokus glanced over his shoulder to see the instant transition in the legionnaire's eyes—from determination to apology; he gagged and exhaled, and then relinquished his hold on both Rokus and his life, and fell back with an arrow sticking out under his chin.

Now the roan streaked. As missiles whizzed past, they tore down the road away from the horde, gaining on Marius and the others; they were all galloping into the end of the gorge. The valley walls had closed in on them, and the only sight at the end was a hollow just wide enough for a wagon. The horses and men shot toward this aperture as if it were a portal to oblivion. Then Marius disappeared, followed by Thonkrik, Bentet and the four legionnaires. Rokus smacked the hindquarters of one of the packhorses, and it jumped ahead toward the opening, scattering unraveled supplies in its wake. He brought up the rear then, careening on his roan into the hollow to a hundred reports of hooves. Incredibly, the passage into the mountain was paved; and just as all light dimmed to a dangerous state, the road broke into daylight on the other side.

The Roman engineers had completed their mountain design here with a majestic arch fording a cataract that filled the air with a roar of white water. The entourage galloped across. Marius kept up the pace as they descended the track at the base along a rock face. Below them on the right, churning water dropped down rocky steps, pooled in narrow flatlands, then rolled ever downward to a great calm body in the distance. Marius pointed toward it and heeled his horse.

They entered a small meadow to take stock. Marius signaled his men to rest and sent one soldier into the wood with the horses.

"The Sequani are letting us get away. This valley must belong to another tribe." Marius unpacked jerky and passed it around. "The young one?"

Rokus shook his head.

"He was a promising young soldier, a good sort."

"How many men must be lost just for my return to Betuwe?" Rokus swept his arm toward the legionnaires.

"It's their job; some have luck, some don't, some make their own." Marius glared back.

"Marius, I could go on with Thonkrik and Bentet, and then you and your men could return to Lugdunum. No more losses."

"Rokus, you know I have my orders." Marius took off his helmet and ran his fingers back through his hair.

"We could ride overland on the smaller tracks," Rokus said. "While you and your men take the packhorses back."

Thonkrik stepped forward. "We will ensure our prince's safety."

Bentet nodded, tearing off a piece of jerky and stuffing it in his mouth.

"Roman uniforms will attract more trouble the closer we get to the Rhenus," Thonkrik said.

"And you know I will go straight to Betuwe." Rokus put his hand on Marius' shoulder.

"It's all part of the Empire; we shouldn't have any more trouble. That was a rogue group back there, outlaws," Marius said.

"Outlaws? Marius, they may have been defending their territory." Rokus turned away and gestured to the hills and mountains surrounding them.

"Rome has treaties with the tribes from Cisalpine Gaul to the Oceanus Germanicus. They were breaking the pact. The people from here to Augusta Raurica won't bother Roman uniforms," Marius said.

"Three of us can make better progress than the whole group." Rokus turned to Thonkrik and Bentet.

Bentet stepped toward Marius. "And he'll be protected by his countrymen."

"I have my orders and I intend to follow them to the letter."

Rokus raised his hands in assent, looked at Thonkrik and Bentet, then shrugged.

Wind whipped treetops, and the men heard the screech of a hawk.

"I'm going hunting for dinner," Bentet declared.

"I don't want to stop until late this afternoon when we arrive at the lake," Marius announced.

"I can't live on that jerky," said Bentet, taking out his bow.

"We let the horses drink, then we go," Marius pronounced.

"Men, there is probably superb hunting near the lake." Rokus jumped on his saddle and then pointed down the road.

"Right," Marius said.

They passed the wine bag around, each man drinking deeply. The rest saddled again; they moved at a trot, Marius spurring his mount several lengths ahead of the others. After several miles of good road flanked by meadow and grove, the terrain changed. Tall pines pressed the road from either side, their towering whorls blotting out the metal sky. Hands jerked cloaks around necks, and all the men tightened up on their saddles, shrinking themselves against the cold. The ground dropped in stages, changing its verdure in descent to the lake. A carpet of gorse and heather supplanted rocky outcroppings, and ferns swayed in pockets between trees. Wafts of cool air met them at turns; and, with the ripples of the lake clearly visible, they entered a light snowfall, crystalline dots feathering down and sideways.

Rokus cantered up to Marius, settled into his trot, and rode with him in a clamor of silence. Marius fixed on the destination seen between trees, the sheer gray expanse looking more solid than the water it was.

"What did they actually tell you—that I was a revolutionary going to stir up the barbarian hordes?" Rokus said.

Marius did not answer but pulled back to walk his horse.

"I never understood the escort but was willing to go along quietly because I was tired," Rokus continued. "I learned you can get exhausted doing nothing. I saw the escorted journey as a diversion, but now I don't see anything. What's going on?"

"Nothing."

"Something. Talk to me."

"All right. But this doesn't come easily."

"This journey is fraught, and I'm not referring to the weather or attacks from rogue tribesmen.

Marius breathed in deeply and then exhaled steam into the late afternoon.

"All right. Some of the senators convinced Galba to release you so that they could use your experience and talents. They are the same senators who persuaded Nero to bring you in for treason. They now want to place you among the Batavi once again to start training camps. When they learned I had fought beside you in Britannia, they chose me to take you where they wanted you."

"What kind of training?"

"They want to produce militias of Batavian-trained soldiers to use for themselves. Since the Batavi are the best warriors, why not have them, versions of them, to use in a political career? That's how they think. The Batavian prince will transform Germans into Batavian warriors, is their idea."

"I want to laugh, but my mouth is numb, the wind is in my face, and my butt's frozen."

"With your experience and reputation, they think the Batavi would follow your direction," Marius leaned toward Rokus. "The first camp would be built near Castra Vetera. The natives of Germania would be lured with gold, you'd run them through the paces, and the senators would get their private armies—if not for free, then very cheaply."

"Do they really think tribesmen are fools?"

"This is what I know; these are my orders."

"To think Germans would subject themselves to Batavian training, it is dreaming." Rokus looked straight ahead.

"Rokus—Prince Rokus—I truly thought there was some merit. The northern Empire would become more stable, all parts contributing." Marius sat up and passed a hand that took in the vastness before them.

"For the betterment of Rome," Rokus sneered.

"I'm just a soldier." Marius pulled his cloak around his neck and over his legs.

"You think so?"

"I do."

"There are different forms of obedience." Rokus turned to Marius.

Marius gestured toward Rokus, Thonkrik, and Bentet. "The Batavi are highly respected auxiliaries."

"Then why use them so?"

Marius was silent.

"You're in a bind," Rokus said.

Marius lowered his head.

"That's what it feels like."

Rokus frowned. "So the loss of that young soldier means nothing?"

"Just one of the costs of the plan." Marius searched Rokus' face for approbation.

"And the loss of that murdering shit in Arelate?"

"Same."

"But now you think maybe the whole idea is a sham," Rokus said, glaring into Marius' eyes.

"I'm not sure."

"What are they paying you? You know I could leave at any moment."

"I'm hoping you will let me complete my assignment."

"Always the soldier."

"Like I said, this is not easy."

They walked their horses farther, while they allowed silence to consume them. Rokus sorted through anger and suspicion, betrayal and revenge—all gross injustices—and soon the snow gathered on his arms, his brow, and the roan's strong neck.

They came to a much-used shore camp worn clear and flat by innumerable boots and hooves. Scarring the clearing was a fire pit, charcoal and ash and snowflakes surrounded by heavy stones, and ringing it were bench logs making a little amphitheater facing the lapping waves.

"Soldiers, gather wood and get a fire going." Marius jumped off his saddle and embraced the clearing with outstretched arms.

"Going hunting," Bentet announced.

"Go left, I'll go right," Thonkrik added, looping the strap to his quiver over his shoulder.

Marius unleashed the stores and slid them to the ground.

They set up a warm camp with food and such comforts that could be created in mid-November at a mountain lake. Rokus took the horses to nearby grasses, attached their fetters, unsaddled them, and began brushing. He consoled them with warm words, and they nickered and nudged until he finished. Next, he spread saddle blankets over their backs and left them to bunch together for their own warmth.

The fire crackled, and the legionnaires had gathered around it holding palms to flame. They had put up two tents, and Marius had put out tin cups full of straight wine and a mound of biscuits.

Twilight descended.

Rokus was far away; the beat had arrived again as he had brushed the horses' coats, and it had continued fireside as plaintive notes, a kind of call from the mists, and he found solace in the fugitive music. It was the pulse of the tribe expressing the memory of marshland and streaking sky, of the smell of humus, the neigh of horses, grindstones working, the village fires flickering, of children, women, men in collective motion. He was cold but refreshed, full of abstractions—pictures rather than words, impulses rather than plans. He took a cup and raised it toward Marius in thanks. Marius nodded.

Bentet burst into camp hoisting a stick filled with fat birds, already gutted and plucked.

"I hope you have salt for these grouse."

The soldiers made room for him. Bentet fashioned two long Ys out of sticks, piled heavy rocks at their bases next to the fire, and then set the stick of fowl on this apparatus across the flame.

Thonkrik returned from the forest and joined them.

"Here, men, warm yourself," Rokus said handing cups to Bentet and Thronkrik.

Bentet threw it back and offered his empty cup for more. Marius chuckled and poured before going to each legionnaire and filling their cups.

Rokus sipped wine, grinning to the music in his mind, and studied the fiery shimmer of his ring. Blood, stone, he thought, different kinds of strength. Blood in the stone means there is life where none appears.

Marius came to his side. His brow creased, and his hand rested on the hilt of his sword. He rubbed the stubble across his jaw and exhaled. "It's a good assignment. They trust me."

"You are a professional." Rokus sat up.

"I waited a long time. Gods, maybe I'm getting soft."

"You're a Roman soldier and I'm a Batavian warrior. We've seen things. We've had many campaigns. We look for some meaning in it all. Our lives."

"Have more wine."

Marius poured and they clinked cups. After emptying his, Marius returned to the fire.

While Bentet told a story about a mountain feast and the bear that invaded his camp, the bear growing in size with each new scene, Rokus went to the legionnaire who had become the new lead answering to Marius. A young man, he had pale skin and wiry hair still showing the impressions from his helmet's inner strapping. He sat off to the edge looking somber.

"I'm guessing you knew him well, the fallen boy."

The legionnaire nodded, the inner corners of his brows drawn up

"We're from the same village in Narbonensis. Since we were little boys," he murmured.

Rokus sat next to him, silent, while Bentet, drawing pictures in the air, told the men around the fire of how the bear began devouring his foodstuffs and how he prepared his spear so he could defend his roast, bread, dried fruit and new wine. Rokus picked up a twig, toyed with it, and then broke it in half.

"It's always like this, never gets any easier." He studied the young legionnaire's face.

The legionnaire looked back to see if that were really true. Rokus' gaze penetrated him. Then the young man's shoulders began to quake.

"We signed up together. Did—did every—everything, together, like broth... brothers we were," he sobbed.

Something broke loose in the young legionnaire; the partition separating soldiers' training and his humanity shattered. He cried deeply now, letting his emotion fill the night air. Rokus put his arm around his convulsing shoulders.

As the legionnaire wept, Rokus ruminated on the nasty business of not just that day, but of the era. Like a torch at the end of a forest track, its light fitful and weak, the resolution to all this seemed distant and uncertain.

"What is your name?" Rokus asked.

"Gaius Julius Val d'Olonzac," the youth from Narbonesis replied.

"That's a fine name. I'm Rokus."

"But, Civilis?"

"Just, Rokus. It suits me better."

"Val is the name I am usually called. Just, Val."

Rokus smiled.

Val nodded, settled himself, and drew back.

"You are a great warrior and commander." He sniffled, wiping his nose with the back of his hand. "I could learn much from you."

"You have your commander." Rokus nodded toward Marius. "I have a different business far to the north."

Young Val looked down and toyed with some pebbles by his foot. He breathed in deeply and exhaled. He tugged at his cloak.

"I signed on and so have made a commitment, but sometimes I wish it were not so. I could change this for the Celtic plaid and follow you."

"Boy, you are young and still learning your profession. Your commander has noted your skill. But to exchange your red cloak for a plaid one now would be reckless, headstrong. Time will give you a better perspective on things. You would be an asset to any army. Best you be a legionnaire for now—and a sleeping one at that. It's late." Rokus patted his back.

The young legionnaire, drained, leaned back against a log. Rokus pulled his cloak around him and patted his shoulder. The young legionnaire nodded, fluttered his eyes, and slept. Rokus found his bedroll near the fire.

❈

The valley had sharp cliffs along its borders, as if the gods had taken a crooked finger and scratched a massive furrow through the mountains. They had been kind enough to leave ample soil for lush meadows and groves of trees that ran into the foothills before the precipitous heights. In their generosity, they had let run streams full of trout, and every few miles they placed a pond. It was country rich in grasses and trees, game, fowl, and fish.

Rokus studied the land as they pressed on, and by mid-morning he realized the tribal beat had begun again. The blood pulse rhythms and strings of soaring notes discomfited him this time, and his senses piqued. Bird songs and bubbling water carried in the breeze, the winter light dazzled on the high rock, and rustling grasses shone with countless greens. The picture was too perfect; where were the people?

He scanned the reaches for signs of homes, fences, domesticated animals, and other vestiges of settled life. He looked low for pens and pastures, the elevations for trails, caves, mines, shelters—some sign of inhabitants or trade.

As the valley cut south, the road, too, bent, and they followed it into the sun. Behind a row of trees, a pond glimmered and the thick meadow ran to its narrow bank. Arrayed behind the pond were black shapes low to the ground, with posts and beams leaning all around. Marius turned their little caravan toward it. They passed the pond, continuing through a field to the black spot seen from the main track.

It was a farm perhaps. Or it was a meat seller's place. Once. Beams sagged in defeat and the walls had become teeth-like points sticking up from the floors. Smoke twirled up from every surface and recess in the tired fashion of a late stage burn.

Strewn everywhere were the bodies of animals, their butchering interrupted by some incursion. Heaps of hides lay scattered among chunks of meat; glistening surfaces of blood turned dark red and black were now being feasted on by flies. Several wild dogs spied them and backed off unwillingly, but when Rokus raised his arm and grunted and heeled the roan toward them, they retreated into the wood. The carcasses were concentrated around the burning structures, but some served as markers to the remains of a pen, its rails string-like cinders suspended improbably between smoking posts. More carcasses lay in the pen, next to a smashed trough, and around a series of smoldering foundations beyond.

Rokus counted quickly: seventy, eighty lumps of animal sides. Again, the disquiet returned as he wondered where the people were and why they had left this bloody harvest of meat. He walked the roan into the pen. She had her ears back and only advanced with his firm heels. Then he located the gruesome touchstone for this event fuming around them: Two carcasses had human legs and next to them four severed arms and next to them Roman helmets dashed beyond use.

It was an outpost of sorts, but what they saw was the gutted residue of fire and force. The count suggested a century of legionnaires.

"Rokus!" Marius called from the meadow.

His chestnut horse stood in the dappled light beneath three trees. Marius looked into the branches. From three heavy boughs dangled the bodies of three men in legionnaire's uniforms. He could make out the centurion's rank on one of them. They had neither arms nor legs, and their faces had been smashed off.

Thonkrik and Bentet sat their horses in front of the main structure surveying the destruction with stony-faced expressions. The legionnaires stayed in their pairs, as if the formation afforded some protection from the exterminating force that did this. Young Val, however, nudged his horse to be with Rokus, sidling to him to hear his analysis.

"What is this place?" the soldier asked.

"Where revenge happened."

"Are they Romans?"

"All. Look." Rokus pointed to a torso shrouded in the eagle flag and pinned to a tree with a standard issue javelin.

"I think I'm going to be sick."

"Go back to the road."

Marius came to them. He held out three braided cords ending in tassels; one was gold, one red, the other purple.

"A centurion, his optio and tesserarius."

Rokus imagined the overwhelming horde required to wreak the havoc around them.

"This was not a battle, but revenge." Marius scanned the scene shaking his head.

"They were crazy with it," Rokus said.

"Let's go."

Departing, they crossed the meadow toward the road until they came to a gulch. Marius' horse reared. The other horses stopped and recoiled, their eyes wide, their nostrils flaring, and their ears flat. As Marius wrestled with the reins, his horse jumped over the obstacle at its hooves, and then the rest saw the heap of severed heads—all men with the military haircut, all with eyes rolled back looking at nothing. Filling the ravine for a hundred paces to the left, these men's identities were piled randomly as rocks might be.

For several miles it was a ride devoid of talk. The men sat slumped in saddles looking down the road, while the animals carried their loads quietly, occasionally shaking a bridle or swinging a tail at flies.

Rokus was blind to the scenic vale now, numb to compassion, stoic. The lush beauty he had seen before had been altered; it was now a sylvan road tainted with cruelty. As his eye studied its bucolic expanse, he saw places to hide, places from which to attack, places to train warriors and horses—all loci transformed to destructive purpose rather than something more fruitful.

He studied his ring; where there is blood in stone, there is hope in the liquid sheen.

The road dropped into a long coulee that graduated a mile on into a wider, deeper trough. This valley within a valley was a good killing field, Rokus thought, but he admonished himself for his disenchantment. They walked on, taking the drop in elevation easily, crossing the lowland slowly, entering the trough bewitched by the memory of that mayhem.

"There is a campsite up ahead," said Marius rolling a scroll map and stuffing it inside his hauberk.

Around a turn in the road they saw the orchard and the additions to the natural set of trees. Randomly spaced and facing all points were crucifixes with bodies hanging on them. They rode toward these executions out of a sense of duty, as if their gazes might acknowledge the end of lives taken so. They sat their horses and looked at the crude assemblies of post and transom and the tribesmen who had struggled against the ropes and endured the ripping nails that held them there. Thrashing marked all the bodies; the men who had inhabited them had suffered further humiliation with their nakedness.

Rokus surveyed the setting to make sense of it. The orchard had been a camp; fire pits dotted the area, and the scorched poles of shelters, long cooled, stuck up from the ground obscenely, their former walls piles of ashes. In the meadow surrounding the orchard, lumps of men and women lay scattered as if the sky had rained them down on a dark and treacherous day. Their bodies had been hacked and now were in decay, and the autumn air swirling over them carried rot and misery. Men's bodies populated the central part of the orchard; elder men and women made a gruesome crescent around these, and heading toward the cover of foothills, women and children lay sprawled.

Rokus had seen many Roman spectacles. In some, death was the entertaining endgame of ritual combat; in others, the legions had systematically exterminated whole tribes to the last child in order to remove future opposition and set example. In still others, the dauntless files of legionnaires overran outnumbered and outclassed barbarians and relished their roles as victors, setting their own examples far from the commanders' eyes. He rubbed his eye, having seen too much that day.

While Marius and the legionnaires explored the scene, Rokus reeled his roan toward a blackened shelter. He dismounted and entered its perimeter of cinders, imagining the terror therein once the Romans began their methodical destruction. At his feet there was a shard in the rubble; he picked it up. It was a ceramic piece of bowl or cup, glazed blue and green with a linear pattern resembling rolling clouds or a woman's flowing hair or sea waves or maybe just exuberance. He blew the ash off it, rubbed it to a shine and polished it on his tunic, and then put it in his pocket with the hand wearing the bloodstone ring.

"Let's move on." Marius thrust the blade of his hand forward.

Rokus studied the grave faces of the young legionnaires. Young Val stared back at him, reconciling the fateful balance of scales he'd seen that day. Would that the world offered his generation something better, Rokus thought.

They gathered on the road a thousand paces from crucifixes and ruins and tribal folk cut down. The horses shook their reins, anxious to move.

"Let's leave this valley now. It's not right. Looks like it will take half a day. Ready?" Rokus kneed the roan onward.

"We must move to the north now." Val turned to his fellow soldiers and fell in behind Rokus.

Thonkrik and Bentet nodded approval. Marius drew up next to Rokus and spit to the ground.

TEN
In Genava, Helvetia, a Lakeside Town

The road climbed in a series of switchbacks that took the party into the higher country. The journey through chasms of radiant light and opaque shadow, towering peaks covered with snow, and roads carved into steep hills had put them at ease. Their voices remained subdued, as if their reticence conferred honor on the Roman and tribal dead.

Late in the day, Genava appeared in the distance as an expanse of pitched roofs and gates arranged around the sweeping edge of the lake. The lake itself was an ocean to their eyes, stretching into the haze of day.

They entered the town that welcomed them with straight and narrow streets, neat storefronts, and sparkling order in every direction. They passed through it and turned north at the main square; along the way, people stopped to look at them, decoding the grime of overland travel, the tribal furs and Roman uniforms, the forbearance etched into brows.

The garrison rose from the bank. It had walls of stone and buildings arranged on a grid. Around it ran deep double ditches with sharpened stakes imbedded close to the perimeter walls.

The corner towers were armed with bolt launchers, big bows mounted on fat wooden braces, aimed at the roads near and far.

The party of horsemen walked through the west gate, receiving pass from the guards who scrutinized Marius' orders then saluted him. Rokus, eager to continue north to Augusta Raurica, the Rhenus River and home, focused on immediate things: clean weapons, oil leathers, shine metals, bathe, eat, drink. Thonkrik and Bentet scanned the grounds for men who might know of their flight. The legionnaires followed, led by Val, who sat straight in his saddle despite being road weary and covered with dust.

Marius tied his horse to a post outside an office, went in, and returned to lead the legionnaires to their quarters. At one end of the fort, an optio drilled a small squad of soldiers, and scattered throughout, legionnaires cleaned equipment, wheeled barrows of grain, groomed horses, and rode out of the gate ten at a time. Smoke swirled up from the livery, joining that of the canteen and the smoldering strands coiling up from chimneys on every building.

"I don't feel safe here." Thonkrik's eyes darted left and right.

"No one knows," Rokus consoled. "You're far from men who'd recognize you."

"How long are we staying?" Bentet asked, unlashing his saddlebag.

"Long enough to rest or replace the horses and get cleaned up is my guess." Rokus surveyed the fort from the barracks, noting fastidious trappings and judicious care of walls and roofs.

"We should leave now," Bentet blurted.

"Stay," Rokus said with an even tone, part command, part entreaty.

"He's right, Rokus. We're not safe until we get to Betuwe." Thonkrik stopped the loosening of his saddle's bellyband.

"Please stay with me."

They took bunks in the legionnaires' quarters, as Thonkrik and Bentet looked in corners and out of windows.

"I don't like this," Bentet announced.

"Just wait a while," Rokus said.

He left the quarters and walked along the arcade toward the principia. He found the veteran there, distress on his face.

"We're going for a meal in town," Rokus announced.

"They're serving in the canteen in twenty minutes," Marius offered.

"We want something different. Join us."

"I want you to stay here."

"We'd do better to find something other than canteen food." Rokus grew impatient.

"You shouldn't go into the town," Marius declared, approaching him.

"Maybe I'll agitate the Helvetii, hand out the swords I hide under my saddle." Rokus stepped toward Marius while glaring at him.

"Not that."

"Maybe I'll become a brigand on the roads of Helvetia. Form a militia, bond with the Marcomanni, start raiding villages. "

"Rokus."

"We just want to get a decent meal, Marius. Join us."

"I don't want any more trouble." Marius looked out the window.

"Neither do I."

"The others." Marius glanced toward the barracks. "They complicate things."

"Follow your orders. You're escorting me safely back to my auxiliary command in Germania."

"But—they've deserted." Marius spun around gripping the hilt of his belted sword.

"Not your concern."

"I should report them to the commander here." Marius gestured to the back office.

"And what would that serve?" Rokus raised his voice.

"Justice. They pledged allegiance to Rome."

"You heard what happened. Would you stay for more?"

"Rokus, you wear the Roman tunic. You're a Roman citizen. It's different. They are outsiders, tribesmen from the edge of the empire. They have to remember what Rome has done for them, what Rome is."

"Gods, Marius, listen to you. I'm their tribesman." Rokus threw up his hands.

"It puts my detail in jeopardy having them along." Marius snapped.

"What did you say when you checked in?"

"That they were kinsmen of my charge, met along the way to your home."

"Good. Then we shall go into town."

"Rokus…" Marius pleaded.

They ducked to enter a tavern that consisted of two great rooms joined perpendicularly. Long planks on support legs ran their lengths, and, many and varied folk sat on benches eating, drinking, spilling news and gossip like magpies. Two men dished up platters of bits of roasted meat and gravy from one end, smoke rising from hot coals and a cauldron; and, at the other, a group of musicians played lyres, zithers, rebabs, pipes and a bodhrán. The assorted strings, plucked and squealing with bows and urged on with the deep thumping drum, conjured for Rokus Batavian land black with minerals, green with supple grass, and gray with the tumbling clouds from the sea; in it he heard water birds crying, the sweet low of cows, and the crackle of the hearth.

They took a bench in the middle, the plank shiny with oils and spillage over years, incised with Latin names like crude petroglyphs. A Helvetian girl came to them and spoke with faltering Latin learned from the garrison, and they ordered platters, with steins of beer. She was pretty, tall, blue-eyed, with waves of blond hair down her back. Their gazes followed her to the sideboard, as she drew their beer from an oak cask. She slammed the vessels on their plank, then hurried to others who called to her.

"Val has been on the road far too long." Rokus looked at the young soldier whose gaze was still riveted on the girl.

Marius ran his hand over Val's head and smiled.

"It will take four days to Augusta Raurica, if we keep moving," Marius announced.

"The sooner the better." Rokus looked each of his countrymen in the eye.

"Wait a minute. Things are looking just fine here." Thonkrik swatted young Val's arm, dislodging him from his reverie. "Right, lad?"

Val remained fixated on the girl.

Marius poured and held his stein out. "To our continued safe journey," he said without irony, to which they held up theirs to clink. They were thirsty, and they poured more.

The girl brought platters of meat and gravy and chunks of crude brown bread. She returned with a bowl of something—coagulated fruit mixed with crusts of bread; it smelled fermented, with the smell of both sweet and sour discard. They poked it.

"I wonder where the women are." Bentet spoke with his mouth full.

"Follow your groin, big man," Thonkrik said.

"Don't get into any trouble, men," Marius warned. He paused and then added, "but if you find them, let me know where they are." The men laughed together.

"She's like a goddess," Val murmured.

"He's smitten".

"Cock in the roost."

"She's busy, boy."

"She's beautiful," Val declared.

As the girl cleared their platters, Val watched her with longing and admiration. She smiled at him. Holding the stack of platters, she looked at Rokus, who pointed at their steins, and she nodded.

A tall narrow man stepped forward from the corner and bowed. He carried three apples in his long fingers. His face was a mask of tiny veins burst under his skin. Shifting back and forth, he adjusted his stance as if he didn't want to fall from a high place. Then he regarded the audience dully and wiped his shiny lips with the back of his hand.

The girl brought more beer, and the travelers drank with zeal.

The juggler's hands went to work, tossing two apples aloft, then bisecting their trajectories with the third. He juggled like a magician, entrancing all with his speed and dexterity. A man in the shadows tossed him a fourth apple, which he incorporated into the routine. He whirred on, effortlessly, flawlessly, with arms and hands athletic and precise. Then a fifth apple came his way, and that one, too, became part of the whole.

Rokus and the men tried to follow one apple but kept getting confused and shifted to another.

"Would you look at that," Bentet said, elbowing Thonkrik.

Finally the juggler threw one apple after another into the space above him. He thrust his hips while pulling an oversized pocket wide, letting the pocket swallow one, two, three, four, five apples from above. He looked sheepish and then bowed.

One, then three, then an entire bench applauded, and then the whole crowd cheered for the juggler. Lean lives of work and obeisance found release in the juggled fruit, and each man cheered at the summary: five things thrown and caught, five things dropped into a pocket clean. It declared talent and control, like straight furrows, a dovetail joint, well wrought cooking pots, or a precise stone wall.

Rokus lost interest. He drifted back to Betuwe where he planted a garden for the first time. He placed seeds just below the surface of the soil he'd worked and nudged dirt over them like nature's blanket, and then he dripped water from a cup onto them until his row of plantings was a series of neat blotches and expectations. All the while he listened to the music of his land, the plucked strings in rhythm to the arcing melody achieved by some ephemeral bowman more magus than man.

"I've had enough of this." Rokus stood and pulled his cloak over his shoulders. "Going for a walk." His fingers toyed with the ceramic shard in his pocket.

Then he realized he had been squeezing it in his palm since the juggler's act had begun. With a nod to Marius, he stepped into the November evening, flurries and bleakness all around.

He vowed to get breeches and then strode across the bridge, leaning over the rail to look at the metallic water already transporting chunks of ice toward Gallia. He turned toward the west gate and lowered his head against the wind. Fifty paces behind him, a legionnaire stayed in the shadows, ducking under eaves and behind columns, darting behind walls and bridge posts, following Rokus out of the town limits.

ELEVEN

Leaving Genava; the Road to Lousonna, Winter Sets In

"What are you thinking, Marius?" Rokus spoke tersely, his fists slamming the air at his sides. "I am not a criminal."

Marius rolled over in his blankets, propped himself up on an elbow, and considered the Batavian. "Just wanted to keep an eye on you."

"Keep an eye on me? Make sure I didn't escape is more like it."

"For your safety."

Rokus charged the Roman's bed, wrenched the covers off, and seized his tunic. He shook Marius once, gripping the cloth as he spoke.

"I gave you my word. Do you know what a Batavian's word means? Do you have any idea how our promise is sacred?"

"My orders are to bring you to Betuwe."

"To blazes with your orders." Rokus released him.

"Did you kill him?"

"Kill a legionnaire following stupid orders?"

"Did you kill him?"

"No. He's still out there, wandering through wood and field looking for the disappearing Batavian."

"I'm glad you didn't kill him."

Rokus grunted his disgust and stomped out of the barracks, while Thonkrik and Bentet looked on. They reached for their scabbards, leaning them against their bed frames, and rolled over to sleep lightly the remaining part of the night.

Rokus walked through the moonlight. The long buildings of the fort lined the main street, and the night watch walked the stockade with muffled footfalls. Horses snuffed in the distance; men snored. At the central intersection, he turned toward the gate. Cold and dark, the night spoke to him in hushed tones; it coaxed him, a plea to action. He drew in lungs full and felt some exhilaration, then stood before the guards with their crossed spears.

"I can't sleep."

"No one is to leave without papers or rank," said one of the guards.

"Listen, puppy," Rokus growled, transforming the cold air in his lungs into a furnace of irritation. "I will walk to see the dawn from the river."

"Sir," the guard said blocking the passage.

"Step aside." Rokus lost sight of the men in his cloud of displeasure. For the moment, he stood in his mind lording over the Batavian lands, waving his staff and watching his people at chores, laughing in groups, or huddled around crocks set on coals. Veleda and his sages and counselors flanked him, and he knew that his command would ripple through his court and into the countryside bringing good effect and prosperity. "Let me pass."

They held their places; Rokus stood motionless. Then the strains of music entered his mind, the quiet pulse of drum and arcing melody pulled by a bow and the strum of tight strings. He rolled the ceramic shard in his pocket, watched the guards, and then smiled.

"If you please," Rokus said simply.

There was a kind of shudder in them. Then the spokesman stepped aside, as did his companion, and both saluted.

Rokus walked the outlying roads and paths for hours without direction; and as the darkness softened, he came back into the town and crossed to the marina. Most of the fisher boats were out on Lacus Lemanus, their sails flecking the distant haze. Shops began to open, shutters swung to, doors invited entrance. Shopkeepers and marketers arranged goods on tables out front; braziers crackled and smoked in the morning air.

"There," Thonkrik called.

Rokus turned to see his fellow Batavians approach in their furs. They grinned; he admired the square Batavian jaws, the clear eyes, the ruddy skin radiating health.

"Countrymen."

"Have you eaten?" Bentet asked.

Rokus shook his head. They entered a shop, and Bentet bought a small loaf of black bread for each of them as well as a cut of smoked pork.

"I wonder if it's possible to get a piece of fruit in Genava," Rokus said.

Thonkrik found a shop on the next street and returned with a selection of raisins and dried figs and dates. Rokus chewed slowly savoring the goodness of the sugars and textures. They meandered through streets and came out on the waterfront which was now receiving boats with decks glistening with fish, the fishermen moving efficiently as they tied down and carried bins ashore.

"Genava isn't bad at all." Bentet chewed with pleasure through stuffed cheeks. .

"They have a lot of food."

Thonkrik threw his head back in a silent laugh and then looked down on the stocky man as if he were a gift to the human race. Rokus observed this and loved them for it.

They turned away from the lakefront and headed to the main intersection where they could turn north toward the garrison. Rokus, now determined to procure breeches, scanned the streets for a tailor. After three blocks, there was a sign depicting a needle and thread spiraling around scissors.

"Can you give me a few denarii?" he asked.

Thonkrik obliged. Rokus took the coins and dropped them in his pocket where they jingled next to the shard.

"Look at that," he said.

Thonkrik and Bentet followed his gaze down the street. Fumbling with his tunic and trailing his cloak, Val scrambled through the streets. His bootstraps flew with his strides, and his hair stuck out in all directions. For all his haste, he still wore an expression of utter contentment. They met at the intersection.

The Batavians watched the young soldier without speaking. Bentet's grin stretched across his round face, while Thonkrik's brown eyes gleamed with collusion.

"The blonde servant girl," Rokus said with a grin.

Val nodded repeatedly, as he stood on one foot, fastened his boots, fixed his belt, and teetered before them. He gushed a kind of silly glee, part joy, part smugness, and returned their looks, the holy fool.

"Your first?" Thonkrik asked.

Val jerked his head up and down again, grinning.

"Better go, you're late," said Rokus.

They watched him struggle down the street organizing his parts for presentation.

"First one is always the sweetest." Thonkrik rested his hands on his hips.

"You think so?" Rokus murmured

They walked abreast to the next street. Rokus pointed to the tailor's sign and left them.

He entered the shop, the inside of which was covered with countless pieces of draped cloth, folded piles, swatches strewn about. The tailor stood at a worktable snipping cloth as Rokus stepped in and appeared at Rokus' chest before the Batavian had a moment to survey the establishment. He was a mole of a man, wiry and stooped, with squinting eyes and hands clinched under his chin as if he were begging. The tailor worked his teeth with his tongue. "May I help you, sir?" he asked with accented Latin.

"Breeches."

The mole scurried back among the samples, piled up like cairns, and rummaged among them, ticking off with grunts the rejects and possible choices. He emerged with a selection.

"What about these?" he said wetting his prominent front teeth.

Rokus felt several cloths, butternut colored stuff, some stripes, a plaid, all course weaves, and wools. He inhaled deeply, smelling tannin and the lanolin of fresh yarn. He stepped away, and explored the rows of cloth while the tailor watched him. Rokus looked back, and the tailor nodded approval enthusiastically, wringing his hands and wetting his front teeth.

The door opened and a man rushed in. He wore the Roman tunic and hairstyle but spoke Helvetian. The mole pulled at his elbow and they scurried behind a loom, both talking at once. Rokus listened to the heat of their conference, the Helvetian delivering news, the tailor finding relevance in every phrase. The Helvetian transmitted anxiety; the tailor empathized and consoled. Finally, satisfied, the Helvetian left.

The tailor returned to Rokus, caressing fabrics as he passed them. He faced Rokus, but the Batavian wasn't sure the tailor could even see him out of those squinched eyes. The tailor moved his head up and down measuring Rokus' size and the amount of fabric it would take to clothe him.

"Lost an eye, eh?" he said wetting his teeth.

Rokus touched the patch covering the socket.

"Pity," the tailor muttered. "Gallia?"

Rokus searched the mole's face for information.

"You're not from this region, correct?" the tailor asked.

"Can you make me some breeches in a couple of hours?"

"Of course," the tailor responded, dashing to the door, opening it, looking up and down the street, then closing it again.

"I'm interrupting something. Never mind." Rokus watched the man at his shop door.

"So where are you from?" The tailor composed himself and assessed Rokus.

"The north."

"Thought so. Belgica or Lugdunensis."

"Expecting someone?"

"The tax collector. They've raised our taxes twice in the last five months. Every week it seems, a new edict. They claim mine are due, again."

He opened the door again, stuck his head out, glanced around, and slammed the door.

"He should come around this morning."

Rokus paused, letting the uneasiness dissolve.

"The breeches?" Rokus presented himself.

"Of course. The material?"

Rokus held out a deer hide, supple and sturdy. What about this?"

"Two denarii."

"How about a jacket with it? For three denarii."

The man pulled out a measuring tape and accosted Rokus, noting the dimensions of his arms, shoulders, chest, waist, and legs. "This will pay my taxes," he said, "and I will stay in business that much longer."

"Who was that?"

"Brother-in-law. Owns a pottery. They're driving him out of business with these taxes."

"The Roman way."

"I don't know what's better, Roman peace and taxes or Celtic wars."

"You don't have much choice."

"You're right about that, but some do."

"Some?"

The tailor checked the street again and came back to Rokus' side. "The Sequani have mobilized. I've heard they've done battle."

"You can't believe everything."

"Whatever the Sequani do, it will just increase our taxes. I hate it."

"Here, pay your taxes," said Rokus, dropping the coins in the man's palm. "I'll be back."

"Thank you, thank you," said the mole, licking his lips and rubbing the coins between his hands while he scuttled into the recess of his shop.

Rokus walked down the street with commerce all about. Fat horses pulled carts, men carried parcels, boys led goats and sheep on leashes, and women flitted from shop to shop like bees on blossoms. Smoke streamed up from fire pits and braziers, and punctuating the bustle were the regular clangs of the smith's hammer.

Rokus stood on the bridge over the last finger of lake, water flowing away from Lacus Lemanus west toward Lugdunum. A girl scampered by with a basket of loaves. He stopped her and offered a small coin. She took it, examined its sides, smiled, and pushed it into a pocket. He took the loaf she gave him and watched her run off, her braids dancing on her shoulders and her tunic fluttering. He savored the bread as he walked along the southern shore, venturing several miles from the town, studying it in the morning dazzle reflecting off the blue slate surface of the vast lake.

Across the lake, small farms dotted the plain and low hills, their patches of brown and pale green rolling up to the forest line. A bank of gray clouds rested on the hilltops, and in that curtain of gloom, he observed the turbulence that would beset their journey. He threw stones into the water and then skipped the flat ones he found. Finally, he returned to Genava drinking in the details of shore and lake, sky and land.

Rokus knocked on the tailor's door and pushed it open. His leather breeches lay on the table next to his jacket, the deerskins transformed into human shape, supple yet sturdy. Then the music arrived like a beating heart, its drum and bowed strings working underneath the soaring flute. Cold air shot up the back of his neck, and his entire being flushed to alert. His music rose in him and gave notice that harm was present.

He called hello and surveyed the place. Several piles of cloth had been toppled, and the chair behind the table was on its side. Men's commands resounded from the back.

Jumping behind the worktable, he saw through two farther doorways four men surrounding the mole, whose slits darted from one to the other. The tailor's hands pinched at some fugitive thing below his chin, and he flinched as if awaiting a blow.

"What's going on here?" Rokus' eye darted back and forth.

"Just some business, just some business," the tailor explained, his voice strained with trepidation.

The men in togas were carrion wolves slaking appetites, Roman administers come to exact tribute. They hunched over the mole to emphasize his defenselessness; they gnawed their demands and clawed at his daily labors with cold words about the law. The tailor nodded more than he needed to.

"Leave us, sir—we haven't finished here," their leader demanded.

"I believe you are finished. Shove off." Rokus strove to measure his voice.

They turned at once. The leader leered at him, and his second lowered the ledger in his hands in preparation of something. The two others, enforcers, stood squarely, baring teeth.

"This man has work to do," Rokus said.

"This man has taxes to pay," the lead toga asserted.

The tailor nodded and wrung his hands, shooting glances from Rokus to the leather bag tied to the lead's wrist. Definitively, he pointed to the bag and then worked his tongue behind his lips.

"I paid my taxes, paid them," he said, emboldened.

The leader swung round and seized the tailor's tunic.

"You paid last year's amount. The rate has increased for fabricators."

Rokus stepped toward the group; the enforcers blocked him.

"This is an honest man, a workingman. Let him do his business."

"This is no concern of yours, citizen. Go about your business and leave us."

"I will follow you out the door," Rokus announced.

The lead toga threw the tailor back. "Let's get on with it," he uttered to the other men, as if precipitating an execution.

The enforcers rushed Rokus, clamping his arms and throttling him. Rokus wrestled them, but they countered his moves, and he realized they were special warriors, trained for patrols, spying, persuading the taxed. He was overmatched. He relaxed in their clutches, and they flung him into the worktable. But Rokus caught himself mid-flight and landed squarely. Turning to them, he set himself ready. They paused. He heard the drum thumping and the bowed melody, and he felt the sea breeze at his back and smelled the salt air and Batavian loam; then, thus accoutered, he mastered his defense and waited.

They fell upon him with arms outstretched. He crouched low and then sprang at them from below with his forearms cutting into them. One took a blow to the neck and faltered, the other to the nose and recoiled. Without hesitation, Rokus repeated the same precision with a reverse elbow jab, dashing the bleeding nose in the temple. The man dropped. Then Rokus set upon the second enforcer. The fury thus summoned aroused a collective revenge in him, and so the first punch was for the tailor, the second for the smith down the street, the third for the parents of the bread girl, the fourth for the tavern owner, the fifth for his servant girl—and so Rokus mauled the man until the town of Genava had been restored in his seething mind and his own hands throbbed with shredded skin. He couldn't stop. He turned and kicked the downed man whose broken nose spattered blood still and whose eyes fluttered just back to life. Rokus' boot caught him full in the face, and his head jerked back as if without link to his frame. Rokus kicked him again. Turning to the other, who slumped, stupefied and bleeding from purple welts, nostrils, and lips that puffed with deformity, he leveled his boot and shot his hobnail sole crushing him against the wall.

Then Rokus faced the tax collector and his second, who both watched with dumfounded expressions, as if some foreign language came at them and they were required to comprehend it.

"Have you paid your taxes, tailor?" said Rokus, panting.

The tailor nodded and pinched the space below his chin.

"And you have received his taxes in your little bag there?" he said to the pair of togas.

"He has paid them, yes."

Rokus' chest heaved, and he ran his hand back through his hair. His eye patch had fallen round his neck, and he repositioned it.

"And the surcharge for this new period?" Rokus studied their Roman faces and the face of the tailor. "Was there an increase as you claimed? Or was that for your own pocket, services rendered, so to speak?"

"He's square," the taxman said.

"So you lied, and were cheating him out of his money?"

Revealed, the Romans cowered before Rokus. The taxman looked him over: his mangled hands, his splattered tunic, his heaving chest, his eye that cut to the core, as if to dig out some justice from the tissue of the Roman's temperament.

Rokus stepped aside and nodded at the door to the street. The two Romans hesitated and then inched passed him. They were too slow, because Rokus reconsidered. Their timidity and smallness made the Empire that much larger and mean; they were stupid minions serving callous law. Rokus raised his arm and smashed it on them one after the other. "Shame," he exhaled. "Get out," and kicked them in the backsides. They scrambled away terror-stricken.

The tailor shuffled over to the enforcers who lay amidst their groans and brokenness.

"You shouldn't have done that. Shouldn't have done that. Others will be back. Back."

Rokus knew he was right. He removed the rest of his coins and gave them to the tailor, who took them as if they were overdue.

"I'll put on my new garments."

"Shouldn't have done this," the tailor said, gesturing to the downed enforcers.

Rokus took the leathers and went to the back. When he emerged from the shadow, he had been transformed into an auxiliary scout or special guard—or Batavian prince. He felt it, presenting himself with the jacket covering much of his tunic and the new breeches running from under his tunic to his boots, all well cut and finely stitched; he stood tall.

Rokus grabbed the enforcers' arms, and pulled them across the floor. He sat them, bewildered and bleeding, and nudged them, one at a time, out the door.

"Their boss can pick them up later."

"Don't like this at all," the tailor whined.

"Thank you for your quick service."

"At all."

❖

Mid-morning, Marius led horses and men in a single line out the west gate and over the river. The animals were full of grass and grain and prancing sassy, snorting and chuffing as they snaked through the town. The men held tight and rode with form, settling into their horses' rhythms, looking straight ahead as the town folk watched them.

Down the block smoke rose as a solid column above the rooftops. They came to its burning source, the tailor's shop, and to a man they turned to consider the flickering in the windows; the sizzling tongues climbing the dry-wood framing, devouring fiber and wind for sustenance; and the merchant's sign, a powerless offering to obstruction. Rokus halted the roan as the blazing fingers snatched the sign from its metal wall trestle and flung it to the feet of the mole standing there pinching his chin.

The train turned on the east road, a track pounded by hooves and feet since before seeds were sown in the lakeside fields, when the caves in the escarpments above them were reliable shelters to live in and not just places from which to watch sheep graze, when flint blades fashioned yew sticks into spears that some naked species threw at fish forms gliding through shifting shallows. They pushed onward in a clatter of hooves, stomping yet another age into the dirt, scarring forever the passage from Genava to Lousonna, and becoming, unbeknownst to each of them, ingenuous players in the sweep of history.

They came to Equestris and halted in front of the stone wall and gate. Roman helmets could be seen traversing the parapet, soldiers' long javelins poking skyward and bits of red cape flashing through openings of the rampart. Marius studied the disposition of his retinue, and, so satisfied that they were hardy, ordered the ride to pass the town and follow the long shore track eastward. They rode for two more hours as the air grew laden with winter. At a meadow with fallen trees, saw cuts and dust everywhere, Marius dismounted and told young Val to pull out jerky and biscuit from the stores while the other legionnaires walked horses to the lakeshore.

"No, I'll keep her here," Rokus explained when a soldier gripped the roan's bridle, and Rokus walked her to a little stream that had pooled behind rocks. She drank while he stroked her flank.

The cloudbank towered in the north sky now, a threatening edifice churning with streaks and opacity. The air was heavy, and flurries had started, whirling white commas cast from on high.

They pulled up their cloaks watching steam from their mouths and the horses' as well.

Marius approached with shiny hauberk and helmet, flashing red cape and tooled scabbard with its pommel ornate in silver interlacing. Hands on hips, he examined Rokus.

"You don't look Roman that way."

"I don't feel Roman."

"Barbarians wear those breeches."

Rokus looked at him, searching for the common ground of their undertaking, and, reaching impasse, turned back to his business stroking the roan and bestowing compliments on her. Marius backed away as if Rokus were some harmful foe and went to divide the food for lunch.

While Rokus sat in the grasses and pulled the jerky apart, Thonkrik came to him pointing down the road.

"Batavi," he said.

Four horsemen approached at a canter, their mounts sleek, their mien rustic. He recognized the oval shields and the fur cloaks and the élan of the riders, the bearing unique to their tribe. The riders came upon them, all dancing hooves, horses' mouths agape with bits; the riders gripping reins, leaning back and heeling with finesse. They sat their horses to talk to Rokus, who stood in the middle of the road in greeting.

"I don't believe it!" cried one rider with high collar and cloak, fur hat and stole. "Prince Rokus, free at last."

"Menfrid, welcome. And who else do we have? Folkbern, Liuppo and Gerulf!" called Rokus.

He surveyed their familiar aspects and grinned. As their horses trotted, the riders glided easily in their saddles. Their clothes and furs, colors and textures were rich with distinction, a melding of nature and the art of the loom, and the brightness of their countenances illuminated memory and the moment.

"We come from the hunting grounds to the south." Menfrid pointed back to the snowy caps on the jagged range hanging above the haze.

The lunch party formed a circle around the riders. They studied the paraphernalia of the hunt and battle that were cinched to the horses' sides. Spears and bows, quivers and slings, and swords of different lengths stuck up from their places at saddle. Bentet, mouth full, stepped forward garbling his own welcome and requests for news from both the north and south.

Menfrid bellowed, "We've heard much, but it would take a mighty mug of beer to remember it all!"

"We have wine," offered Marius.

"Sit with us," Thonkrik said, "and rest your bones."

Folkbern stroked his bristled chin and then slapped his hands on his thighs.

"Gods, it is great to see you, Rokus, we've all been afraid you shared the fate of Habo, that is, Claudius Paulus. But here you are."

"I am free and returning to Batuwe," Rokus said, glancing over to Marius. "And my brother is avenged."

"Your eye, prince?" Folkbern leaned to examine Rokus' face.

"The small price for revenge." Rokus touched the strap to his patch.

"And the killer's eyes are permanently closed," Liuppo said.

"Your people await you; your father is quite ill," Menfrid said.

Liuppo dismounted, pulled off his felt cap and scratched at his bald scalp. "Where's that wine?" he asked and then unbuckled a wide belt with loops holding knives and slings, metal tools designed to clutch and snip.

The others unhorsed, their mounts stamping, sleek with sweat and salty froth at the straps. The Batavi were thick, wearing bear and wolf fur and woven breeches, either plaid or broadly striped, and Roman legionnaires' boots. Their hats bespoke their tastes: a practical fur dome like Rokus wore; a soft beret; a bronze helmet from Germania; a wolf's head with snout and teeth, quartz eyes, pricked ears. But massive fur cloaks draped them all, now standing amid the Romans like some new genus emerged from the deep forests of Germania.

"This way," Marius instructed, leading them to the stores and makeshift table of a tree stump. He put out metal cups and filled them from a leather wine bag.

"What do you hear?" Bentet asked, glancing at Thonkrik. "Anything from the northeast?"

"Not much. We did come upon a party of Roman horse making way to Rome from Germania," Folkbern said. "They were riding to support Otho."

"Otho?" Marius exclaimed.

"Former governor of Lusitania. He's in Rome stirring it up. Some say he wants the Emperor's throne. The legions love him, though; he understands them."

"He's generous," Menfrid added. "One of them told of the riches available with a show of allegiance to Otho."

"And you didn't join them? You are auxiliary, aren't you?" Marius asked.

Bentet gulped and ate more biscuit and went round topping up cups.

"We did not," Menfrid said. "We seek something else after being with the Legio XIII Gemina in Vindonissa."

"Rome has cut benefits," Folkbern explained.

"And added mindless detail—digging trenches, building walls, setting pylons in rivers," Liuppo said..

"But it has always been so." Marius looked at them with suspicion.

Gerulf stepped forward. He was an exemplar of a Batavian warrior: solid, trim, erect, a shining youth with experience, open and circumspect. He removed the wolf's head and scratched his thick hair, then fingered a large garnet amulet set in silver.

"Not for Batavi. We are auxiliary to legionnaires who do battle, not work beside slaves constructing whimsical things for generals. Isn't that right, uncle? We left our positions to return home."

"Yes, nephew," Folkbern said. "We set out for Betuwe a month ago. Thought to make the solstice festival after trading meat and pelts for awhile."

"You will come with us," Rokus said. "Won't you?"

"I am for it." Liuppo drank his cup.

"I, too," said Gerulf, finishing his wine.

"To Betuwe." Folkbern drank, adding, "I am for this as well."

Bentet took the wine bag from Marius and made the rounds while Marius stood absorbed in the prospect.

"Wait," he declared.

Then he looked them over as he digested this proposal. The Batavi returned his scrutiny, and for a long minute a gulf of silence separated them. As the snow flurry descended, they cinched their cloaks around their necks. Marius squeezed the hilt of his sword.

"Our train grows longer every day," he said finally, and they held up their cups to toast to his agreement.

They restored the cups in packs on horses and fell in line down the north shore of Lacus Lemanus, skirting the few farms and pastures dotted with sheep and goats and pigs and horses. The road changed from dirt to stone, the Roman engineers laying blocks and fillers with precision, so that their numerous hooves clattered as a din that echoed in the groves they passed and trailed over the hills. They eventually paired to talk, except the legionnaires who, trained so, maintained formation and silence.

The creation overhead grew in complexity, its gray opacity battling the mean streaks of black, and soon lashed them with furious hail that hurt and spooked the horses and drove them to the cover of farmers' trees. After watching the ice balls explode in the naked branches and bounce all around them, they set forth through the hard snowfall angling from the southern high country.

When Lousonna appeared along the ashen shore, they heeled their horses, and collectively their pace quickened; man and beast sought cover and warmth and food. They entered the garrison with quick salutes, and while Marius checked with the commander, the others dismounted and pulled the ice off their brows and crammed their hands under their arms.

Val took his men and all horses to the stalls. Marius called to the Batavi and led them to a long building with many chimneys sending curling smoke into the wind. As the Batavi stomped warmth into their legs and slapped feeling into their arms, Marius stood in the barracks looking grim.

"The commandant said I'm to be on the lookout for two Batavi deserters from Massilia who may be heading to Germania," he said.

TWELVE

On the Aventicum Road, Where Snow Falls and Smoke Rises

In the morning Bentet and Thonkrik had vanished. The remaining Batavi took the morning meal in the canteen. Marius, silent and brooding, sat away from them and the legionnaires. After awhile, Rokus left his plate to join him.

"You are free of them now." Rokus looked Marius in the eye.

"I want to get to Castra Vetera and be done with this." Marius stared past him.

"Why don't you turn back now and leave us for the rest of the journey? You know I am going back," Rokus said.

"Can't do that."

"Thonkrik and Bentet were no business of yours."

Marius slammed his spoon down. "I am a Roman officer; they were my business and I failed to carry out my duty."

"They are gone; I am your duty."

"Roman law is my duty."

"Calm yourself, Marius, you are carrying out your orders. You will be promoted with my delivery, and you can return to Rome to make your mark. Become a magistrate."

Marius stared ahead tapping the table.

"The army wants only obedience. You are following orders. Something greater is not expected," said Rokus.

"That's just it, Rokus. After so many years…"

"You are a great warrior. You will distinguish yourself again. But this time your respect for the Batavi outweighed some notion of Roman law. You will get your moment."

The Batavian saw fatigue in the Roman's eyes, the career worn into the leathery skin, the uncertainty. "My tribesmen did nothing wrong, really, and you know it." Rokus slapped Marius on the back. "Come, Roman soldier, escort the Batavian prince all the way home."

The five Batavi, five Romans and two packhorses trotted north into the cold central plateau of Helvetia. The lake extended far behind them like another land, flat, gray, glassy. They passed single huts and low-slung barns, small wattle and daub things with meager chimneys releasing streams of smoke, and plots cut by wooden plows pulled by struggling horses.

Wild fields and groves of trees separated these homesteads. Brambles and knotted trunks awaited another wave of settlers to alter the growth of countless seasons; their hacking blades and new carved plows would work the land during their short lives of privation.

Marius kept a trotting pace, moving the train unremittingly across the land. They passed forlorn outposts of life nestled against far hills and by abandoned shelters undefined, derelict, insufficient for the clime. Three hours elapsed.

Young Val rode up to Marius to report a lame packhorse. They looked back to see the limping animal with the net full of parcels and cloth wrappings lurching across its back. Marius stopped the file of riders and rode back to investigate. Rokus heeled the roan after him.

Marius lifted the fore hoof and dug at the sole with his thumb. He ran his hand up the leg slowly over the pastern and fetlock joint. When he reached the cannon bone the horse flinched and kicked and began to buck. Rokus, at the halter rope, pulled the horse in and patted the neck and crest while issuing calm words.

"It's swollen. Very sore," Marius said.

"Better stop." Rokus wrapped the reins around his hand.

"Can't."

"The horse has a bad leg."

"We need to keep moving."

"This horse will not make it."

"I say we go. I'll slow the pace."

Rokus dismounted and went to the lame leg. He passed his hand over the long thick bone without touching it. He did this three times. "There's fever. Needs rest, more, in fact, until there is no heat."

"We have to go on." Marius was emphatic.

"Listen to me."

"Doesn't seem so bad. Let's go."

"It will cost you a horse if we push on," Rokus said as distant cries wafted in the wind.

"Then we leave it." Marius signaled to the legionnaires to re-pack supplies on the other horses.

Rokus took the halter and led the horse away from the train and across the meadow as the music entered his awareness like a mist of sound, indistinct at first, then coalescing as units of melody and rhythm, the heart thumping of a drum. He disappeared behind a stand of barren trees that clutched the side of a hill. Soon the melody was broken into metallic noises, harsh screams riding the breeze.

"What are you doing?" Marius called.

Beyond, in that direction, columns of smoke rose, and they all saw this.

"Where's he going?" young Val asked.

Marius threw his leg over the saddle, heeled, and followed Rokus. The others studied his horse's lope through the field, keeping their eyes on Marius' cloak and helmet and, farther, the smoke strands; then they listened for the lame horse's mercy killing.

❦

Impartial to the development, Menfrid and Folkbern dismounted and stretched. Gerulf pulled out jerky from his saddlebag and tore off a piece and began the chewing. He heeled his horse toward Liuppo and offered it. Then he reached over to Val with the chunk of dried meat. Val tore off a piece and returned it. Then Gerulf circled back to the other legionnaires who gripped their cloaks tight around their necks. He sat his horse and held out the dried venison while reaching into his bag for more. They sat stroking horses' necks, adjusting their warm cloaks, and scanning the field next to them.

They heard the shouts of attack, screams released from the bosom of fear, the menacing timbre and high volume that accompanies havoc. All reached for swords instinctively. Menfrid and Folkbern jumped into their saddles and the group bolted for the place beyond the hill.

They entered a flat surrounded by low hills dusted with snow. A hut leaned away from prevailing winds and an animal shelter stood tired with rot. The posts and rails of a primitive fence encircled the shelter, and a fire pit bereft of anything combustible pocked the ground near the hut. Farther in the flat, the arrangement of hut, shelter, and pen was repeated at least five times over, creating a hamlet.

The clang of swords cut the air. Men yelled. Women screamed. In a far field Rokus fended off a swarm of men bedraggled of fur and greasy leathers. They wore horned helmets, and with each swipe at the Batavian, strands of bone ornaments flew helter-skelter.

Rokus fought reactively, using each attacker's broad stroke for a thrust of his own. In the Roman fashion, he lunged in the trail of a blade and cut home to screams and fatal groans. The swarm became one, and the two parried as Menfrid arrived wielding sword overhead. As his horse galloped by the two, Menfrid's blade disappeared in glittering motion, and Rokus jumped back as the attacker's head and arm fell with violence and the man's neck and shoulder spewed blood in the air.

A woman's cry rose from the trees; tribal yells came from behind the hut. Marius issued sharp commands, and the terrifying chimes of swords and earthen thumps of hooves resounded throughout the proto-village. Men attacked men; innocents cowered or attempted pitiful defense.

Rokus ran into the grove, sword poised, senses sharp. A man stood straddling a woman, his tatters resembling some diseased hide burned black with use. His knotted hair fell in tormented ropes past his shoulders, his bare arms blotched with filth flexed at his sides, and his erection braced his greasy kilt. He lorded over her, watching the life drain from her gashed throat. Her arms were frozen above her as if she were shielding bright sunlight.

Rokus pounced with a windmill of strokes that severed manhood, then scalp with vulgar mane, then one hand at the wrist. The savage dropped, dying just as he learned of his gory wounds.

The woman gone, Rokus doubled back to the vortex of trouble. Marius and the legionnaires held their ground against a host of savages, the Roman javelins serving as deadly quills that kept attackers at bay. Frustrated, one barbarian jumped into the points yelling false victory in some German tongue as Marius cut him down. The others discovered that one of their kind might deflect the Roman javelin as another brought his long sword into the fray. One legionnaire lost his shield to such a blade and stood defenseless as Rokus swooped in from behind, dispatching two barbarians quickly and drawing the others' attention.

As they turned to this intrusion to their death feast, legionnaires threw their javelins to shrieks of men impaled, and then Marius and his line of soldiers pounced on them with their short swords, renting their ranks until the raiders fled.

Rokus pulled a javelin from its target and launched it at a bear cape in flight, and it found its mark. The man froze in stride, gripping the javelin point as it protruded from his chest.

More war shrieks thundered in the farmyard, and then they saw Folkbern, Gerulf, Menfrid and Liuppo engaged in battle with a squad of barbarian horse. The German numbers and long swords forced a Batavian retreat, which summoned demons in the attackers' chest.

Crazed, they bore down on the Batavians, but Folkbern and his comrades resisted, swiping, plunging, hacking, thrusting, until the raiders' own cuts and impalements grew too numerous to ignore. They reined horses, blood flowing from arms, thighs and heads, spattering withers and neck; and the animals themselves suffered in the exchange—sliced ears, random incisions across heads and necks, and the few fatal blows that collapsed their legs in their death throes.

Gerulf then slew the raiders who wrestled under their fallen horses, leaving lumps of former life twitching in the grass.

The remaining group followed their leader, a muscular raider sitting tall, who reared his horse and yelled, splattering spittle and venom, and drew his men back and across the field toward the trees. Folkbern would not have this and spurred after them; then his nephew Gerulf followed, then Menfrid slapped a long rein on his horse's sides galloping it.

Rokus' roan horse had drifted into the farmstead and watched the chaos from along the edge. Her Batavian rider called, and the resounding color of his voice jarred the horse from her trepidation, and she came to him, and he to her. Mounted, he spurred, and they chased them.

The raiders broke overland, careless of landform and obstacle, following neither track nor path. Their wide eyes focused only on the sky beyond the hills. Their pursuers raced after them and soon felt the muck kicked in flight descending upon them. The raider leader cheered another terrible call to death and hit his mount's rump with the flat of his sword. Hunter and hunted plunged down a ravine and up its side, trampling brambles that lashed out as they barged through.

Rokus followed the other Batavians galloping down the narrow dell. But then the roan committed herself and flew over land as if winged, gaining ground as if supernatural. Presently, Rokus flanked Folkbern, their mounts charging, their boots touching, and they could remember similar pursuits and outcomes; Folkbern yelled, and Rokus answered him.

Then Rokus leaned into the roan evermore to say, Can you go even faster? Folkbern waved at his back, a warrior's benediction.

Rokus advanced to the lead raider galloping among his men. The barbarian horsemen shied away from him in their galloping as the roan leaned ever forward, speed incarnate. Rokus smelled the raider, a fetid cloud of human animal, and drew close enough to study the Bructeri fur yoke, the Roman chainmail, the Chatti horns, the Tencteri sword—a barbarian made of parts, traces of men Rokus had fought beside and against.

The roan drew near the raider and Rokus reached for the sword he'd taken from the homestead massacre; he pulled it from his waist belt and held it out, poised to strike. The raider saw this and pulled away. The two horsemen plunged down a hollow, Rokus and the roan half a horse length behind. They galloped hard, dirt spraying, the stench of the raider conjuring primal times of fearful and wretched survival, and gradually the roan, with Rokus riding her high on the shoulders, arrived.

Rokus swiped and missed. Then he heard the thumping of his tribe's bodhrán and the bowed melody running quickly across a range of notes, repeatedly, heatedly, in time with the frenetic pulsation. The notion flashed in his brain to break protocol, to release his weapon and thereby have none. It seemed to him like the destiny of this chase; it was risky but perhaps right. He wound back and swung his arm and released the sword as if it were an assassin's dagger. The blade passed through the bear fur, true to the mark. The raider flinched and pulled at the annoyance sticking out of his chest, then rolled to the side.

Rokus pulled the reins. With proud steps and heaving chest, the roan circled back to the raider who lay in a heap of limbs. Rokus dismounted and, kneeling next to the corpse, pulled on the sword. It wouldn't draw. He stood, then, boot to bloody back, yanked on the weapon until it squeaked and broke free of the body's bones. He turned the body over to look at the German with his heart blood pouring out across chainmail and scrambling grass, his odor mixing with the blood that was fresh to the outside world. He was seasoned, scarred, and tattooed across his forehead and down the bridge of his nose and around his lips in a grotesque blue muzzle now silenced.

Rokus spat, as if he could expel the bad taste of killing. He turned away and walked into the dell, overcame the raider's horse, cut off the strapped leather pad, and returned to the roan. Saddled and spent, he walked her back with the other horse trailing after them. When he heard the whimpering, he stopped.

Carried in the wind, the sound fluttered and dove as an invisible bird. It came from the wild shrub; it came from the treetops; it came from the gullies. Rokus scanned the site looking for its source. Through the rattling branches the mournful call whisked, faded, then sounded again, frail in its evanescence.

He turned the horses into the tall brush and ducked under some limbs. Grief sounded in the breeze, and there she was, pitiful and stained with blood: a girl.

Rokus dismounted and approached slowly. He circled round to face her, then, seeing the soiled limbs and the scratches across face and naked shoulders, he dropped to his knees to help. Her eyes were profound hollows of disquiet, and except for the breeze fanning her long thin locks, she was utterly motionless. Rokus searched her face, but she looked through him. He thought maybe she was blind.

He unclipped his cloak and covered her, but she didn't respond. He daubed a bloody smear on her temple, but she didn't acknowledge him.

"I won't hurt you," he said.

He picked her up and placed her sideways on his saddle, unsure about her injury. Mounted, he cradled her with reassurance and heeled the roan back to the hamlet.

Marius and his men gathered in the pasture by an animal shelter. Among the carnage was a legionnaire sprawled in death with Val tending to the lifeless form, weeping quietly, stroking the hair. Marius touched his shoulder, and Val stood up, wiping his cheeks.

It was a vile harvest; bodies were strewn throughout the fields, around fire pits and the wattle and daub structures that leaned pathetically throughout the grounds. Men's bodies were aberrant forms, injustices to their husbandry. Women's bodies lay discarded after atrocious deeds against them, and the children— boys and girls, toddlers and youths—lay scattered like cut flowers, hindrances to men's atrocities.

Signs of brave defense were everywhere, and their bodies bore witness to its futility. The men and women of the hamlet clutched swords and rakes and hayforks and scythes, and even the older boys gripped shovels and poles to their last breaths.

Though in Celtic lands, they were not Celts; the men and boys wore tight breeches under tunics and leather boots. Crude, the boots consisted of single pieces of hide turned in and stitched, slipper-like, with the fur inside. Some breeches had broad bars of contrasting colors or checks in natural browns, reddish or blue dyes. The women and girls wore long skirts, short jackets and full shirts with open necks. Women's hair was folded in long braids or twisted and knotted into elaborate forms on the sides or backs of their heads. The mean cuts and brutal ends eradicated any sense of tribal identity; all people lay rigid in the redness of slaughter.

Rokus drew the roan to them, clutching the girl's face to his chest lest she see. The other Batavians arrived next, cantering in with victory and a line of horses. They brought a homesteader who leaned in the saddle. A gash shone deep red across his thick dark hair, and his back was a map of red blotches.

They set him to the ground just as Rokus unsaddled the girl, and soon the homesteaders lay side-by-side. The man's rustic garb was soaked in his blood, and his face implored them for water. His head wavered, delirious and weak; he turned to the girl and emitted a silent scream—she was his daughter. She stared into the sky above, her eyes two disasters in a garden of light, closed to the men around her.

The man struggled to sit up. He screamed a silent alarm as he looked at his daughter, his muzzle forming words that became knotted in his shock. The man tried again and again to expel his message, and they observed the character of the man; he was dying and had but moments to settle.

Rokus lowered his ear to the man's face. "Tell me, sir."

The man moaned a word, two syllables hidden in a whisper.

"Again." Rokus cradled the man's head. "He's German, too," he said turning to the others.

"The raiders were Tulingi," Gerulf said.

"Had their markings," Folkbern added.

The downed man exhaled, then, as best he could, drew in a last breath of strength from the air above his farm.

"Ulla, my little Ulla."

Rokus felt the man's vitality wane and placed his head in the grass. The man stared emptily at the coming of winter, and Rokus imagined the man's life here, the chores, the reward of carving a life out of raw nature, and then passed his hand over the man's eyes closing them for his final rest.

"How many dead?" Rokus asked.

"Thirty or forty," Marius said.

"A pyre, then.

Half the troop piled wood and brush in the field and dragged the remains of the hamlet people, old and young, while the other half butchered a pig and a goose. Rokus had the entourage gather around the pyre before they lit it.

"These were noble people making their way in this mean world," Rokus began. "Pray to our gods, of sky and wind and sea, but mostly the earth, sweet goddess that nurtures us, to anoint their lives and deaths and take them back in this November breeze, in this Helvetian soil. We acknowledge them and cherish their glorious labor."

He nodded to Gerulf, who lowered a torch to the tangle of dried grass and branches at the base of the pyre, then stepped back as the heap hissed and crackled and then roared. They watched limbs and torsos and lost faces as flames consumed them. After awhile, some dropped their gaze in thought, others turned to finish packing.

With the cuts of pork and goose wrapped in found cloths and leathers and cinched in twine and roped to the new horses, they were ready to depart; given a day off from traveling, they would preserve the meat with smoking.

At sunset, they sat their horses at the edge of the vale, watching the pyre smolder. Rokus held Ulla in his arms; she sat sideways across the roan's back and continued to gaze at something horrible. He walked his horse to the front of the line next to Marius. He turned the roan to face the line and then raised his arm.

"Thus we celebrated the deaths of the farmers with such a fire, offering their smoke to the gods for lives well lived, for love shared, for the hope they carried until the end. The brigands we leave for the vultures and crows and wolves," Rokus stated in a measured voice.

Marius led them on, following the track northward until they came to the huge lake. He led the string of riders and horses along its shore; they saw the distant flickers of the Helvetian village. Inured to saddle and pace, they arrived at the place before long and without discomfort. Marius left them and went into the village to an office flying the Roman eagle. When he returned, he said they would camp at the lake and thus instructed young Val and the legionnaires to water the horses at the tributary stream nearby, to set up tents, to start a good fire.

Rokus and Ulla watched them; now Ulla's eyes had shifted from her visions of terror. Her frame had lost its tension, and she glanced at things, as if her burning memories were fixed straight ahead and deviations were taken only suspiciously. He placed her on a rock and covered her. The bear blanket engulfed her completely and her wispy blonde strands and tortured eyes seemed more vulnerable next to the wild fur.

"I will bring you something to eat," he said as he backpedaled toward the fire.

He returned with a tin plate covered with biscuit and roasted beef and three dried dates from Judea and a cup of beer.

"This isn't much. You should eat. You're weak from everything you've been through." He said this twice, once in Latin, once in the Bructeri tongue learned from Veleda.

The girl didn't move, but he thought he detected another glance at the firelight. He left her to get his own dinner, but when he returned her plate was untouched. He sat beside her and ate his meal and sipped the beer brought from Lousonna.

"My name is Rokus of Batuwe," he said glancing at her. "Betuwe is at the mouth of the River Rhonus far to the north of here." He paused. "We will not hurt you. In fact, we will find a safe place for you with people who will care for you."

Her gaze remained straight ahead. Flickering light defined her cheekbones and fair skin, the feathery hair, and lips that seemed on the verge of forming words—or weeping.

"Girl shouldn't have to see what you did. But you are safe now. Ulla, is it?"

He faltered, remembering the farmyard strewn with her kin.

"So what else? I'm talking in Bructeri so that you may understand. Your father spoke in a German dialect. I am so sorry about your family, the farms back there. Let's see? What can I tell you?

Two years ago my brother and I were officers in the Roman army—that is, in an auxiliary of the Roman army. An auxiliary is when extra support is brought in to help, like asking your uncle or somebody to help with the harvest. Rome uses armies of tribesmen to make their army bigger and better. The Batavian auxiliary is one of these, and Rome values us because we are good warriors. In fact, many years ago my great-grandfather, Uulfnoth the First, secured Roman citizenship for his line, and so I am called Gaius Julius Civilis by Romans—except by these fellows here; they know me better, and so use my Batavian name, Rokus."

Rokus studied Ulla's passive face. The bear fur had slipped so he pulled it up against her jaw, touched her hair with his fingertips.

"I am the Batavian prince. My father is old and frail and will die soon—maybe he's dead already—and then I will be king. Being king means nothing, really, because, in effect, the Batavi have become vassals of Rome. Do you know what that means?"

An owl's hoot came from the nearby trees, and a breeze rattled branches, and the cold air stiffened in response.

"Batavians give to Rome warriors; in exchange, Rome doesn't tax the Batavi—doesn't ask for money, taxes. Betuwe is small, but unto itself. Nevertheless, Batavians are beholden to Rome because we give up our boys to be left alone. Does this make any sense to you?"

Rokus stood up and looked at her and then left the girl to get more beer. He imagined life in the hamlet, where the demands of survival preempted education; where education was a series of chores executed ever more efficiently so that more chores might be done. Then she would be married at a young age, have children, do more farm work. How would she have any concept of the Roman Empire, Batavian sovereignty, a major river, kings, conscription?

He remembered his father bringing in Roman tutors, the rigor of study mixed with martial arts, and then his kiss to his mother and his departure for the Batavian auxiliary in Britannia.

He sliced a piece of beef, filled his cup, and returned to her. He sat and ate the beef, sipped the beer. He held her plate up to her again, but she remained fixed on far-flung pain.

"Two years ago I gave a speech to my auxiliary that upset the Roman general of the army of the north. He arrested me for treason. Treason is speaking out or doing something against your government. Government is a group of people who lead a country. I gave a speech about how unfair it was for Rome to take our young men in numbers far out of proportion to the number of Batavians there are. Listen to me go on about these things; how could you understand? During the arrest, a soldier killed my brother. I was sent to Rome for trial before Emperor Nero, then put in jail for two years. Galba, the new emperor, released me last month, and now these men are escorting me back to Betuwe."

He leaned forward to see her better out of his good eye.

"Not hungry, are you?"

He put the plate down, and they sat in silence for a long time, listening to the owl.

"My face. My eye. Must be wondering about it. A few weeks ago I met the man who killed my brother. During a fight with him, I lost my eye. Not too pleasant to look at, is it?"

She did not respond, so he stood up to leave.

"I don't know what conditions are in my homeland, but much turmoil is brewing somehow. At all events, I am taking you to a safe place; you do not have to fear me."

Rokus returned to the others and sat staring at the fire for an hour, watching the flames eat away at the logs and the burned chunks break off and drop sizzling into the white and orange coals. The men around him spoke about the day, but their voices were distant to him; his music had returned, carried on a slip of breeze from across the lake. It thumped and soared, rhythm and melody, to the searing flames, and there was solace in it.

He had to settle Ulla into her sleeping place. When he got to her, grease and crumbs covered her plate. He picked up her cup and offered it. "Beer," he said, "or would you prefer water?"

He took his own empty cup to the lake's edge, washed it, and filled it with the alpine water. Returning, he saw her cup emptied.

"Here's some water if you want."

He went to the packs piled near the camp, and by the firelight fetched another fur cloak and a satchel full of cloth and netting and bunches of fire-starting grass. He returned and laid the cloak on the sandy soil and leaned the satchel against the rock.

"A bed for you. We leave early."

"Did you kill him?"

Rokus looked at her staring straight ahead.

"I did."

"Good."

THIRTEEN
On the Roman Road from Aventicum to Augusta Raurica

Their train entered the high plateau surrounded by hills. The lake was ever present with its damp wind and gulls, and the horizon grew broad and promising. Marius kept a quick pace, heeling his lead horse to trot for fifteen minutes, then walk for as long, then trot again.

Ulla rested her head on Rokus' shoulder, except during the trotting times when she sat up and settled into his rhythm. When the horses walked, Rokus closed his eyes and held her firmly, because in her body he felt something essential that reminded him of his sons when they were so young. The young getting strong always inspired and delighted him. Ulla was strong in spite of her thin frame, and she began transmitting her confidence in him by clasping the big stone of his ring, draping an arm on his, squeezing his wrist.

As they crossed the flatlands, there was perfection in the landscape, gentle rolling hills and streams spread under the wide sky. Distant cliffs and outcroppings marked ancient washes and the wear of time, and he was sure such a plain would be farmed someday soon. Green patches indicated fecund places to plant, and high ground at the perimeter would make superb grazing, and rock formations good shelters for herders.

The paved road became more refined, with the flat stones precisely configured and the filler gravel and sand pounded almost solid. Milestones grew taller, more ornate. The road widened also, ushering them to Aventicum. Here was the hand of Rome, beyond the Alps, far from the Forum and Circus Maximus, a place where Celtic resourcefulness and invention coexisted with Roman power and engineering.

They smelled the town before they saw it beyond hills that broke the plane. Wafts of roasting pig melded with the aroma of roasting fowl, and infusing both were bouquets of herbs, savory notes that caused them all to heel their horses onward. The road dropped into a swale, climbed, and swung round a hill; the clatter of hooves resounded where they passed, and then they saw the rooftops peeping above the wall.

Ulla sat up to the canter and leaned forward as they all did, and Rokus held her tightly as the roan loped with the others.

The people of Aventicum scurried around the main square putting up tents and booths and stages. Fire pits had been constructed at the corners, and each billowed the piquant smoke of boar, grouse, partridge and thrush. Mummers gathered to the side, their brightly colored costumes in majesty against the gray stone and beams and whitewashed buildings.

"What goes on here, friend?" said Rokus to a mummer in a tall pointed hat.

"A festival, my lord, to the gods that protect us."

"Gods?" Marius asked.

"We offer fire today to Belenus and to Brigindo. There," said the mummer pointing to women and children and old men piling scraps of wood and straw at the base of a pyramid form made of poles lashed together.

"I know them," Rokus said.

"Your gods!" Marius blurted.

"Tell us what you are doing." Rokus looked down at the mummer from his horse with Ulla in his gentle grasp.

The mummer motioned to another to join him, and then he hopped foot to foot, screwed his face, and trumpeted his voice. The second mummer danced to the first's words, miming god and goddess and earth folk in turn.

"First there is Belenus, he of light and the power of the sun. To him we owe our health, our crops, and our pastures. And then there is his consort, Brigindo, goddess of fertility and all things crafted by our hands. She ensures we produce our children and the things we need to survive and that all these are bounteous and pleasing. But more, she lavishes qualities of beauty on all, so that our children are well proportioned and fair, and they grow more attractive, and thus promise that life goes on."

The second mummer jammed a stick between his legs and thrust his lusty groin, and the first mummer mock-smacked him on the side of the head, and the second returned the false blow and tweaked his nose.

"Let's move on," Marius commanded, spurring.

The file of riders and packhorses crossed the square near the pyramid. Fastened to every cross pole of the structure, figurines with decorated faces looked back at them, wraiths in multiple colors and malevolent smiles. This choir of apparitions, leering, wide-eyed, summoned in them a doleful silence.

Ulla squeezed his arm. He steered the roan past this night-marish construction, and they came to booths full of pies and cakes, toys in carved pine and twisted willow, ceramic cups and bowls, bits and bridles and leather halters, and bronze castings of Belenus and Brigindo. Women arranged talismans on planks while children darted among them earning swats and warnings. Men carried platters of apples and squash and dried beans and einkorn to special benches, filling bins arranged on them and placing placards with prices per libra.

They turned a corner and encountered musicians walking to the square—costumes of red and maize checks, green and gold stripes, blue and red diamonds—followed by a squadron of legionnaires shadowing them.

Marius called over his shoulder for his group to wait. He spurred to the first legionnaire, and they talked. The legionnaire pointed down the street. Marius turned, called out, "Wait here!" and then trotted his mount down the street and around a corner.

Their line broke, and they clustered together. Horses stepped in place and shook their bridles while the men watched the town folk hurry by with their bundles and platters and colored streamers and signs. Through it, Ulla gazed ahead as if lost in the memory of her hamlet.

"A festival or something," Gerulf observed.

"To their gods," Rokus said.

"Smells good around here." Menfrid sniffed while he twisted left and right in his saddle.

"I've got to eat something," Liuppo declared.

Liuppo, Menfrid and Gerulf dismounted and tied their horses to poles supporting the overhangs. Limbering side to side, they twisted and stretched the long ride out of their muscles, then concentrated on the boar that sizzled on a spit nearby.

Marius rode back and sat his horse next to Rokus.

"Commandant will see us."

"Folkbern, will you?" Rokus adjusted Ulla in his arms.

Folkbern drew his horse closer while Marius scowled. Rokus lifted Ulla and handed her over to his fellow Batavian, who, holding the girl as if she would break, duplicated the sitting on his own saddle. Ulla only stared at some unseen horror. Satisfied with her placement, Rokus nodded to Marius and they trotted down the street, around the corner, down several town blocks, passed a wooden amphitheater, and into the garrison.

Two legionnaires met them. Their breastplates and helmets shone in the sun, and their belts, straps and scabbards gleamed. They stood erect, turned with precision and, lockstep, led the arrivals down a corridor of the principia on the fort's square.

Rokus and Marius stood before the commandant, a career man with a stone face.

"Sir, my charge, Gaius Julius Civilis; Julius Civilis, this is Lucius Verginius Nerva, Consul of Helvetia."

Rokus nodded once and held his hand up.

"Hail."

"Hail," Nerva said. He turned to the legionnaires standing at attention. "See to our meal."

Nerva pushed away from his desk. He walked to the window with his hands on his hips. Seasoned in war, he showed its vestiges: a lean frame, strong forearms, scarred leathery skin, and an upright bearing that was, at once, ambition, achievement, solemnity.

"Marius told me about the raid on the farmers to the south. Ever since Vindex's revolt we have experienced such invasions," he said, glancing at legionnaires drilling. "What do you make of it?"

He studied Rokus. The Batavian prince returned his gaze, and they locked eyes like this until Marius stirred.

"I had them for Alamanni, sir," Marius said.

"Alamanni!" Nerva exclaimed. "They've been subdued for a generation."

"Defeated, not destroyed," Rokus corrected him.

"And we encountered Sequani east of Lugdunum. Ambushed us on the road first, then we found the aftermath of a raid. Loss of a century," Marius reported. "The commandant at Genava has been informed."

"Tribes have become bolder. They think they can defeat us," Nerva said. "Are there not paved roads from here to Rome? Are there not similar roads from here to the northern ocean? Are there not roads from here to Lugdunum and farther on to Narbonensis, Aquitania, and Hispania? Are there not legions in garrisons like this throughout these lands? That means the territory belongs to Rome."

"Roads and forts mark lands, not hearts." Rokus corrected him again.

"Our roads bring commerce, prosperity."

"And armies."

"To protect the people."

"To defend Rome."

Nerva returned to his desk. He leaned on it, hands spread like spiders on the oak. "Rome conquers and improves. The roads facilitate this," he said, looking at Marius' scroll left unrolled before him.

A long silence ensued during which Marius shifted his weight and Nerva finished reading and rolled the scroll with one hand.

"Sequani ambushed us, but the Tulingi did the rest." Rokus rested on one leg and draped his hand over the hilt of his sword.

"How can you be so sure?" Nerva asked. "The Tulingi chiefs have made peace."

Marius searched the Batavian's expression, then the commandant's.

"They left their distinctive mark." Rokus stepped to the window where the soldiers drilled.

"Mark?" Nerva followed Rokus to the window.

"Heads," Rokus answered, turning to the consul.

"Do we have a confederation against us, then?"

"I believe these raids are by rogue tribes, sir," Marius interjected.

"Rogue tribes?" Nerva asked, turning back to Marius.

"Unrelated attacks. Roaming groups looking for gains, anything," Rokus added.

The commandant went to a wall rack housing javelins. He selected one, tested its weight, then presented it.

"This pilum is a tried and true weapon. But it is also a symbol. It is perfectly weighted to assist the thrower. A man can heave it thirty yards with accuracy. The sharp point can penetrate most shields if the weapon is thrown correctly. The barb prevents withdrawing it; the iron shaft is designed to bend on impact, preventing its reuse against us. It symbolizes the army's methods, its battle strategies, its success, its invincibility." Nerva hefted the spear while he lectured.

Nerva then tossed the pilum sideways at Rokus, who caught it, then stood it by his side without examination.

"This pilum is made of tempered yew and iron," Rokus responded. "It is strong, man-made from materials of the earth. The iron the tribes of Germania possess is made of different stuff: the will to freedom. This is not of wood or metal but from the spirit. Roman ways are imposed, not elected; dissent is punished, never given audience. The tribes desire what is best for them in their eyes, and so they implore the spirits of the forest and sky, the running waters and the grasslands, the rain and sun—fertility, bravery, clanship. They summon their spirits' aid and pitch for battle, whenever, however. You can't see it, but it is there with

the Sequani, the Tulingi, the Alamanni, the Vindelici, the Marcomanni, the Chatti, the Tencteri, the Bructeri, the Frisii."

"And the Batavi? Civilis, I am aware of the charges that put
you in prison. You are treading a dubious path here, now."

"Nerva, I only observe."

"When my brother defeated Vindex, he had to set an example.
Here was a governor of a province opposing the Emperor, the will
of Rome. When Vindex allied himself with Galba of Spain, it was
against the order of the Empire. Do you understand? If a governor revolts, he is destroyed. If a tribe revolts, it will be destroyed."

"These are words. I am talking about something that cannot
be eradicated; something that runs so deep, you, Nerva, cannot
fathom it."

"Insolence!" the consul shouted, crashing his fist on his desk.
"Do you not understand, Civilis? We will crush them, as my
brother crushed Vindex, as I will crush the Tulingi, Alamanni,
the Chatti. And I will go deep into the forest and destroy the
Marcomanni if I learn that any of these raids are theirs."

"There is a new Celtic strain, different from the tribes of Gaul,
even Helvetia. The forest spirits and sea spirits and those of the
mighty rivers and the wind that touches all—these are the new
elements mixing with the genius of the Celt, producing something different, stronger," Rokus rotated the pilum as he spoke.
"You do not understand because you have not seen it yet, but it
is out there: along the Rhenus, in the great forest of the east, in
the delta plain next to the northern ocean. It is new—the re-
sult of consort, not confederation. Like mixing iron with carbon

to produce steel, two different elements make something new, something stronger. I know this."

"You've been in prison; what do you know?"

"I watch. I listen."

"Then there is a confederation of Germans who plan an attack?" Nerva asked, approaching Rokus from around the desk.

"No. It is in the blood of children. A girl grows up to couple with a boy from another tribe; their children do the same, and two tribes merge into one. Two elements combine to produce a stronger third element."

"I thought you tribesmen kept to yourselves." Nerva stood close to Rokus and looked him directly in the eye.

"It was once so, and it may still be so in many territories. But change is in the wind. Steel folk are emerging from the forests and river deltas."

"We'll see about your steel people."

A legionnaire appeared in the doorway. He snapped to attention and they all turned. "Yes?" Nerva demanded.

"Your meal is ready in the officers' dining chamber, sir."

"We'll be there straightaway."

Nerva turned back to Rokus. He filled his chest and slowly exhaled a deep threat: "You speak like a king of a powerful nation, Civilis, but you are nothing of the sort. If you fail to complete your assigned task, I will personally see to your end."

Rokus heard the music of his tribe, the soaring strings and the thumping bodhrán. He entertained whipping out his dagger and burying it in the man, but that was the Rokus of thirty years ago. He had a bigger plan, and the music was the anointment from the spirits.

"I'm sure your spread is hearty, but I have to check on little Ulla," Rokus explained, handing over the pilum.

They stood fixed with the unresolved threads of their conversation dangling all around. Rokus turned to Marius, gentled his voice.

"I'll be in the square showing Ulla around. She needs some joy in her world."

He left them without another word, leaving hostility suspended. The winter sun hit Rokus as he entered the garrison square. He paused for a cavalry unit passing by and then made for the hitching post. He nodded at the legionnaire stationed there, mounted, and trotted through the gate and back to the town square.

Ulla sat alone on Folkbern's saddle. Rokus came to her from the front to avoid startling her from behind. He waved; she did not.

"Let's get you off that animal and walk around, shall we?" he said.

He set her down and put his hand on her shoulder, an overture to a kinder realm. He took her hand, leading her into the square that now teemed with townsfolk and foreigners milling around booths, performing mummers and jugglers, displays of wares and oddities. They walked into the latter, vessels with strange rodents and reptiles preserved in fluid, stuffed wildcats and bears growling in unbearable silence, and assorted physicians' tools and soldiers' weapons that looked about the same. Several men from the garrison worked the booth, and they explained the different parts of the empire from which each oddity came. Part of this concession included a ride on an ostrich in a pen set up on the edge of the square, the pavers there covered generously with straw. A horde of children, mostly boys, pushed into the pen to ride the freak bird.

The creature fascinated Rokus, and he assumed she shared this feeling, so he led her through the boys to the pen. He leaned against the makeshift rail and watched, smiling broadly. Ulla stood next to him watching something in the distance, some scene insisting itself on her memory. A legionnaire lifted a boy on top of the ostrich while another legionnaire held back the bird's paltry wings, and a third soldier muzzled the bird with his hands. After positioning the boy's legs under the wings, they released the strange pair to the guffaws of the crowd, and the bird shot across the enclosure, wide-eyed and gamboling.

Rokus laughed and turned to Ulla, who gazed into her memory. He knelt beside her, studied the side of her face, the soft skin still smudged, the wispy strands of long hair, the frailty. He knew she was frozen in the horror of that day; the scene would forever be a crucial aspect of her constitution. Would that he could bury this memory with better ones.

He picked her up, and she did not resist. He faced her to the spectacle and then pivoted so that she could see the town boys and girls yelp and point and taunt. Then her gaze skittered, and she watched the ostrich also. The young rider bounced on the bird's back as the bird stepped quickly along the railing. As the boy clutched the thick of the bird's wings, his soft hat worked itself to the back of his head and flew off. Delighted, the crowd launched a wave of jibes, and when the bouncing threw the boy, they exploded with scoffing and twenty different brands of glee.

Rokus jiggled Ulla as he laughed, and she groped for his hand, and her fingers seized his bloodstone ring by happenstance. This seemed salutary; she looked at him without the haunted expression, and he felt some mutual understanding.

"There now," he said, offering a trace of mirth.

She examined his face and then touched it with her fingertips. They caressed his temple and cheek and then hovered over his eye patch like beacons from the hand of some child savant healer. He hugged her gently, and they turned to watch the next boy roll off the ostrich's back to another roar.

The legionnaires lifted another boy, who cockily removed his hat and whirled it over his head.

"Where is this big chicken from?" Rokus called.

"Upper Egypt, sir," a legionnaire responded.

"Can it hold a man?" Rokus asked.

The legionnaire stepped back to regard him entirely, then nodded. "Want to try?"

"I do."

Ulla flinched in his arms and stole a glance, alarmed.

"Don't worry, I've ridden nags and stallions and everything in between. I just have to try this."

He put her down. She clung to his ring as if she were falling.

"I will be right back; just don't laugh too hard, Ulla."

Rokus stepped into the pen as the last fallen rider ran past him trailing straw and chaff. The legionnaires held the giant bird steady as Rokus positioned himself, grabbed the long neck, slid his hands to the bases of the short wings, and jumped on. His weight seemed to check the bird's advance, but quickly the bird recovered and set off. They circled the pen several times, and during each circulation Rokus bounced as the boy bounced, but his years of riding showed, and he fell into a rhythm with the ostrich's scuttering.

The boys sent kudos above the pen and banged on the rail with their fists.

As Rokus circled the pen, he watched the ostrich's head, the huge eyes bulging from the flat hairy head, long eyelashes waving up and down, the beak opening and closing with agitation. He came to the legionnaires and slid off the back of the ostrich to a fanfare of youthful cheers. He bowed deeply and acknowledged the ostrich's part in his jaunt by holding out his arms to it. The second wave of cheers erupted, and a gaggle of boys pushed into the pen's gateway to be riders, too. They pushed past Rokus and fell into the arms of the legionnaires while Rokus inched toward Ulla.

"We should have a cavalry of these creatures in the auxiliary," he said. "They would either frighten the enemy or set them laughing to distraction."

Ulla pushed into him with her arms up. He lifted her and held her securely.

"Let's get something to eat, shall we?" he said.

"Looked silly," she said, putting her head on his shoulder.

He clutched her and followed the smoke billowing from the square. They came to the fire pit with skewered fowl roasting high above the coals, juices sizzling and running down the long sticks fashioned for the occasion. When he reached into his pocket he remembered his circumstances; he looked around for Folkbern.

"Maybe there is something else we can buy," he said, palming the small coin he'd found.

Ulla was pliable and looked where he looked, smelled the same game birds as he, turned with him, and conveyed assent. They crossed the square through a thickening crowd. Nudging close to another booth that emitted fine aromas, together they saw pastries shaped like little animals.

"How about one of these?" he said.

She pointed to a round cake with rabbit ears shaped from it and currants for eyes and nose. He paid, and they meandered through the crowd while she held the rabbit cake to her chest.

They walked hand in hand around the square. The mummers entertained a small crowd, poking, slapping, kicking in a spree of pratfalls; the musicians played a tune that reminded Rokus of his Batavian theme; one of the four played a narrow stringed box with a bow, one a bodhrán, another a psaltery, while the last's flute fluttered in the wind.

Ulla paused in front of them, and when Rokus tugged to move on, she resisted; her face, he saw, found something soothing in the sound, and she insisted on letting it wash over her. They lingered through several tunes while the musicians smiled and winked and played with grace.

Folkbern appeared next to them carrying haversacks brimming with oilcloths full of fowl and cakes, dried fruit and roasted grains. He looked sheepish, his eyes darting from Ulla to Rokus and back.

"I asked you to watch this little one," Rokus stated.

"She wasn't there when I came back," Folkbern explained. "Then Marius told me your meeting was over. I bought her—us—some food."

"But you left her. We have to take care of her." Rokus took Ulla into his arms and held her firmly to his chest.

"You're right," Folkbern answered, lowering the haversack so that Ulla could view the food. "The Roman is foaming at the mouth. What happened?"

"I will take care of her," Rokus asserted. "She will be cared for. Ulla."

"The Roman is worked up, he wants to leave immediately." Folkbern reached into the bag for a small cake.

"Our Marius is hearing things he'd rather not hear."

Folkbern looked quizzically.

"He suffers from divided allegiance—the warrior's, and the soldier's."

"They're different?"

"Very."

They all turned to walk back to the horses. Rokus draped his arm over Ulla's shoulders while she nibbled at the rabbit's ears.

Crumbs fell down her tunic. Folkbern listened to the prince as a student hears a teacher.

"He has served the army for a lifetime, and its ways have become his ways. Still, he has a warrior's heart that recognizes bonds formed when battle rages all around. He's a brother more than a rank. This is an aspect of the spirit that army discipline has never beaten out of him. He's a man, not a command. Folkbern, this is a class of man that is beyond boundaries; it is in him to cross over to the Batavians or some other tribe, but years of the Roman system have conditioned him. And he's been touched by ambition, and it clouds his thinking. That's it, I see now, this desire to advance; he is lost to us. And now, I do not trust him."

They came to the horses. Gerulf held the reins of one mount while stroking the coat of another. The other horses rested side-by-side with reins wrapped around posts, stamping and snorting. Just then, Liuppo and Menfrid arrived from the opposite direction. They, too, held bulging saddlebags, and Val the legionnaire walked up to Gerulf, took the reins, then signaled to the other legionnaires trailing him to prepare the train. The Batavians and Val formed a circle.

"I see you've replaced the legionnaires' biscuit," Rokus observed. "And now we have to get to Augusta Raurica—and to Batuwe. Let's mount and wait for our guide."

"Too bad we can't stay," Liuppo said holding a partridge leg and licking his fingers.

"Better to go home to eat at a Batavian hearth." Rokus looked back at the packhorses and the legionnaires.

"But the Helvetians are friendly," Menfrid said nodding to a pair of girls strolling by with baskets of loaves.

"You best return to Betuwe and mend the broken heart you left there." Folkbern leaned over and tapped Menfrid on the back of his head..

"Rokus, look." Gerulf pointed across the square.

Down the street they saw Marius speaking to a horseman. His right hand gripped the hilt of his sword, and his left gestured emphatically. The rider wore the clothes of a tribesman from the east. His soft red hat had earflaps hanging low, and his tunic was bright yellow with checks; his ruddy cape had edges of fur, and his breeches were blue with stripes. Leather boots climbed snugly up his legs. He sat well in his saddle, his brown hair falling down his cape; and then he leaned low to Marius, nodding and pointing toward the north gate. They came to an agreement, and the rider whipped his horse around and galloped away.

Marius stepped into their brittle silence. Glances. Suspicion. They stood together like that until Ulla offered the remains of her rabbit to Rokus. He took it and ate it. He looked over Marius' shoulder at the horseman's dust cloud and the townsfolk arriving to the festival. Marius surveyed the group, the saddlebags, Ulla.

"Let's ride now," he said.

Young Val jumped to, bringing the packhorses about, adjusting the stores under their ropes and netting. He gave his reins to a legionnaire so that he could help Rokus with Ulla. Rokus mounted and reached down for Ulla, and Val hiked her up to the saddle.

"There you go, girl."

Rokus nodded his thanks; and Val, the legionnaires, the other Batavians, and then Marius, mounted their horses.

Liuppo tore at another leg of partridge as he rode. Menfrid and Folkbern grinned as they saw this penchant and with Gerulf, put their horses in trot behind Marius. Rokus and Ulla followed; out the gate Rokus inhaled deeply, savoring the pleasure of the road and their movement northeastward.

Throughout the morning they crossed meadows, following the Roman road as it traversed the high plain. Forests followed the waves of land flowing to the road from the hills as if this vegetation were liquid spilled from the heights. Blackbirds darted from the shrubbery by the streams, and the frequent hawks swooped into the brush and shot out with talons filled. The grasses, dried from the cold season, bristled along the road; and puffs of clouds hovered high above, a network of same-sized vapors that dropped their shadows upon them. Rokus sat satisfied with his world. He knew such moods were temporary, the wiser to extract the most from these occasions.

In the afternoon the sun bore hard from the west sending their shadows far across the flats. Their fourteen elongations were strange things stretching eastward, and the entire train watched versions of themselves and their bizarre horses, blackened and disembodied, dance through glade and grove, climb tree trunk and outcrops, and shoot down slope according to the countryside. The distant hills turned purple and wan and the sky exhausted itself with a gush of orange that tinted cirrus and tufts of vapor until all riders gazed up as if spellbound.

Soon the dark merged with the ghostlike shapes of the trees and consumed the silhouettes of hills. Immersed in the blue-gray twilight, they continued on the Roman road, clattering, and pulled up collars and pulled down hats and sank deeper into their saddles. Infinite pinpoints filled the broad sky as if treasured dust had been spilled in ink, but then they felt the ice in the air and saw the stars vanish behind a mantel weighted with winter.

Rokus heeled the roan to Marius' side. Ulla had settled into sleep beneath a fur, and so he cradled her head in the bend of his arm. Marius scowled.

"Everyone is hungry and tired," Rokus said.

"We can stop at the next milestone," said Marius, pulling his cloak across his legs and spurring his horse farther on.

Rokus drew back, listening to the hushed strains of the tune, the cry of bowed strings, the bright jangle of strumming, and the heart thump of a drum. He looked at Ulla, so innocent, and adjusted the cradle of his arm and the snugness of the fur around her. Something swelled in him, filling his chest with pressure, until he realized he'd come to a decision: Upon arrival in the north, he would bring Ulla to Veleda, because that was the only way to protect her from what he was to do. He pictured an expanse of field and the brave Batavian warriors trimmed for battle. He saw their formations and Roman legions facing off, and imagined how he would maneuver them to victory––Batavian horse would plow into the Roman ranks, and as the tribes pressed against them, his best warriors, having swum the river behind the Roman position, would route his enemy .

They arrived at the milestone with its clearing and fire pit near a stream. As Marius commanded the legionnaires to set up camp, the snow fell.

"And we'll need the tents tonight," he said, kicking two logs in place at the fire pit. Marius motioned young Val over, and then offered him the flints and a ball of dried grass. "Get this started immediately."

Liuppo pulled his saddlebag down, and Folkbern his, and they set up a meal near the pit. Marius brought the stores of legionnaires' food—the einkorn fry bread, the dried fruit, the jerky, the barley wine.

As the fire crackled in the pit, flames feeble against the cold sky, Rokus cinched the fur cloak around Ulla's face and kissed the top of her head. He pulled back, surprised at himself, and then smelled the earthy perfume of her person, apples, honey, wheat. Standing, he watched her sleep—he, the worldly guardian, she, something pure.

Menfrid held a metal cup of barley wine to him; Liuppo, Gerulf and Folkbern all held up theirs, spilling the overfilled vessels.

"We covered many miles today, so here's to the same for the morrow," Menfrid raised his cup.

"Same," they toasted.

"The faster we get home."

"We'll see Raurica then, and it's just a few weeks to Betuwe."

"Eighteen days if we keep up the pace."

Marius came over with young Val.

"The weather will be milder along the Rhenus, and the road is flat," he noted, taking a cup. "I think we can get to Castra Vetera in less time."

"Agree," Liuppo said, drinking.

"But we must remember the horses." Rokus stroked the roan's neck. "They need to rest."

"We have our schedule." Marius looked over the group, "So we will get to Castra Vetera when we are supposed to."

"We have to consider our charge, as well." Rokus glanced at the mound of fur that was Ulla.

"There's only one charge in this train," Marius asserted, "and I have a schedule to keep.

"The girl would have died."

"Maybe that would have been better for her."

"Good Donar, help me." Rokus raised his voice. "We don't kill innocents."

"She should have been left behind." Marius' voice was barbed.

"I'm taking her to safety."

"I didn't sanction such a thing."

"I didn't ask."

"She's holding us back."

"She needs a home."

Marius threw down his cup and turned to leave. Rokus grabbed his sleeve, spun him back round.

"Forget not, Marius, I'm letting you take me to Castra Vetera."

Each stood his ground. The pressure Rokus had felt in his chest had vanished, anger the unguent for its dissipation, and he now saw the Roman clearly.

"We have four hundred miles to go, Rokus, so let's get on with it." Marius pulled away and walked into the darkness lurking around them. As the Roman disappeared, Rokus heard the cries of predator and preyed upon in the mountain wind. He followed him into the night.

"We can move swiftly, at times, but we can't drive the horses to death, and this little girl needs a gentle ride. The fast pace will take its toll," Rokus called after him.

Marius snorted. He paced along the edge of the firelight, vaguely shaking his head.

"Who was the horseman in Aventicum?" Rokus asked.

Marius stopped. He seemed to weigh different responses, then he turned to Rokus. "Just a messenger."

"With what message?"

An owl screeched, and they heard wings flap and the rustle of underbrush and a pitiful squeak.

"What message?" Rokus repeated.

Marius looked up into the fire and smoke. Rokus waited, then spat to the ground.

"Is he going to Raurica? Vindonissa? What are you mixed up in?"

"I owe you no explanation."

"You're taking me to train men for private armies. I got that out of you. You just sent an expert cavalier north. I want to know where, why."

"Sure you do."

"What's his word; where was he going?" Rokus positioned himself in front of the Roman.

"I cannot say"

"Say it, man."

Marius stepped back into the night, but then Rokus blocked his way. His eyes shot through the Roman, who twitched as if wounded.

"Something about the armies of the north?"

"Vitellius."

"And the rest of it?"

Marius looked at him, and it was the battlefields of Britannia all over again, one beholden to the other. Rokus felt his power over the Roman and the Roman's respect. Marius sighed.

"His name is Torix, a Tulingi scout for Nerva. He is to work up the troops of Vindonissa for Vitellius."

"That's a formidable force, both southern and northern legions for Vitellius. Unstoppable. So, Marius, you are against the man who freed me."

"He is not good for Rome."

"Who is good for Rome?"

Marius turned to the fire, listened to the men talk about the hunt. His eyes grew dreamy, focused on some distant place. He stood up straight, as if at attention.

"Vitellius."

"There is much more. Whose armies will I be training, really?"

"Clever, Rokus."

"Well?"

"It's as I said—the senators."

"There's more."

"The senators who back Vitellius."

Rokus stepped away rubbing his beard and running his fingertips across the long scar concealed under his wavy hair.

"This Vitellius will bring destruction on Rome as soon as he arrives. You must know that. His way with the legions is his way. He will bring that same indulgence with him. A fine example."

Still Marius stood at attention.

"And you and Nerva will be there for part of the spoils."

A burst of laughter came from the fire pit, with Liuppo's cackle above all.

"The Emperor should be more than a glutton."

"We shall see."

"So it's Vitellius."

"So it will be."

Rokus shook his head and returned to the fire, bundled Ulla in his arms, and brought her to a tent.

"Everything well?" she asked.

"Fine, just fine. Sweet dreams." He touched her forehead and cheek and then left the tent. He looked across the night sky.

"Or is it?"

FOURTEEN
Augusta Raurica and the River Rhenus

They crossed wide meadows and hills the next day. Every rider closed himself off from the others, as if the estrangement between Rokus and Marius had infected them. They passed clusters of houses and barns without looking at the animals grazing or the furrows from harvest. They forded streams without studying the bracken and darting fish in the watery shadows. They looked at the road, solid and level and well paved, and kept moving.

Late morning they encountered a farmer and his son at an intersection. A nag pulled their cart, its bin piled high with turnips, bulbous and tousled with tendril roots. The rustic waved as he watched the train clop by, but each member of the train rode immersed in a troubled yet sensate world so real to them they didn't notice that the man was weary with labor and maybe anxiety, or that the boy was racked by the evil fire—red blotched, black-fingered, stuporous.

By afternoon they arrived at the mountain range outlying their destination. They knew that after climbing the mountains they would descend into the river valley and find Raurica perched above the Rhenus. They sat their horses and studied the long slope climbing into the forested pass. In a long lazy turn, the road ascended and disappeared far above where they stood.

Rokus dismounted, lifted Ulla to the ground, and stretched. Ulla reached to the sky and yawned, then looked to Rokus for something to eat. The Batavians pulled out pieces of fowl and roasted boar and dried fruits, and Marius and Val brought out hard cakes and barley wine.

They ate absorbed in the reticence they'd known all day, and nothing seemed to be able to lodge it from their minds. The wine bag passed from hand to hand, and even Ulla drank with gusto, wiping her mouth before handing it to Rokus. He drank and gave it to Marius, uttering no words, sharing no glance.

Mounted again, they put their horses to the climb. Rokus wrapped Ulla in his arms and hummed the melody that always came to him. She stared ahead and hardly moved but once laid her head against his chest. By late afternoon, she slept across the saddle and held tight the bloodstone ring.

The road climbed toward the sky. On their left and right, stands of forest pressed against the road, but where the road straightened, the view ahead was spare: no farther mountains, no clouds, no trees along distant pass. They headed for the sky, trusting that they would not fall off the earth, because there was nothing at the end of their view.

A mile from the summit, the roan faltered, dropping her ears, widening her eyes. Rokus heeled her gently, and she put forth but shook her reins and bridle to announce her reluctance.

Then Rokus smelled smoke and, beyond the end of the visible road, saw an opaque wall, gray and black. He sat up, listened. Birds chirped around him at their afternoon feeding, but that was all. The sight of the smoke, telling in its billowing, quickened his pulse, and he heeled the roan firmly. She trotted, waking Ulla.

"Hang on, Ulla."

He held her between his arms while working the roan into cantor. He clicked his tongue and then demanded the roan to run. They flew past Marius, the legionnaires and the Batavians. As they reached the summit, the Batavians galloped just behind him, and then together they lined up abreast and walked their horses to the edge of a lookout.

The valley far below smoldered. A row of fifteen triremes, looking like a child's toys, burned; orange flashed under the weight of smoke, and each great column connected to its neighbor and formed a great wall. Along the river, buildings that served the waterfront business were black skeletons spewing streams of cinder and ash.

Out on the river, long black shapes gushed thick smoke, rolling up on itself, climbing, swirling down the river way.

Men ran in the streets—specks, frantic and confused. Down every street rode tribesmen brandishing swords, long hair and capes flying.

Rokus stiffened at the prospects— yet again, he thought— blades thrusting into bodies, gushes of blood, screams of the vanquished and cries of the victorious. Again, it was the mayhem of close battle, heated spirits igniting muscle and reflex, the desperate hacking for survival. He searched for the legions up and down the streets but could not see them.

But he did not have to act; this was Marius' affair. Let him see this disaster and decide what to do.

The wind shifted bringing with it the cries to attack and the cries of the maimed—horrible notes full of dementedness and pleading. Ulla snapped out of her trance and craned forward to see. She seemed fully informed of not only what she saw, but also the understanding to take action.

"Help them."

"It's a Roman town."

"Please."

Rokus looked at Folkbern to his right. The comrade moved his hand to the hilt of his sword and nodded. Gerulf did the same. To Rokus' left, Menfrid and Liuppo drew their swords and pointed them toward the town.

"Awaiting your command, Prince Rokus," Menfrid said.

Marius and the legionnaires drew up to them, and then Marius walked his horse to the edge. He studied the chaos below before leaning back. He remained silent.

"Can't see the legion," Rokus observed. "Probably went after some of them."

"Maybe to Valhalla." Folkbern reached into a long sheath-like bag for his bow.

"How many do you make?" Gerulf asked the group as he touched instinctively his spears, long sword, bow and quiver of arrows.

"Few hundred." Rokus studied the riverside town and mayhem and then enveloped Ulla, kissing the top of her head.

"Too many; we wouldn't have a chance," Marius surmised while tugging his reins to back his horse.

"Help them," Ulla spoke as if in a trance.

Menfrid pulled his horse out of the line and circled behind them. He strung his bow and loosened arrows in his quiver.

"Create a diversion." Gerulf pulled one of his spears from its sheath and held it at his side, a menacing barb glistening in the sun.

"And attack from the flank," Liuppo added.

Marius, facing away, turned to survey the scene once again: the gathering horsemen by the waterfront, the others charging down the lanes. A large group of tribesmen whipped their horses, attacking victims he couldn't see. They streaked down from the town, past the temple, the amphitheater, the basilica. This charge through the town captured all observers' attention. As the tribesmen disappeared behind a wall, they heard the clash of swords, cries, the bark of commands, more cries.

He shifted in his saddle and gripped his sword. His movement aggravated his mount; it stepped in place, sidestepped, backed up, and began to rear. It snapped at young Val's horse, and then Marius reined forcefully.

Below, legionnaires emerged from behind the wall, closing ranks but giving ground, hacking and thrusting at the horsemen who bore down on them even as some fell with their wounded, bloodied horses. From above, the travelers saw it was a noble but lost fight.

"Help them," the group heard. Not a whisper but a haunting utterance that bespoke lamentation. "Help them," they heard again, and then Ulla emerged from Rokus' arm and spoke again, "Help them," but with the timbre of command.

Rokus looked around and then pulled out of the line. He walked the roan past Marius to the packhorses grazing by the road. Putting his arms under Ulla's, he lifted her onto one of their backs. She sat between bulging stores that hung on the horse's sides and gripped the netting for balance. He gathered the loose reins from the lead packhorse and gave them to her. She looked into his face, and he saw that she understood.

"Let's get in closer to see before we become dead heroes," Rokus called to his countrymen.

He kicked the roan and led the Batavians down the mountain road. Val spurred on, as did Marius and the others, followed by Ulla towing the packhorses.

The road dropped quickly; after plummeting down a series of switchbacks, they galloped pell-mell down the long slope to the floor. Rokus led them physically but not with a full measure of intention. He had neither plan nor purpose, and he did not like the odds. Still, as they charged to the bottom, his instincts took over, and, arriving there, he created a picture in his mind that dissolved misgiving. He drew his sword and pointed to a grove just outside of the town.

"Ulla, there."

She pulled the packhorse to the left, and the string of horses followed.

Marius rode up to young Val. "Arm the men with pila and follow me."

Val and the men extracted javelins from one of the packs drawn by Ulla and rejoined the party.

"To that wall," Rokus called.

They heeled their horses to the foot of the road leading up the town's high position. Turning the corner, they came upon the aftermath of what they had seen from the summit; an entire century had been cut down. Scattered shields mixed with eighty legionnaires' bodies and ravaged horses in a carpet of death. Slaughtered men lay strewn in their throes, slashed, impaled, chopped. Lumps of horses clogged one area, javelin shafts protruding, their chests heaving in final struggle. A lake of blood gathered beneath them and had begun to flow in awful channels down the pavement.

Their horses reared, protesting, and they spurred them around the melee. At the end of the confusion, they came upon ten bodies beheaded, and nearby the legionnaires' swords were planted, hilts holding heads or vacant faces.

"This is their revenge," Rokus declared.

"Of what slight?" Folkbern said.

"Find the rest of the legion and you'll find the answer. Now, up to the town."

They pressed onward to the plateau on which Roman buildings stood in formal arrangement. Dead men in tunics blanketed the streets and steps and central intersection; their naked arms now offered vain protection while the gross smears of their blood anointed the stone.

Rokus trotted the roan into the square looking for signs. Smoke rose from the waterfront, smoke rose from the shops, smoke rose from behind the temple; men screamed, and at every turn there seemed to be tribal horses crashing through barricades, citizen men wielding sticks or useless daggers, as they, flailing ineffectually, met their ends.

Down the river was the fort besieged by barbarians shrieking like animals. Smoke rose from behind the walls; swarms of tribesmen crossed makeshift bridges across the moats and bashed gates and leaned pole ladders up for the assault. The flicker of Roman helmets lined the top of the walls; inside men ran every direction.

"Gerulf, diversion!" he cried, pointing down a street.

Gerulf swept an arm by Menfrid, who lashed Liuppo's leg, and the three of them shot down the street bawling their own screams of victory. Gerulf yelled as they passed the first marauding horsemen encountered. These raiders were butchering innocents gathered at the forum, the detritus of women and children piled around them in gory disarray. One of them growled, and together they abandoned their hacking feast, jumped onto their horses, and chased the Batavians.

Gerulf drew them away with his flight. Batavians and raiders galloped twenty horse lengths apart as they hurled down the street. Rokus, meanwhile, signaled to his group to follow him, and he heeled the roan down a parallel street, leaning forward, urging the horse to fly. Marius and the legionnaires raced closely behind.

After several blocks, he turned sharply at a corner, sword flashing, and crashed into the raiders. They hadn't expected the broadside and caromed into a building in a tangle of arms and legs and horses. Several raiders, recoiling from the collision with Rokus, the Romans, and the wall, were knocked from their saddles. They groped for balance in their tumbles, fumbled swords, and thrashed and snarled at each other as they righted themselves.

Rokus reacted swiftly, swiping at one after another. His blade sliced deeply across a face, then cut wide a chest, and then, leaning over, stabbed through a cheek and skull. He heeled his horse, dragging the man, blade through head, until his blade slid out of the mangled face.

He whipped the roan around, heeled and charged after the stragglers of the mongrel cavalry. In his wake, the Romans laid into the other raiders, so surprised by the ambush, and hacked off hands, stabbed into faces, and chopped at shoulders until the barbarians lay spurting from severances and gapes across their heads and torsos.

The Romans finished their own slaughter and caught up with Rokus, and they all galloped after the marauders, catching them at the end of the long street. Their horses reared and a fight there flurried, brutal, desperate, crazed. With these engagements, the marauders lost the advantage of surprise and intimidation and now attempted to retreat or reconsider even with their greater numbers. Breaking away, they left themselves exposed, and the Romans threw the remaining pila, piercing both horse and man at odd angles, and both species screamed in agony. Then Rokus and his men stabbed and slashed two and three per man as the rabble scrambled away.

Rokus sat up in his saddle to survey. "Take that road down there. Attack!" he called to Folkbern, Gerulf and Liuppo, point-ing to the right. "We'll get them from this side."

The three Batavians plowed down the hill and around to the harbor, and Rokus and the remaining riders charged down the other road.

"Marius!" Rokus called through the din. "Take three of your men and attack first. I'll take Val and Menfrid."

Marius ignored him, whipping his horse to speed. They gal-loped together, leaning forward, holding their swords out, spur-ring. Rokus turned to Val and another soldier, "Follow me!" he yelled and heeled the roan. Moving as one, Rokus and the Roman horse turned the corner of the waterfront street and swooped in, yelling.

Rokus then signaled to his legionnaires and Menfrid, who followed him as he turned down a side street. They galloped be-hind the row of river front buildings, reining after two intersec-tions, then turned toward the river and charged.

The shrieking marauders rushed Folkbern, Gerulf and Liuppo who kept them at bay with uniform swipes of their long swords.

Marius and the legionnaires crashed into the marauders' rearguard, turning them. In the wild swordplay, many maraud-ers struck their own men, and with the Roman attack, they lost thrust and momentum and began to retreat in all directions.

Just then Rokus' contingent struck the middle of the ma-rauders' confusion, and they were easy targets without discipline. Rokus and the Romans attacked the raiders where they spun, jabbing into them from saddle perches, slashing, cutting. It was a chorus of groans and wails that followed and—mixed with the clang of metal, the rent of leather and skin, crunch of bone, and the piercing cries of horses gashed—an afternoon of fatal noise.

First five, then ten and more of the marauders fled behind rows of amphorae and stacks of pallets. As the Batavians began killing these tribesmen, they broke for the street and disappeared behind the buildings.

"Let them go," Rokus called as Menfrid shot an arrow at one.

It hit the marauder full in the shoulder. He spun and tumbled to the pavement, rolled and jumped to his feet grabbing at the arrow sticking out. He ran down the street as he struggled to extract the shaft.

Marius chased after him, sword overhead, and, galloping by, swung mightily across the man's back.

"Enough!" Rokus yelled.

Folkbern walked his horse among the dead and dying. Men gulped mouths full of blood as they gasped for air, others groaned in delirium. Bodies lay slumped in death at this intersection of streets.

Gerulf leaned over in his saddle, blood smearing his arm, and put his horse to Rokus and the legionnaires.

"Bad?" Rokus craned his neck to see the wound through the blood.

"Don't-think-so," Gerulf sputtered.

Rokus took his wrist to examine the arm; a slash across the forearm had cut through cloth and muscle but not bone. He jumped off his horse and dug a strip of leather from out of his saddlebag. He had Gerulf lower his arm so Rokus could cut and tear the sleeve off. After cutting away the bloodiest cloth, Rokus wrapped the shreds around the wound tightly and then secured this cloth with the leather strip. He tightened it until Gerulf winced.

"We'll unloosen this in a little while, for now," Rokus said positioning the arm in Gerulf's lap.

Rokus surveyed the riverfront, the surrounding hills, and the fort.

Then the faintest strains came to him, the crying strings soaring over the drum, the drum driving the rhythmic jangle of chords. He could barely sense it, but it was there.

"Ulla," he blurted, jumping across his saddle. "I'll meet you at the fort," he called to the men.

He whipped the roan with the long reins. Young Val saw this and ran to his horse and followed.

Rokus galloped down the road that fed the town, made the last turn, and saw the grove at the base of the mountain. The packhorses grazed nearby; Ulla was gone.

As he burst into the grove, snapping branches and twigs, Val halted quickly behind. The roan pranced in place.

"Ulla!" Rokus' shout trembled, commingling doubt and despair.

He whipped the roan about and shot past Val, galloped up the hill toward the forum. A thousand paces on, he came to a scraggly horse pulling at its reins tied to a tree. Fresh wounds covered its back and sides, and the saddle was rudimentary and poor.

He heard a yelp from the brush and bounded off the roan, drawing his knife, and crashed through the tangle of leaves and limbs into a man standing over her. The impact sent a knife flying from the raider's hand, and Rokus and he fell next to Ulla, who lay splayed in the grass.

In a blur of arms, Rokus sliced the man's throat. And as Ulla whimpered, the man sighed.

He looked directly at Rokus, his bushy red eyebrows shadowing his complete understanding of what happened. He smiled exposing rotting teeth and faded into death.

Ulla rolled to her side and vomited. She held her sides and her crotch, spewing bile, and yowled her pain and fear. Purple swelling closed her left eye, and her bottom lip had become a gross adornment on her face, fat, red, bulging.

"Oh no, oh no, oh no!" Rokus pleaded to the gods.

She glared into his eye as if to transmit her horror and outrage, while the good side of her mouth quivered to form some words to scream.

"I'm so sorry, girl, I didn't protect you! Oh, I'm so sorry!"

After wiping grit off her forehead and daubing her seeping cheek, he tugged at her tunic as if fewer wrinkles would undo her rapine; then he cradled her, forming a shield between her and the world.

Val met them at the raider's horse.

"See if that horse can go on." Rokus gestured with his head while his arms supported Ulla.

She fell out of his arms as she doubled over wailing. He engulfed her and pressed her gently, but her frail form shook uncontrollably. His cheek was against her temple, and he felt the pulsating stress throughout her being. How could he have let this happen, he thought, and tears of his failure brimmed over and streaked down his face. Wispy blonde strands stuck to her mouth, nose, and eyes. Then her body quaked in a fit of despair. He held her tighter, but she pushed away; he stepped back, but she fell into his embrace, bawling.

Rokus handed Ulla to Val and, after mounting, lifted her from his arms. He cradled her as he had before, and she bellowed into the afternoon.

"Let's get out of here," he said.

They walked their horses back to the grove, tied the packhorses to the marauder's horse, and turned down the road toward the waterfront. While Rokus held her, young Val watched the girl weep; they approached the town through an ache of misery. Ulla's crying gave form to her nightmare, and the black cloud of her horror struck a position over them. Rokus believed something had died back there.

Most of the biremes and triremes had burned out and sunk, and there were blackened frames of merchantmen hanging from stanchions along the river. Farther upriver, a line of barges smoldered, and the carcasses of horses lay slumped in rows, orderly except for their twisted necks and legs.

Rokus covered her face. He frowned at Val. "Where are they?"

Val shrugged, then handed Rokus the packhorse rope and spurred his horse toward the fort; Rokus watched him climb the hill and disappear behind trees. Liuppo returned on foot from the town, dragging his sword.

"Where are they?" Rokus asked again.

Liuppo jerked his head back as Folkbern emerged from a side street leading Liuppo's horse and another.

"This one had a time of it." Folkbern pointed at Liuppo. He stopped and stared at Rokus and the girl.

"Find Menfrid and Gerulf; we're leaving for Betuwe," Rokus ordered.

From the fort in the distance, the cheer of a thousand men echoed in the blackened sky; it rumbled again, and then again. Rokus walked his horse past the slaughter of men and horses and the charred barges and settled in a clearing beyond it all.

He jumped off the roan and carried Ulla to the water's edge; she cried still and had drenched the front of her tunic with tears and slobber, and her hair stuck to her cheeks. He cleared her face of hair strands and tears and began rocking, then realized he had not done such a thing in twenty years, since his sons were so young, and he, too, was different. Then he shuddered with the idea of children in the men's world of fighting, and, cradling her, he wept with regret.

After Ulla calmed, he bent his knees and sank into the river with her. She dropped her head back releasing her hair into the water where it flowed with the contradictory currents. He cleaned her forehead and cheeks, then clasped her firmly and twisted left and right allowing the water to wash her torso and between her legs. He held her still, wishing he could have the afternoon again. After she splayed herself under the surface, she pressed his chest with her cheek to signal she was done. Then he carried her to the grasses by the river road, and placed her down gently. She convulsed still with little cries and groans.

After touching her forehead, Rokus covered her and then went to the river with the roan. He led the horse into the shallows, splashed water on her legs and barrel, and stroked the tinted water off her coat. Again and again he washed the animal clean of the blood that glistened across muscle and bone. Then he washed himself and shivered as he returned to the girl.

He turned as he heard the drumming of hooves.

Rokus helped Ulla to her feet. He squared her to him and looked into her eyes. They reassured him with a clarity that had replaced the vacant gaze of before. He smiled encouragement, then tipped his head to the trees.

"Do you have to pee? We will depart soon."

Folkbern led the Batavian horsemen into the clearing, where they sat their horses. Liuppo slumped low in his saddle looking bedraggled; Gerulf protected his bandaged arm and tugged the ropes to the packhorses and new horse with his good one. Menfrid smiled.

"Was an army of them," Folkbern recounted.

"From the far northeast, hear tell," Menfrid offered. "Bastards."

"Marcomanni, then?" Gerulf asked.

"Likely," Menfrid answered.

"Prepare to leave," Rokus announced as Ulla returned from the trees. Rokus ushered her to Val to hold while he mounted. Thus in the saddle, he took her from him and directed, "Keep an eye on that raider's horse. We may have to put it down."

"Our Roman friends?" Folkbern looked down the quay, up to the fort, and at the acquired horse, the packhorses, and Ulla. He saw Rokus' impatience and took the packhorses' reins from Gerulf.

Rokus spat. "They can figure this out."

Rokus led them at a trot along the river road. On the hill east of them stood the fort with its united roars of men delivered from death once again.

"Should have avoided this place," Rokus declared to Folkbern, who rode at his side.

"It was a massacre." Folkbern kneed his horse to keep apace while watching the mortal remains of raider and horse scattered across the area.

"But not ours to fix." Rokus stared straight down the river road.

FIFTEEN
Along the Border of Gallia and Germania

They rode in silence, the clopping hooves soothing in their rhythm. Ulla whimpered and trembled, though Rokus held her. He closed his eye and listened to the hooves and allowed the irregular sound to assuage his own inquietude, even as he imagined her terror. After two hours, her distress seemed to reverberate through the land that now spread wide and rich in all directions, and he wondered if she would ever find a homeland, or even survive.

At the ten-mile marker, they turned north, and the paved road that had run from Latium changed to dirt track. They fell into a formation: Rokus and Folkbern side-by-side, Menfrid and Liuppo following the packhorse towed by Folkbern, and then Gerulf. The silence that prevailed assumed its own presence and traveled lockstep with them. They all acknowledged it pervading their retinue, but after so long weighing the bloodshed of the morning and the solemnity of death, they sent overtures into the air.

"Cold."

"To the bone."

"Getting colder."

"It is."

"Solstice festival soon."

"Yes."

"Going?"

"Most likely."

"Be good to be home."

"Arm all right?"

"Been better."

"Change the bandage."

"Yes."

"How's your leg?"

"Hurts. And your neck?"

"Shoulder."

"How's it?"

"Bleeding stopped."

"Who were they?"

"Don't know. Marcomanni, they said."

"Burgundians, I'd say."

"No, Marcomanni are smarter."

"Liuppo's sagging."

"Just needs rest."

"And barley wine."

"Or beer."

"Or mead."

"Pretty country."

"Nice."

The land flattened and the similarities to Betuwe manifested and brought unspoken respect and fascination.

Four hours northward, they stopped. Rokus put his horse off the road to a meadow, and the entourage followed. He dismounted and pulled Ulla to him; he wished she had been asleep, burying fear with slumber, but she stared at the unspeakable.

The group wordlessly tended to the horses, watered them in a stream, and fettered them in the meadow.

"Let's build a fire and wait for the Romans," Rokus said. "They're most likely on their way."

Liuppo gathered twigs and brush and a few broken branches and made a pyramid. Gerulf produced a wad of dried grass and flints. Shortly, a fire crackled in their center. And they held out their palms, stomping the ground. Rokus rummaged through the stores from the packhorses and spread a meal on a little berm; they ate deer jerky and grain cakes and dried dates. He filled six tin cups with wine and handed them to each of the party, and they drank them silently as the battle shot through their beings. One by one, they sat back into blankets and bags of gear to let the fighting abate.

Rokus covered Ulla with the fur cloak. She had retreated into some web of fearsome memories, her little body attempting to reconcile the evil forced on her. Divorced from the sort of language that had betrayed her, she wouldn't talk now.

The blanket of cold air weighed on them, and they tucked their furs tightly around themselves. Blinking, yawning, they rested their heads and closed their eyes.

Presently, the ground trembled; Rokus woke and jumped to his feet. Five Romans approached at a gallop, their dust cloud rising like a phantom mountain.

Marius reined fiercely, and then Val and the legionnaires drew up, their horses' eyes flashing, mouths agape, and hooves digging in the dirt as they skidded. Marius slid out of his saddle, straightened his cloak, and marched over to Rokus.

"You missed the feast at the fort," Marius declared. He surveyed their camp.

"My men took a beating." Rokus asserted.

"Commandant rewarded handsomely." Marius gripped a leather pouch dangling from his belt and shook it so that all could hear the jangling coins.

"Batavi had no business there," Rokus explained. "We were at risk when we should have bypassed the place."

"They won't be back." Marius reasoned.

"The Marcomanni will be back." Rokus spoke with conviction and his knowledge of the tribes east of the Rhenus River. Restless and land-hungry, the Germans, as a people, were in flux.

"Not if we kill every one of them. Legio XIII Gemina of Vindonissa came to help," Marius' voice had a tinge of arrogance that Rokus found ill-advised.

"Where were the commandant's boys?" Rokus asked.

Marius looked at the Batavians one by one; Rokus studied the ambivalence in Marius' face.

"Couldn't have been more than two centuries there. Where were the rest?" Rokus pursued.

"A foray," Marius replied, assessing Rokus' line of inquiry.

"Against...?" Rokus hung his thought in the air.

"The Marcomanni," Marius answered.

Menfrid elbowed Liuppo, nodded, put his hand on his sword.

"Rome fooled by the Germans again?" Rokus turned his back on Marius and began to pack things into the stores.

Marius scowled, removed his helmet, and ran his hand through his hair. He glared at Rokus, then the others.

"Should've gone long ago," Rokus stated.

"You know my orders."

"You're a liar."

Marius seized the hilt of his sword, but before it left its scabbard, Folkbern and Menfrid locked his arms in theirs. Young Val jumped forward, hand on hilt. Rokus raised his arm in front of the young legionnaire, who stopped.

"Hear the truth," Rokus insisted.

Marius struggled in vain.

"Val should know."

"He follows orders, doesn't need to know." Marius strained against the Batavians at his side.

"All should know." Rokus stepped back, scanned the men before him. He put his hands on his hips. "Roman senators want me to run training camps for Germans. Start militias for senators' personal use. Germans trained by Batavi warriors."

The Batavians looked at each other, perplexed.

"Get Germans from across the river?" Menfrid asked, pointing to the opposite shore.

"And teach them our ways?" Gerulf asked, incredulous.

"Let's teach fish to fly." Folkbern laughed. He eased his hold on the Roman.

"Be easier," snapped Menfrid.

Rokus stepped up to Marius and examined the face he knew well.

"We leave you now," he announced, nodding his head at his countrymen, who released him.

Rokus strode to the horses. "To Betuwe."

He swung his saddle across the roan's back. The horse dropped her ears with disapproval, circling away from him, but he slapped her rump and she submitted. He bridled her, after which she shook her head. Folkbern and Menfrid followed suit, while Marius fumed and stamped.

"I'll come after you," Marius threatened.

"Go back to your senators, Marius," Rokus directed, as he tightened the bellyband.

"I have to come after you, Rokus."

"You follow your orders, Marius; I'll follow my calling." Rokus went to Ulla who still stared into the cloud of her torment.

He picked her up and placed her across his saddle and then slung his leg over, signaling their departure. The Batavians gathered knives and blankets, saddlebags and cloaks. They unfettered all the horses and put saddles in place; then, after cinching saddle straps, they mounted and put their horses to his side. He guided the roan to the road.

The Romans watched them break camp and line up on the track. Marius remounted and appeared ready to strike.

"Here, don't need these nags," Rokus called out, pointing to the packhorses. "And have a safe journey back to Rome."

"Watch out for those Marcomanni," quipped Menfrid, saddling up.

The Batavians spurred, and as they departed, Rokus called over his shoulder.

"Tell Galba or Otho or Vitellius I'm home."

"I'll follow my orders. I will." Marius' voice had the tautness of a threat.

Rokus dismissed him with a wave. They cantered away in a clatter of hooves. He held Ulla tightly as the horse bounced in its rhythmic gait, and as they rounded a bend, he drew back to a trot. He listened for the Roman horses, but there was only the breeze and somewhere, water rushing.

The road narrowed by evening; hard-packed loam and sand coursed near the river for the first time in miles. The Rhenus now spread wide through steep banks choked with forest. On the west side were landings every few miles, small clearings cut into the trees, and feeding these were tracks from the road. The villages they passed or stopped at for food and drink were made of wattle and daub, whitewashed; the generous folk there gave what offerings could be spared. On the east side of the river, the forest was a dark green wall along the shore that extended far. They could hear bizarre squawks and screams, drumming, and growls from unnamable beasts coming from behind the wall.

At twilight they stopped at a clearing to sleep. They ate fried bread from a hamlet and apples picked along the way. Rokus fashioned a rudimentary lean-to from thin branches and twigs and dried leaves. He settled Ulla inside, covered her with furs, and joined the others for mead.

"Did he mean business?" Folkbern asked, raising the prospect of a confrontation with the Romans.

"He did." Rokus drank from his cup, savored it, and drank again.

"There are five of us; he doesn't have a chance." Menfrid leaned on his bow.

"Let's hide and wait for them," Gerulf suggested, gesturing to the woods behind them.

"There will be no fight. He's not a fool."

Liuppo pulled his cloak over his shoulder and winced at the pain from his wound.

"Do we just let him take us?" he offered, poking the fire with a stick.

"Tail us," Rokus corrected.

"Like we're animals." Gerulf took out his knife and stabbed a branch reaching into the clearing.

"He'll not bother us." Rokus looked into the bottom of his cup and then held it up to Folkbern, who held the skin.

"Rokus, he meets us or we meet him," Folkbern issued his ultimatum while pouring into Rokus' cup.

"No. We cross tomorrow." Rokus looked at each one of them in turn and stood.

"Cross?" Liuppo asked.

"The Rhenus," Rokus clarified while stretching. "The River Rhenus."

"Romans would never chance it over there," Gerulf agreed, nodding.

"Brilliant." Liuppo passed the skin filled with mead.

Menfrid took it from him, poured into his cup, and drank. Wiping his mouth, he passed the bag to Rokus and examined Gerulf's forearm.

"If this old fellow is up to it, we cross," he said.

"I can fly with this wing," Gerulf reported, moving his arm up and down.

Rokus took a deep draft of the mead and passed it to Folkbern. They all then shared a collective nod and found places to sleep.

"I'll take first watch," Rokus announced.

"And I will take second." Folkbern pulled his cloak to his chin and closed his eyes.

At daybreak they collected a pile of reeds and straight sticks from the shoreline. They braided long blades of autumn grass into twine, bundled reeds, reinforced the bundles with the sticks, and then wrapped them in three places with the twine. They made many of these and lashed them to straight branches they'd cut from small trees. By mid-morning they'd made two small rafts and piled all their saddlebags and saddles on one and prepared a saddle in the middle of the second for Ulla.

"Wonder if she can swim." Menfrid lashed an upright saddle in its place.

"Give her a line to us," Rokus instructed.

He led the bareback horses to the shoreline, tethered them, and checked on Ulla, who lay speechless as though possessed by forces powerful and fearful; she quavered.

"This is asking much, little one."

He pulled her shoulders gently away from the roll of fur cloak she'd put her head on. "We're crossing the river."

Ulla began breathing heavily and then spun around to him.

"Afraid," she whispered.

"Don't know what those Romans will do. Best we go where they won't."

She lunged at him, squeezing his neck and clinging there.

"Be leaving in a few minutes. Ready?"

She grunted a sound that could have been, "No!"

He took the fur cloak away and placed it on her raft. Then he picked her up, gave Menfrid a sign, and padded into the shallows with her. Gerulf waded in to steady the raft, and Rokus set her down.

"On the saddle, that's right."

"Here, little one," Menfrid coaxed gently.

Ulla grasped the line like reins, adjusted her placement, and looked at Rokus fearfully.

"That's it, Ulla, nothing to be afraid of."

The men peeled their outer garments, and Rokus removed his deerskin breeches and jacket. They placed them on the first raft and led the horses into the water, little eddies tumbling between their legs. Grasping the halters at horses' cheeks, they pushed off.

The cargo raft rode low in the water on one side. Menfrid swam to it, pushed the saddles closer to the middle, and then pulled and lashed bundles tighter. It bobbed and spun in the current but cleared the surface.

Ulla's eyes darted left and right looking for the disaster that did not come. She gripped her reins and scrunched forward as if cowering in a storm, but her raft was sound and rode the current as the raider's bay horse towed it across.

The men lay prone in the water, kicking for balance and gripping halters as the horses used their trot-like gait to propel. Their tunics floated like watery flags pulling downstream, and their long hair lost all shape as it, too, drew north with the current.

As they made headway, the Rhenus carried them downriver so that their landing place was not certain. Horses flared nostrils at the water line and raised open mouths gasping as they kicked and kicked some more.

Ulla's raft had floated far down, its line to Menfrid taut and dotted with droplets quivering and flying off. She was separate from them, riding the current that had the weight of alpine lakes, the breadth of the valleys she'd seen. She clung, always looking back to Rokus for a sign.

Rokus waved in between stabilizing strokes and kicks. His horse had pulled ahead, and he saw from that vantage that they would make it, that Menfrid would land second, that they would pull her to shore.

After thirty minutes they felt the muddy bottom, kicked and thrashed for solid footing. Rokus pulled at a low branch and hoisted himself to shore.

The dark forest was a physical force at the landing place, looming, dense, forbidding. It offered no clearing, no paths. Crows laughed from the treetops; a hawk dropped into the sludge nearby, seized a fish, then waved its broad wings, lifting off gracefully.

They forced themselves into the forest edge, stamping down brush and pushing between trees to rest. Like some itinerant band of mummers exhausted with performance, they sprawled haphazardly with their heaving chests and dripping forms and sodden clothes. The horses, too, rested; dripping, snorting, they looked at the troupe skeptically.

Rokus climbed the embankment to explore. He followed animal trails to a glade and continued far into the forest through other glades and came to a track worn north-south; he noted scat from wolves and bears, and then returned for the others.

They had dismantled the rafts, saddled the horses, and lined up waiting for him.

By mid-afternoon, they had advanced north on the eastern track and found a place on a bluff overlooking the Rhenus as it swept to the northwest; they broke out jerky and breads. Rokus unwrapped the greasy cloth from the chunk of jerky.

"Try this," Rokus offered it to Ulla.

"No," she mumbled, turning her face.

"Haven't eaten much these days."

She gazed over the ledge.

Rokus made a little setting on the cloth: a piece of jerky, the cup of mead, a chunk of bread, and an apple.

"Come on, good Gallic fried bread." He stood, touched the top of her head, and stepped back.

She glanced furtively at the bread.

"See. Help yourself." Rokus walked over to Folkbern, who studied the river and opposite shore.

"See Argentoratum?" Rokus asked.

Folkbern stood poised over the bluff, scanning, eating. Steady and calm, he turned to Rokus, sat on a rock, and leaned back against an elder tree.

"I see their road but not them," he shared while picking up a handful of berries.

"Marius will put in there." Rokus pointed upstream to a settlement tucked behind trees. A dock ran along the bank.

"What's he trying to do?" Folkbern picked a berry from his palm and aimed it at an overhanging branch. He tossed the berry but missed his target, a leaf, dried brown and wavering.

"A promotion," Rokus explained. "He's grown ambitious. Has a new love for denarii."

Rokus picked up a handful of elderberries and positioned himself next to Folkbern.

"And what's this about training camps?" Folkbern tossed another berry at the leaf but missed.

"It's as I said: lure the Germans with gold, train them in Batavian methods, hand them over to some senator," Rokus continued.

He lobbed a berry toward the leaf, but it flew far to the right and over the cliff.

"Are they daft?" Folkbern exclaimed. He fingered another berry, examined it, and flicked it at the leaf.

"No," Rokus answered, "Roman." He tossed another berry at the leaf, this time getting very close.

Folkbern adjusted his posture, selected another elderberry, and flicked it past the leaf. He quickly threw another berry, and another.

"Doesn't matter—no Batavian would go for it." He nodded to Rokus, acquiescing.

Rokus fingered an elderberry, then arched it just as a breeze vibrated the leaf. His berry disappeared below, while the leaf quivered in the breeze.

"Of course not," Rokus agreed.

"Rome can't control everything," Folkbern mused, aiming again.

"They're trying." Rokus watched Folkbern's next berry fly wide to the left.

"Good plan, swimming to this side," Folkbern said.

"Good plan to go home." Rokus spoke carefully as he aimed his next elderberry. He flicked it and missed, barely, yet again.

"Well, the woodland is beautiful, peaceful," Folkbern observed looking all around.

"And the spirits are abundant," Rokus said following his gaze.

"I feel that, too." Folkbern tossed another berry, which hit the branch above the leaf, shaking it.

"Little Ulla worries me, though. She's been through much," Rokus shared as he launched a berry at the leaf, missing.

"Will Marius keep after us?" Folkbern took another berry from his palm and flung it at the leaf, missing to the right.

"Yes." Rokus threw his next berry but missed to the left.

"He wouldn't cross?" Folkbern rolled another berry around with fingertips, inspected it, and approved of its roundness and weight. He tossed it, but it flew over the bluff.

"No, Romans have a sour memory of dark forests," Rokus pointed out. "They'll never forget Teutoburg Forest." He cast his berry, which hit the overhead branch exactly where Folkbern's berry hit.

"We're safe here," Folkbern concluded, aiming, waiting for the breeze to subside.

"We're safe anywhere," Rokus added, and as he aimed with Folkbern, the leaf trembled, and broke free, swirled and gyrated over the bluff and into the river's mist.

They watched the river's timeless course, the green jewels dancing on the surface, the trees hugging the shore, and together tossed their berries over the edge. They looked at each other and shook their heads, smiling.

Rokus heard the strains of music in the back of his brain rising from dormancy in woven melodies propelled by the thumping of a drum. He welcomed this and closed his eyes and let a new element, a chorus of voices, enter, and the beating drum propelled this like blood surging before combat.

He opened his eyes to a whistle. As he turned, an arrow shot past Folkbern and shivered into a tree. They ducked.

"Watch out," Liuppo called needlessly.

The troupe dropped to the ground as yells echoed through the forest canopy, and they heard cries of intimidation and the wild rustling of combat, the clang of swords, the dreadful crunch of killing.

Rokus crawled to the edge of their clearing, peered through the underbrush.

"Tribes," Rokus pushed the bushes back. "A skirmish."

"And Romans?" Folkbern narrowed his eyes for focus.

"Just Germans. Chatti, I think," Rokus said. "And somebody, Tulingi." He checked his knife and sword in his belt.

"Chatti've come far," Gerulf whispered as he joined them behind the bushes.

"They want this forest," Folkbern surmised as he reached for his bow and quiver.

"To move into?" Gerulf asked.

"To expand," Menfrid announced, crawling on all fours to the cover of the bushes.

Ulla whimpered. Rokus crawled to her and covered her with his arm. "They fight among themselves, little one; they don't want to harm us."

Rokus signaled to Menfrid to protect the horses. Menfrid jumped to his feet, ran around a screen of trees nearby, and brought the horses down a slope to a ledge below them. He looked up at Rokus and nodded. Rokus nodded. Soon, Menfrid was among them, and they listened.

"Someone just got reinforcements," Folkbern whispered.

They lay low while the battle raged. In crashing waves, tribal yells broke through the glades and groves that rolled away from the river canyon. Ebbs of violence followed, metallic clashes and pitiful groans, screams of assault and screams of impalement. Ulla shook.

The cacophony subsided into a stream of inarticulate misery as one group finished off the dying—grunts, the swoosh of blades, skin and bones sundered. By twilight it had quieted, and they poked their heads up to see silhouettes, arms and legs and torsos in disarray. Rokus entered the reddened battle zone to witness that which he knew already. Men had been reduced to pieces of meat; to the victor, a hectare of forest that they would leave in half a generation.

Returning to their cover, the bodhrán of his dreams propelled him, and to its pounding he moved more swiftly and found himself running through the thicket that snapped at him with its fingers.

To his relief, his company lay in their places, and in the shadows he detected Ulla, who sat up with an ear to the wood.

"Better to move at night," Rokus whispered

"I'll get the horses," Menfrid offered, feeling his way from tree to tree.

"Ulla?" Rokus studied her bearing, puzzling over her condition. He knelt to look into her eyes.

She sat bolt upright, then held up a finger. Her eyes goggled and she gaped, and he thought she had the fever or worse.

"What is it, little one?"

"More coming." Her dispassionate voice trailed over them.

Rokus looked back into the forest, but nightfall now reigned and the moon was still low.

"They come for us," she said.

Rokus reviewed the afternoon and remembered no time when they revealed themselves to the battling tribes. He studied her face, went to her, and touched her chin.

"What is it?"

Ulla reached for his knife, withdrawing it halfway before he stopped her.

"Let me look at you," he said, and searched for some blush or blotch of sickened skin.

"Leave. Now."

"Yes, we are."

"Now."

"Rokus?" Folkbern whispered, charged and urgent. He faced the darkness.

They studied the forest together, black trunks holding up the darkness, a backdrop of infinite shadows, and blue-green shafts of moonlight now angling through.

"Something moved," uttered Folkbern craning into the night.

"Seven," Ulla whispered.

They all turned to her, astonished at her speech and message. She then closed her eyes and began to rock back and forth, humming. They looked at each other. Her humming grew more modulated, and a chant emerged, words repeated in a conjuring effusion, and they felt its power even in a dialect they did not know.

"What's she doing?" Gerulf asked, bewildered.

Ulla swayed and chanted in time, and as Folkbern scanned the moonlit forest and the others sensed the enchantment, they heard the crack of a broken branch. Gerulf drew his bow, and the others drew swords. As Menfrid arrived pulling on the reins of horses, another crack came from the opposite direction.

"Down," Rokus commanded with a hush.

Menfrid darted behind a tree while the others fell to the ground. Rokus pushed Ulla down and shielded her. Leaves rustled at the perimeter, and as Folkbern raised his head to look, a spear cut through underbrush and hit near him. He rolled to the side, grabbed his bow, loaded it, and hid behind a tree.

"Flints," Rokus whispered.

While Gerulf explored his pockets, Rokus extracted the spear and pulled out handsful of dried grass from all around. He then wrapped the spearhead with clots of grasses forming a padded tip that he wound with twine. He reached to the side and retrieved the greasy cloth that had coated the jerky and covered the spearhead with this and then with more dried grass and encircling twine.

"Here," he offered Gerulf.

Gerulf dropped his bow and struck the flints together. On the seventh try, a spark flew into the mass on the spearhead; Gerulf let it sizzle, then blew on it gently.

"Bows ready," Rokus alerted them.

Gerulf fanned the smoldering spot, and as the smoke became denser, blew several times coaxing flame. It popped into a small tongue, and he continued feeding it by rotating the spear until the torch-like end was ready to fly.

Rokus stood above the flickering light studying the shafts of moonlight playing through the trees. He waited several minutes until he saw movement not twenty-five paces away—a helmet, shoulders, an axe. He readied the spear, its tip now aflame, and motioned the direction for the bowmen, who stood up slowly, strings pulled taut, arrows pointed that way. He looked back and nodded. "Shoot, then go for the horses. Ulla, ready."

She swayed in place; her eyes were now closed, and her mouth fashioned a silent chant.

He jumped into the clearing they'd made, then wound up and released. The spear arced into the trees, landing with a burst of fire among the silhouettes of men. The Batavians released arrows. Rustling and shouts followed as the attackers fled the flames and arrows that ripped through autumn scrub and thicket.

The Batavians scrambled to the horses. Rokus carried Ulla under his arm, but she struggled against him, so he put her down, and she ran abreast and even passed him. At the roan's side, she vaulted astride the animal, and he followed. They all spurred down the trail to the road, turned away from the river, and galloped into the forest.

Brutish yells followed them, and they heard the clamor of pursuit.

The road was wide and well traveled, tamped down with countless hooves and soles. They shot onward, trees blurring past, the cacophony of flight filling the woodland. Yelling followed them.

Narrowing, the road dropped into a gorge that led to the moonlit river; at the bottom, a black stream poured over rocks into pools and flowed down several steps into the dark mass of river that they felt but could not see.

Rokus halted their progress to test the depth. He dismounted and plunged a stick into the stream. He found no floor, and other testing spots also proved too deep to cross safely. The moon opened the sky after a bank of clouds lumbered on, and they could see the imposing wall opposite them; there was no road, and the water passage had cut deeply over time.

"It can't just stop!" Rokus exclaimed. He mounted the roan and wrapped his arms around Ulla.

"So, there were seven of them back there; now where is the road?" he demanded.

Ulla looked over her shoulder at him. Her eyes had lost fragility and instead had the steely resolve of a warrior.

"Over there." She pointed to a brake of boughs and shadows.

In the fold of trunks and limbs was a void; the road made a sharp turn and disappeared into it.

A familiar sensation overtook Rokus—well-being mixed with trepidation. He'd only felt it with Veleda, when she would sacrifice. She'd leave the altar with fingers dripping entrails and chant to the forest, and from the wall of branches and trunks and leaves and the limitless space would come a reply. Her singing repeated the spirit's message and, both frightful and beautiful, soared throughout her tower. She would look at him with the same shrewd expression.

"Go," Ulla commanded.

Rokus heeled the roan and they led the men into the black hole, through a narrow tunnel of twisted branches, and along the shelf that cut above the feeding stream. Level and smooth, the track afforded speed, and they cantered without impediment until a formidable log—rotting, immoveable—blocked their way.

The horses reared, snorting, clattering on the forest floor.

"No room here," called Rokus, jumping from the saddle.

"Don't hear them," Menfrid reported.

"Doesn't mean a fig," Gerulf replied.

"He's right." Rokus stalked back on the track.

Ulla watched from the saddle. As before, she began to sway, humming and moving her mouth to form words. Rokus went to her and studied her face as she discovered the chanting words, and when they came, her visage assumed authority.

"Seven," she repeated several times, as if her audience were deaf or disbelieving.

Rokus smacked the rump of the roan. "Dismount," he commanded.

They jumped to the ground, shooing horses into the forest up the hill. Ulla grabbed Rokus' sleeve and pulled him behind the fallen tree, and presently the others entered the redoubt.

"We just wait for them?" Menfrid asked as he pulled out his sword.

"Wait for something," Rokus answered.

Ulla scratched a handful of dirt and studied it as it spilled from her palm. She smelled it; she tasted it. She sat up straight and cocked her head to listen. Then she fell to hands and knees and gathered dirt and bracken that were under them into a mound between her legs. She inhaled deeply several times.

"What's she doing?" Folkbern stared at her.

"Quiet. She's got the gift," Rokus proclaimed.

They all watched the swaying and listened to the humming that sounded like water flowing or breeze filtering through trees.

Then they heard the rattling of beads, like necklaces or ornamental strands, and the grunt of exertion and the swoosh of missiles in flight. Next the spears landed, staccato thuds on their barrier and the brush beyond, followed by a taunt from the darkness.

In a Germanic tongue they didn't literally comprehend but with challenge infusing it, the cry roared over them again. The forest rattled with movement, and they all drew swords and loaded bows.

"What is it, Ulla?" Rokus asked.

Her head hung low while the humming became deeper and resonant. Her arms grabbed at the dirt and scraped it toward her as she hummed and breathed more frenetically. Then, another savage cry from the forest shot through the air at them, itself a kind of deadly missile, but it was answered when Ulla sat up straight again, filled her lungs, and sounded a freak call.

Her sustained cry from the depths of the earth echoed all around them. Both melodious and incongruous, it seemed to envelope the barbarian howl. Ulla sounded it again, and so her call surrounded them and flew beyond, as if flocks of birds had burst into the sky.

The Batavians leaned away from her, astounded at this demonstration, and the forest gathered impetus and shook.

The air grew heavy with moisture as if it would rain, but, smelling the succulent earth and feeling the mist all around, they saw the moon and clear night sky, then turned to her to understand these sensations.

After ten minutes of night sounds that conjured the equilibrium of temporal and mystic forces, Rokus touched her cheek in gratitude and then left the shelter to explore. He circled far above their position, creeping slowly, and secured a place he knew to be down the track from the redoubt. Pressing on, stepping over branches and rocks, he came to the location that produced the spears.

There were broken twigs and a few thin branches snapped above a matted path, but that was all, except the musk of forest dweller, which lingered in the air like butcher's offal.

SIXTEEN
To Moguntiacum and Colonia Agrippina

They traveled north for many miles, dark forest to the east, the river to the west. Squawks and growls announced their passing as the lattice shadows fell across the track, small animals darted across their path to hide, and the river, jewels flickering on liquid green, flowed inexorably on.

At the end of the second day, they looked for a campsite. The road had turned toward the river and a place with a wider shore; as they headed there, smoke drifted veil-like across their vision.

Menfrid and Gerulf loaded their bows; Folkbern unlashed one of the new spears they carried and held it ready. Rokus adjusted his arm around Ulla while he rested his hand on the hilt of his sword.

"Can't tell if they're friendly," he admitted.

"Friendly." Ulla spoke with the force of insight.

"How can you tell?"

"Smoke, friendly," she contended as she brushed strands of hair from her forehead.

"You're feeling better?"

She leaned back into him.

"No one should have to go through what you did. You're doing fine. Just fine. And you have the divination like Veleda. Didn't see it at first. How could I? You were so distracted with, well, you know. Veleda, I don't think I've told you about her. She's a friend. More than a friend. Going to introduce you. You can stay with her. She's a priestess for the Bructeri. Neighboring tribe. Good people."

"Friends," she said pointing.

They came upon the fire pit still smoldering, with gear scattered around it. Several fish were stuck on poles leaning over the pit. A scrabble of footprints skirted the water's edge, and several fishing lines stretched from drooping rods growing from the gaps between rocks.

Folkbern dismounted to inspect clothes drying on branches— breeches, tunics, cloaks. Menfrid followed, holding his bow loaded and ready. Liuppo went to the fish, smelled them, and turned to the others, smiling.

"So these are friends?" Rokus asked Ulla.

"Prince," Folkbern called, "they're Batavi."

Wide plaid patterns in blue covered the breeches, and the tunic was double stitched. He held up a buckle with horse rampant.

"So they are."

A horse snorted. They all looked into the jungle of tree shadows. Emerging, Thonkrik was putting his sword away and picking up a skewered fish he had cast aside. Bentet followed him, his smile pushing his cheeks wide.

"Batavians." Thonkrik approached with outstretched arms.

"Kinsmen," Folkbern answered, sheathing his sword.

"Prince Rokus." Bentet strode toward him with skewed fish as an offering.

"Friends," Rokus answered, grinning. He tucked Ulla under his arm and kissed the top of her head.

After embracing and slapping backs, all of them shifted into movements and tasks as if they had traveled the seven hundred miles together and made many camps. The fish were roasted, the lines were pulled in and more fish saw the fire pit, and mead was passed around. Bentet folded and stored the dry clothes; Liuppo cut up cakes and bread and spread dates, apples and wild raspberries.

Thonkrik knelt by Ulla and held out a doll made from willow and dried grass, bits of fabric and leather twine. She held it as if it were fragile, turned it around with both hands, nodded approval. Thonkrik nodded back and smiled.

"Have it. Picked it up along the way. For somebody."

Ulla examined it as a precious discovery.

"Fair girl, where'd you get her?" Thonkrik asked touching Ulla's cheek.

"Helvetia," Rokus said. "Invaders raided her family's farm. Tulingi. She's all that's left. Had a rough time of it."

"It is so." Thonkrik shook his head and pursed his lips.

"Taking her to Veleda." Rokus ushered Ulla to the food, resting his hand on her shoulders.

Thonkrik went to the fire, withdrew a burning stick, and watched the strings of smoke curl up from its charred tip. He nodded without facing Rokus. "Good place for her."

Folkbern and Bentet went to the logs placed for seats. Then Menfrid, Gerulf and Liuppo sat, all eating skewered fish, wiping beards, drinking mead.

"You see we've taken our sweet time getting back," Thonkrik declared.

"Tell me what you know." Rokus picked a skewer for Ulla and a piece of bread.

"The Chatti are active," Bentet reported. "Protecting their forest like madmen."

"Stay out of their forest," Rokus advised. "It can only come to no good."

"We're in it," Thonkrik pointed out, gesturing to the tall trees.

"This far south?" Folkbern's voice jumped in pitch.

"Wounded guy came through yesterday," Thonkrik explained. "Going someplace to die. Wouldn't let us touch him. Said the Twenty-Second Primigenia has a new commander. Real bastard. Raids into the forests. Harassment. Revenge, and for what?"

"He's mobilized the Chatti, just happenstance," Bentet observed. "Wounded guy said the Chatti were building more villages, settling down. Planning a solstice festival just like the Batavi."

"Then the legion comes crashing through, taking leaders, killing," Thonkrik added.

"Let's swing wide of Moguntiacum. I'd like to avoid that." Gerulf rubbed the bandage on his arm.

"How close are we to Moguntiacum?" Rokus stood and walked to the water's edge and looked downstream.

"Close. Half a day," Thonkrik replied.

"Let's stay together but leave before dawn. We'll be by them before they wake." Rokus turned to them.

Bentet poured from a leather bag, and they drank. Rokus spread a cloak on the ground and settled Ulla down, covered her with a fur.

"You heard. We leave early. Let's sleep," Folkbern concluded after their meal.

They broke camp by torchlight and returned to the north road, walking horses under a crescent moon. The music had entered Rokus' head again, putting him on edge as much as consoling him with the bowed melody and thumping drum. He scanned the woods for movement and found it everywhere in the breeze-caressed branches, the rattling canopy, the hungry night birds. He rubbed his eye and listened to his theme.

They made a train of seven with an extra horse, laden with supplies, trailing them. Gradually the music soothed him, and the early morning created its own benediction of dew and warbles; and, without their perceiving it, the stole of chill night lifted as trunks and foliage solidified and the horizon assumed its distant place ablaze with new sun. But more, the air had the aroma of humus and pine, all fragrances of growth and becoming, of hope. He filled his lungs with these things as the birds scattered from them and animals slipped into the remaining shadows.

The road turned west with the river, and he knew they approached Moguntiacum. Across the river he saw the Roman road leading there and, more than anything, wished to avoid confrontation with their forces. The train, on the edge of the German forests, was a fragile thing, really, susceptible to dangerous winds from both Italy and the northeast.

He knew the Romans but had only heard about the Langobardi and Burgundiones from the East. If the Chatti moved, others would follow, and the ripples would affect all tribes. Without homelands, tribes would seek better places. And restless tribes were like dogs foaming at the mouth—to be avoided or destroyed.

He drew comfort from the girl, who now rested her arm on his and clutched the blood ring. He smelled her hair and wondered how it could have the fragrance of lavender so far north.

Farther along, the forest thinned as the ground sloped to the river. As they crossed the watery flats, the sky opened up, vast fissures of clouds poised above the plain, gray, blue and pink in easy tonal symphony. It was a familiar sky, redolent of sea, and contained the paradox of solid light. He studied its permutations and felt something loosen in him, a promise perhaps, that the euphonious melody haunting him might have a counterpart within his people.

Then the melody changed color. The drum beat faster—a heart, a system, on the brink. The bowed melody quickened, pulse-like, breath-like, sawing into a place grave and dark.

He looked far down river to a point of land and, sensing Moguntiacum just beyond it, kicked the roan.

"An observation point. To cover," he called.

The train swerved off the road, overland, into distant trees. They arrived in a line, their horses lathered and panting. Rokus followed a ravine of branches and foliage that led them to another track, where they took stock.

"Dreaming. Shouldn't have gone out there," Rokus admitted.

"It's just turned daylight," Menfrid reasoned. "Don't think they could've seen us."

"But daylight, nonetheless." Rokus looked back at the entourage and felt assuaged. All riders had been swift and could not have been exposed for very long.

He studied the train curving in on itself in the narrow clearing. He found the bright spot of sun at the base of the eastern trees and, to the west, the promontory without figures.

"To Betuwe."

He heeled the roan, and they set off again. Their forest journey was quick on the trampled track that cut wide through the rolling terrain. Still, the sky ahead drew him strongly, and he heeled the roan again until they were at canter, moving briskly through the trees.

The track turned west again, as if it were a tributary to the river road and led them to a point near the water several miles up from the Roman fort. Concealed in trees at the edge of the reed-choked flats, the lazy sweep of the Rhenus glorious in the sun, they watched a column of Roman horse advance opposite.

Folkbern put his horse to Rokus' side.

"Looks like they mean business," Folkbern said.

"Not a pleasure ride; they are on maneuvers," Rokus observed.

"They won't come over." Folkbern spoke more from hope than knowledge as he craned to see through the branches.

"Don't make any bets." Rokus assessed his group, checking their spread and weighing it against the tree cover.

"We could backtrack," Folkbern suggested.

"I want to go home." Rokus leaned over to his countryman and patted his back.

The Roman cavalry, a mounted half century accompanied by auxiliary horse, rumbled with conviction, its golden eagle flying over the leader, red ribbons flashing; and they filled the river road from the walls to a distant point to the north, then disappeared around the bend.

Rokus led the train slowly along the German side of the river. Now running east and west, it caught the sun and shone like silver. It mesmerized everyone; all heads turned to it whether their track dropped or turned or climbed some scarp. After two hours, the river widened and turned again northward. The terrain, too, changed, as steeper hills pushed from the east. The track became a trail, and the river disappeared behind wooded hills, and their way became a series of steps to higher ground.

Rokus found intimacy with the land because he had traveled it as a young man and led men in battle there. He recognized whole swaths of wood and shoulders of hills, the sharp rises of small mountains, the thick valleys and ridges one after the other, and the sky lording over all. Gratitude overwhelmed him, and he squeezed Ulla as he closed his eye and uttered an invocation to Donar: Powerful one, protect me and bring me home. And then he thought of Veleda.

"Veleda, powerful one, protect me and bring me home," he said.

Ulla stirred from her reverie and looked back at him.

"You will meet her shortly."

They sat their horses on a mountaintop. The trail widened and there was a clearing. Below, dense forest dropped in waves to the river line, a meandering break in the green texture three miles away.

"We might cross at Confluentes," Rokus told them. "Less mountainous and quicker."

"Many Romans there." Menfrid frowned, drawing up his horse to Rokus' side.

"But a market town; we'd blend in," Rokus said.

"And we've done nothing wrong," Bentet insisted.

"Except desert." Thonkrik shook his head.

"Rest the horses and eat. Gerulf," Rokus called. "Come with me."

Rokus handed Ulla down to Menfrid.

"What do you see, Ulla?" Rokus asked.

The girl scrutinized his face, seriousness her veil. Then she lifted it to smile tentatively and nod. He bobbed his head acknowledging her meaning.

He clicked his tongue and heeled the roan, and Gerulf spurred, and they set off down the path that plunged down the mountain in sharp turns. They crossed a ford at the bottom and began to climb up the next mountain. At the top they surveyed the river basin, now broader and full of details: a settlement, a harbor, columns of smoke. Gerulf reached into his bag and extracted a chunk of jerky that he gave to Rokus. They ate this and other pieces and hard cakes they washed down with water.

"What are we looking for?" Gerulf asked, wiping his mouth.

"Anything."

"A place to cross?"

"A sign that the gods favor us." Rokus reached to pull a branch out of his vision and scanned the terrain.

"What will that look like?"

"Anything. But not like that," Rokus pointed down the mountainside to thick smoke rising.

"What is that?" Gerulf strained to see through the bunches of leaves.

"Something put to the torch, not natural," Rokus observed.

Gerulf drew his sword and unhooked his shield from the saddle.

"Put those away; we're not going that close. Don't want a fight."

They descended toward the river. The path had been worn into the hillside and switched back many times until the incline became less severe. Rokus reined off the path and into unbroken brush. Gerulf followed him, and together they cut into the wood slowly. They ducked low limbs that swiped at them, and they urged their horses where the animals sensed no egress, but after half a mile of tedious passage, they had circled around a hamlet carved into the hill above the river. Rokus held up his hand as he studied the site.

Horses neighed down on the river road. They heard men talking, and slicing this drone of voices was a woman's plea, high-pitched, incredulous, hysterical. Her entreaty stopped abruptly, and the men continued to talk, and one barked orders.

Rokus and Gerulf dismounted, tethered reins, and inched down the hill to a wall of brush edging a pasture. A cow ate grass and a pig snorted and groveled. Gerulf tripped on a knoll and stooped to clear it.

"Rokus," he whispered.

They lifted a long sod-covered hatch covering a deep hole. Gerulf swiped at webs and dirt to reveal a cache of arms, swords, spears, axes, hatchets.

"Not simple farmers, are they?" Rokus muttered.

"What do we do?" Gerulf gripped the hilt of his sword.

"Watch."

Time passed. They heard more than they could see, but finally forty horsemen pulled away from behind the bank of trees, following the leader who carried the golden eagle and red ribbons flying like festival streamers.

"Let's go down," Gerulf whispered.

"No. There's nothing in our favor."

"Those people need our help."

"They're beyond help." Rokus felt the familiar dread he had in the face of overwhelming numbers. He listened to his melodies that consecrated his intuition, but all was silent except the commotion below.

An officer entered the backyard of a house, hiked up his tunic, and peed. When he finished, he looked around and then kicked the wattle wall as he returned to the front.

Now a squadron of horses departed, this time auxiliary. Rokus flinched; they were Batavi. Long blonde or red hair flowed from underneath simple helmets, cloaks in assorted patterns and colors flapped behind them, and most wore blue plaid breeches.

"I know them!" Gerulf exclaimed under his breath. "One's Salaco, and there's Meginward. Both married Cananefates."

"You can call them Romans now, by the looks of it."

They heard hammering as legionnaires came around the houses with fire, touching thatch and woodpiles and mounds of straw. Others joined them, dragging several children.

While legionnaires held them, an officer drew his sword and stabbed each child quickly, their chests bubbling blood as they went limp in the men's grasps; he wiped his blade on unburned straw and walked away. The legionnaires kicked the back door down and then flung the children's bodies, their little limbs flopping independent of anatomy or purpose, their doll-like heads hanging as they disappeared into the darkness. The fire burst through windows and door, consuming the implements of simple lives.

Legionnaires mounted and left.

"Can't see," Rokus said, slinking across the pasture and hiding behind an outcropping. Gerulf followed.

Horses stood at rest; a squadron of auxiliary and five soldiers faced a point behind the houses.

"What are they doing?" Gerulf asked.

"Waiting for something, somebody. The houses to burn."

The men on the road stood motionless, as if to witness something monumental or strange, and as the flames and smoke belched, they still watched the phantom drama behind the burning houses and barns.

Presently, the feeble structures crumbled in the conflagration, and as the smoke and cinders settled and blew in the breeze, the object of their attention was revealed.

Two crosses loomed over the ashes, bodies drained of resistance slumped from the transoms, their skin caked with blood, slashes announcing their trials. Flames licked the bases of the posts now and began climbing up to the dangling feet.

Finally, the officer tossed a stick at the smoldering heap and mounted his horse. It was Marius.

The other soldiers also mounted, and Rokus identified young Val and the other escort legionnaires from the southern part of his journey. They galloped away, leaving eight Batavians.

"So now we're murdering German settlers," Rokus snarled as he clenched the dirt at his knees. "Curse this Empire."

One of the auxiliaries wrote something on a placard and dropped it on the road near the crucifixions. He addressed the other Batavians as if he were their leader; they seemed to agree on something, then they mounted.

The leader wore a Roman hauberk and cape but also the blue plaid breeches and royal tribal helmet with flared wings. Flourishing the cape and raising his arm that displayed an ornate wristband, he signaled the direction back to Moguntiacum.

His wavy hair blew in the wind, ripples of blond now streaked with gray. And there it was, the long scar that started at the ear and shot over the jaw and down the neck. Wide and shiny, it rode the skin like some snakeskin permanently fixed.

"Gerulf," Rokus began but became tongue-tied with the words to describe this rival, pretender, tactician and enemy.

"The one leading is a Batavian prince as well," he managed.

"You know him?"

"Claudius Labeo of Betuwe." The words nearly choked him.

The auxiliary trotted south for a hundred paces, then broke into a canter and disappeared around the bend.

Rokus and Gerulf contemplated the waste below. The farm situated near the river had been a perfect little settlement, but now the houses and barns and fences were seething sticks leaning against each other, vanquished.

Rokus nudged Gerulf and led him across the field and down a hillock, rousting several chickens pecking there; they walked behind the roadside trees to the ruins, steaming heat and death. They stepped around the body of a woman whose neck had been almost severed, head twisted improbably the wrong way.

The wooden crosses burned now, cooking the men's bodies like some sordid meal delivered to forgotten gods of history. Rokus stood over Labeo's sign.

"Roman symbols," Gerulf observed, standing at Rokus' side.

"It's Latin writing."

"You can read that?"

"Oh yes."

The wind shifted; it wafted burned flesh and blood, charred dogwood and hawthorn, scorched hope. The weight of it pressed

Rokus, and he thought of Ulla and all the settlements whose toe-holds had been demolished.

"Says, 'We helped the Chatti.'"

"I don't like this place," Gerulf mumbled.

"Nor do I."

SEVENTEEN
In Colonia Agrippina

The band of Batavians and the little girl entered the gate as the sun washed liquid orange over the Rhenus and her wide banks, the river basin and far hills, the watchtowers and blocks of buildings buzzing with commerce. Thick walls surrounded the city, and legionnaires walked the parapet above the entrance and streets. The gate was a massive arch with reliefs of Julius Caesar and Tiberius vanquishing Germanic tribes. As they crossed squares and intersections and followed streets, the riders gawked at the magnitude of things, the temples and monuments, the amphitheater, the excitement.

"This is safe?" Folkbern asked, looking left and right.

"It's got to be safe; they expect me." Rokus secured his arms around Ulla.

"We've all deserted," added Bentet.

"Far away, another time. Just blend in," Rokus advised.

Folkbern, unconvinced, examined Rokus' face. "I've a mind to keep riding."

"Let me check in. Then I'll join you," Rokus said.

"So how did the Romans cross the river back there?" Folkbern asked, pointing over his shoulder.

"A bridge. Your nephew and I followed them far enough to see it," Rokus explained as he tucked his cloak around Ulla's shoulders.

"Thought that was destroyed years ago," Folkbern said.

"The southern one was, not the one at Moguntiacum," Rokus clarified.

"What's next? They're going to invade Germania again? There's another Arminius to deal with, no doubt." Folkbern shook his head and reached into his saddlebag for a small stale cake.

Thonkrik rode on Rokus' other side. He'd been listening. "Romans won't invade soon. You've heard that Galba was killed in the streets and the Senate approved Otho, the governor of Lusitania?"

"Really?" Folkbern exclaimed with his mouth dry and full of cake.

"Not everyone is satisfied with this," Thonkrik continued. "It is said some senators believe Otho is ambitious. Looking around for someone else."

"If there's civil war, what will happen up here?" Folkbern asked.

"Troops will take sides, do the fighting for pretenders." Rokus adjusted his arms around Ulla.

The riders turned a corner and rode in silence for two blocks; Folkbern caressed his bow, Thonkrik the hilt of his sword. All of them altered their position, sitting straight and true as if preparing for attack.

They maneuvered the streets, around merchants and folk who scurried about on errands and tradesmen pulling or pushing carts laden with wares or tools.

They passed the marketplace as it was being broken down by Gallic farmers come to town. And this dismantling after a day of labor and dealing possessed a melancholic flavor, like twilight marking day's end or the pathos of harvest time when things die and winter has the prospect of hostile and hungry days. The farmers and wives moved in ways that revealed such notions, and it wasn't fatigue but apprehension of the imminent struggle against cold and want.

Gradually music rose in Rokus' awareness like a tide, imperceptible waves of sound growing until heard in the full of itself, careening rhythmically with the bowed voice heaving in time. He looked around for its source but saw nothing, though it continued; he remembered the music as that which came when the spirits of night spoke or the face of day rose in the east, or the god of war whispered his warning, or when Veleda cast her spells of oneness.

He scanned left and right again because it got louder. Its melody and beat swelled, and now each turn of phrase from the bowed voice and each thump of the bodhrán held ripe associations.

Rokus secured his arm around Ulla and closed his eye. He let the music conjure. He saw in his weary blackness a rapid succession of images: green marshlands and thick waterways and a vast sky wet with rain. Easing circumspection, he smiled.

As they turned another corner, they came upon musicians playing in a square. A band of four stood in the center of a small rapt crowd, and as they performed the changes and wove a spell with melody and rhythm, Rokus watched and listened with pleasure.

Then he knew them; Batavians, all acquaintances from the island.

"I know these musicians," he whispered to Ulla.

"I like it." Ulla nudged his cheek with the side of her head.

They sat their horses for two tunes before the nature of his business urged him on.

"Can you stay with Folkbern?"

He put the roan next to Folkbern for the transfer. Folkbern dismounted and reached up.

"I want that one," she blurted, pointing to the bay gelding that carried parcels of supplies.

Folkbern walked her to it, hoisted her up, and she sat in front of the cargo, holding tightly the horse's long mane.

Rokus nodded approval and walked his horse down the street. He came to the fort, informed the guard of his business, and received an escort inside to the principia and the commandant's office. The legionnaire snapped to attention inside the door.

"General Aulus Vitellius."

Rokus raised his hand.

"Hail, general," Rokus declared. "Julius Civilis, just arrived from Rome to take charge of the Batavian auxiliary in Castra Vetera."

"I'm new here as well."

Vitellius sprawled on a chaise longue in a fine tunic and toga, both of which pulled tightly around his girth. The scarlet border meandered over his corpus, disappearing in folds and reappearing over the crests of shoulder or hip. A tray of sweetmeats and pastries sat on a table at his side, and his arm returned to it mechanically as if it had its own mind.

"You have papers?"

"No."

"How can I know anything?"

Rokus studied Vitellius. His head emerged from the cloth, bulbous and pale, evolving from a fleshy stump of a neck into a giant fruit, swollen and blotched with exposure. Vitellius' features were mere accents among the puffy undulations that constituted his face, and his hair, preened forward, glistened with vanity.

"Gaius Marius Camillus has the papers." Rokus remained erect.

"And he is where?" Vitellius demanded as he dropped a sweetmeat into his mouth.

"Moguntiacum," Rokus reported as he suppressed his revulsion.

"Why?" Vitellius insisted, chewing.

"I don't know. Ask him."

Vitellius jumped to his feet, an agile move that surprised Rokus. "I am the general and proconsul of the northern legions and lands, and I expect more respect from a fellow commander."

Rokus stood motionless while Vitellius circled the room.

"You're the freed prisoner?" he asked, standing behind Rokus.

"I am."

"Treason, wasn't it?" Vitellius spoke as if he knew all the answers to his questions.

"That's what they said."

"An extreme form of insubordination."

"A bad habit," Rokus admitted without concealing his sarcasm.

"I've got to see the papers."

"Marius will be here tomorrow. A guess."

"A guess based on what?" Vitellius came around Rokus and plopped back onto the chaise longue.

"Saw him north of Moguntiacum yesterday. And he wants to find me."

Vitellius studied the platter, selected a pastry, and bit into it, sending an avalanche of crumbs down his toga.

"I need to see the papers before I deal with you," Vitellius mumbled with the pastry filling his mouth. He looked at Rokus while his fingers wandered to his oiled hair.

"Be going, then."

"Where?"

"To my men."

"Don't leave Colonia. I'll talk to Marius Camillus when he arrives." Vitellius reached for the platter, picked it up, and held it below his chin.

"Hail." Rokus raised his hand and turned to leave as Vitellius scrutinized him over the selection of sweets.

The sun was low as Rokus walked through the gate. He followed the road for ten minutes watching the orange glow of the sky and the red highlights on all forms. For the first time in weeks his damaged eye socket ached. He touched the patch like a connoisseur of fine things, felt the jolt deep into his head, and sought a place to sit down. A grove beckoned, and he went to it.

He studied the walls of the city and the Roman engineering that built them. This far journey had reaped so little.

"Veleda," he whispered with a raspy voice. "So long. Too long."

But, no, he told himself, he was doing what he had to in order to be under the Batavian sky, to walk across the familiar marshland and through the settlements, to sit among friends around the fire, to invoke the gods in the sacred groves.

His men awaited him—and what then? Had he any fight left in him, let alone lead men in battle?

He heard the strains of music again and looked up. A bearded old man stood before him in long robes and wearing a hood. He studied Rokus' face, his own registering information with raised brows. His beard flowed luxuriantly, and his two fine lips moved.

"Is this my prince?" the old man exclaimed with a thin voice.

As he regarded the old man, Rokus weighed the timbre of voice with the stately bearing and remembered his sage counsel from years ago.

"Erenbrecht." Rokus smiled.

"So I am."

Rokus stood. "Erenbrecht, Erenbrecht." He embraced him and held him out to behold.

"Been an eternity!" Rokus exclaimed.

"Of tears." Erenbrecht smiled.

"Missed you all. Been two years, at least," Rokus declared.

"Great changes afoot now, Rokus. And I see you've had a big change yourself," Erenbrecht observed, reaching up to Rokus' eye patch.

"Yes, well, I punished Habo's murderer, but he got to me before his own end. What are these changes you mention?"

"Some of our people have died, crossed the great river. We honor them and wait." The old man shook his head, lowering it in a momentary benediction.

"Come, old friend, let us walk." Rokus took his elbow, and while he shuffled, Rokus' mind revisited childhood times when Erenbrecht—Uncle Erenbrecht— ran after boys among the penned horses in a game of chase; or so he thought until he became a warrior, then he realized Erenbrecht had been teaching them how to communicate with the animals in times of duress and anxiety.

"It's getting dark; my steps aren't sure."

"We have an hour yet, it's a straight road, and the moon will rise," Rokus comforted.

"Let me clutch your arm that I do not fall."

They took the road that fed the big town, strolling down the tree-lined way, their shoes crunching grit on the paving stones in the otherwise hushed twilight."

"Who has died and what changes stir the air?" Rokus pressed.

"Uulfnoth, your father. He changed after Claudius Paulus was killed, our dear Habo. Then Geret. Then your mother, Thilde."

"Geret? And Mother?"

"All gone."

Rokus considered his younger brother. He remembered Geret's skill with the sword, vanquishing his brothers with wooden training sticks early on, then progressing to master level before his siblings. And his riding was smooth and adept, and they all admired this artistry. But he was brash and thought himself invincible. For all the petty rivalry, at root, a tight bond held them all together, and his admiration for Geret filled him to the brim and informed his own actions in the field.

"Geret and his auxiliary were ambushed in Dacia. Messenger brought home a few effects in his satchel."

"Geret..." Rokus' voice trailed off.

"One day your mother decided to die," Erenbrecht recounted. "Called me to the house. Your father was in the North meeting with the Frisii. She said she wanted to go away; and she did that very afternoon. Formidable woman but taxed by these violent times. Returning home, your father's group was attacked by the Cherusci, and he received a wound that wouldn't heal; and then his heart, too, wouldn't heal, and thus he passed."

Rokus pictured his mother, a rock of womanhood, giving her sons to the Roman world, "Know you are the prince, to be the king some day," she had told him. "Donar, watch my son."

They ambled through the tunnel of trees. They overtook a bent farmer pulling his cart away from the city and passed an old man sitting on a rock, resting.

"The evening to you," he said, looking them up and down suspiciously.

"To your good evening, sir," Rokus offered, dipping his head in obeisance.

"Kill me if you like," groaned the old one who sat.

"Why would I do such a thing?" Rokus queried.

"They all do," the old one bellowed.

"The fields have yielded, the woods are full of game, and the town is prosperous," Rokus said, in an inspiring tone.

"And full of murderers," the old man countered, his voice full of tension.

"On our way. I offer peace," Rokus said, taking Erenbrecht's arm.

"Murderers!" the old man called after them.

They let the trace of his words dissipate as they walked through the line of trees. Rokus took a deep breath and exhaled.

"I have a sense of things to come," Erenbrecht mused, breaking the silence.

"And is it good?"

"Oh, it is good but only after upheaval."

They walked several paces farther. Those words worked on Rokus, and in the innermost regions of his mind, he detected the thump of the bodhrán and the cry of the bowed string.

"I'm tired of these mixed fortunes," Rokus said, leaning into Erenbrecht so he would hear.

Erenbrecht stopped and contemplated Rokus' face. "Prison has changed you, prince."

"It has, my old philosopher. I wish to use my sword to protect my ground, not invade another's."

"You are coming home, then. Say it is so," Erenbrecht's thin voice assumed a greater substance, like a wispy cloud that halts midair to pour rain.

"I am. I am assigned to the Batavian Auxiliary at Castra Vetera and to train German recruits." Rokus delivered his account, and it felt false. "But I will not comply."

"Then Veleda was right," Erenbrecht stated; his voice vibrated with revelation.

"What did Veleda say?"

"She said the gods would have you return safely to your homeland, and you would lead your people."

"Lead them? Where? I wish to stay in Betuwe." As Rokus uttered the words, his destiny became clear to him. Notions turned to dreams, dreams to plans, plans to visions.

"All great people have a great leader," Erenbrecht observed with gravitas.

"Veleda said that?"

"I say that," Erenbrecht corrected. "She said it would be a new era when you returned at the time of the winter solstice."

"I intend to be there. To celebrate my freedom with friends and family around the solstice fire."

"Splendid."

They had walked far from the city walls. Forms began to dissolve, and the swifts and bats flashed in their dives and turns. A winter chill settled on the ground, and they turned around spontaneously together. The indistinct shape of the city walls beckoned them.

After five minutes, the ground trembled, and they heard the rumbling of hooves, the clatter of arms and the groan of leather.

Looming in the twilight the golden eagle and a brace of horses and helmets grew quickly into a long line of paired cavalry. Rokus took Erenbrecht's elbow and led him to the shoulder of the road, and they watched from between two maple trees as the line grew in size and detail. They could see that half the contingent was Batavian Auxiliary.

Junius Lepidus Crassus of Lugdunum and Julius Verginius Nerva of Aventicum led the force. Marius followed in line and then Val, the young legionnaire.

Rokus waited for Claudius Labeo; and sure enough, Labeo trotted by, his head held high, his mouth twisted in self-satisfaction.

"The cauldron is brewing, Prince Rokus."

"A bitter drink I think."

"Let us return at once, my young friend," Erenbrecht suggested.

They entered the cloud of dust, waited, and continued down the road listening to the clatter of horses.

"More every day, but this is different. Did you see the officers? More than usual," Erenbrecht noted. And now the wily philosopher emerged: "I know why—they've come to keep track of you."

When they reentered the city, night had settled with the faintest afterglow. Rokus found his band still at the square, leaning against posts, slumped against gear—human shapes in the torchlight.

"Ulla got away. One minute she's just there," Folkbern pointed to a ledge, "and then she's gone."

"You all know this old fellow," Rokus said, ushering Erenbrecht into their midst.

"I do!" Folkbern exclaimed. "Men, look who is here!"

Menfrid and Gerulf, aroused from uneasy naps, went to the old man, then the others appeared from the shadows; Thonkrik, Bentet and Liuppo formed a circle around him.

"We have waited for this day. Waited so long," Erenbrecht reported.

"Tell us of Betuwe, Erenbrecht, we need to know," urged Folkbern, touching the elder's shoulder.

"Yes, old man, brief us," Bentet insisted.

Rokus backed away, circled the square, and then entered the dark streets looking for Ulla. He walked carefully into the void, sensing where she might be, head cocked, hands out.

He faced a silhouette of buildings above which a residual glow filled the city sky. Then he heard men shouting, goads and guffaws overlapping in crude celebration.

He groped his way around the building and came to a stockade; the noisy event unfolded on the other side, and he could see some of it through vertical gaps, stripes of illumination in the urban night. Peering through, he witnessed the spectacle triggering such a rabble: a huge black bear and a wolf fought for a crowd of soldiers sitting high in a wooden amphitheater across from him. Mounted every ten feet along the seats and along the stockade were huge torches atop ceramic oil urns, and in the middle of the arena was a fire pit with flames devouring a pile of logs.

The wolf slunk around the bear, showing his teeth, growling; bubbling saliva ran off his gums as the wolf tightened his circle. The bear, giving ground, kept his face to the wolf. Then the wolf pounced, digging his teeth into the thick fur of the bear's back, but measured against the bear's might, it was a feeble attack. The bear shook off the wolf, sending him sliding across the dirt arena on his side. Then the wolf righted himself and began his stalking again.

The bear roared with indignation—slobbery strings swinging from its jaw, gaping mouth of outrage—then reared, thrilling the soldiers who howled with delight. Rokus could see several of the men placing bets, pointing, raising fists of encouragement to one or the other of the animals, and whooping for the sake of it. Drunk on mead and savagery, they fed on the fatal drama as it played out. And each swipe of claw and every flashing fang produced hurrahs; and when the wolf cut the bear's face or the bear slashed the wolf's rump, when blood spattered and flowed, the hurrahs became vicious and promised death to both animals, somehow, some time soon.

As the wolf attacked again, the bear reacted with a round swing, catching the wolf full force and tearing its side. At once, the bear collided into the stockade as the airborne wolf crashed nearby. The soldiers roared approval, and through the din came a plaintive gasp.

Rokus looked down the sequence of slotted light and saw Ulla's shape leaning forward against the fence. Dragging a hand across the stockade, he came to her. She looked through the gaps and didn't notice him.

"There you are!" Rokus exclaimed, crouching at her side.

Ulla jumped, saw him, and smiled.

"Wrong," she said, sticking a fingertip into the gap.

"Yes, it's not right."

"They will die."

"That's just what they want."

"No, they will die."

"Yes. Just a question of how soon."

"No, the men will die, the men will die."

"Yes, they will. We all do."

She turned to him, a blade of illumination striking her head to toe. She grabbed his sleeves and tugged. "But you will be the one to kill them. All of them."

"Don't know about that, little one. Let's go back to the others."

"No. You will."

Returning to the square, Rokus felt the weight of her words. When he added this prediction to her preternatural knowledge of their attackers in Germania, their numbers and whereabouts, it was a burden.

"Come, Ulla," he urged as they found Folkbern and the others.

"Decided to pamper ourselves," Folkbern announced when Rokus looked around for the horses.

"At the livery, Rokus, and we are booked over there," he continued, nodding toward an inn.

Menfrid and Thonkrik stood next to them carrying saddlebags, haversacks and gear.

"Couldn't stay at the garrison after that century arrived. Did you see that legionnaire, what's his name?" Thonkrik asked.

"Marius," Rokus stated.

"Never a good idea, staying in the fort," Bentet chimed in.

"Food there's from the sty," Liuppo added, sticking out his tongue.

"And they put deserters in jail," Thonkrik warned.

"Or worse," Bentet added, mock-slicing his throat with a forefinger.

"What are we waiting for?" Rokus insisted.

They collected gear and traversed the square in the fading torchlight. As Rokus opened the inn's door, a roar sounded over the buildings, followed by three other blasts of bloodlust.

"Garrison's having a time of it," Gerulf observed.

"Reward for securing the empire," Thonkrik said, sarcasm soaking his words.

"Reward for murdering children and farmers," Rokus corrected.

Entering, Ulla began humming her chant of prediction, a singsong repeated like urgent breath.

EIGHTEEN
Leaving Colonia Agrippina for Castra Vetera

As early light peeked over the walls, Bentet and Liuppo brought armfuls of einkorn cakes to the others standing with the horses in the square. Gerulf arrived with dried fruit. Each received three cakes and a palm of dried dates, apples, and raisins, and they stood there eating, watching men wheeling carts and market folk carrying baskets to fill. Horns blew high notes from behind the garrison walls, and the Batavians looked knowingly at each other. A tide of people flowed into the square, and presently they established their commerce; storefronts opened like great eyelids awakening, and tables offered wares, and the merchants, hoarse with sleep, called out for customers. A goatherd and his dog worked goats to some cross-town destination, he tapping his staff coaxingly on the pavement, the dog dashing around the herd snapping at cloven hooves; a woman passed carrying a yoke from which dangled wooden buckets of milk.

Bentet approached the milkmaid with a coin and four cups. They watched his transaction; he returned with fresh milk, offering the first cup to Ulla.

"There's a healthy girl."

"Reminds me of Batavorum," Thonkrik said, smacking his lips.

They savored the cakes and the moment, settling dreamily onto their benches or leaning into the horses' flanks. A bar of sunlight hit the far reaches of the square, and the day seemed anointed with promise.

They all turned when a squadron of cavalry entered from the garrison street, helmets glistening and red capes a stark contrast to the stonework and butternut clothes of the city folk. The eagle flew above them trailing streamers and carried by a stone-faced standard bearer.

Marius led them; they rode right up to Rokus and halted. Horses snorted and pranced, and the mass of them all seemed to encircle the Batavians.

Marius sat his horse, towering over Rokus with the authority of Rome.

"Got to complete our journey," Marius announced.

"I don't ride with child killers," Rokus glared back.

"Saddle up," Marius commanded.

"Eating." Rokus turned to his small entourage and held up a cake.

"We leave now," Marius insisted.

"When I'm finished, I'm going to join my regiment at Castra Vetera. With these Batavi, not those legionnaires."

"I must escort you, Rokus."

"Stern words now."

As Rokus spoke, he saw his childhood rival, now an auxiliary officer for Rome. Claudius Labeo smirked at him, just like he always did. Labeo put his horse beside Marius; he sneered down. A peacock of a soldier, Labeo wore his Batavian helmet with metal wings flared, and his red Roman cape featured white bars running along its edges with the Batavian blue horse intermittent on the bars. Underneath cape and leather cuirass were his leather jacket and breeches made from pale human skins that had the dotted patterns of the Celt. His gloves, too, showed the Celtic dots, and as he rested a hand on the hilt of his long sword, Rokus saw the necklace of fingers declaring audacity and prowess.

"Let's go, Rokus. Now," Marius ordered.

Rokus turned to Ulla, bent to her level, and handed her his cakes. She accepted them, and, intuitively, stepped away.

In one flash of movement, Rokus spun round, grabbed Marius by the sleeves, and jerked him out of the saddle. Marius crashed to the pavement and struggled to free himself. Rokus had him by the shoulder and neck, slammed his head down over and over, and then stood up over him, waiting.

Marius staggered to his feet, groping for his sword and looking back and forth at Labeo, at Rokus, weighing options.

Rokus backhanded him across the face and quickly countered that with a fist to the bridge of his nose. Marius bled now, as Labeo and young Val jumped off their mounts. Rokus flew into Marius before any hands could subdue him, and the two former comrades tumbled into the square. Marius found his wits and struck Rokus on his eyepatch. Rokus reeled.

Just as Labeo and Val entered the circle of strife, Folkbern, Gerulf, Thonkrik, Menfrid, Liuppo and Bentet formed a barbed partition with their swords. Several legionnaires dismounted and drew swords, but Labeo held up a hand for them to stop.

Marius approached Rokus who writhed on the ground. The patch and string dangled from his neck, and his surroundings appeared and disappeared in pulsations of pain.

Ulla cried out, her tinny girl's voice assuming the power of forest and river, and Rokus heard the cry as if goodness and grace struggled against cruelty and hers was the clarion call.

He stood to face Marius. The Roman officer brandished his blade. Ulla's cry ceased. Then the music visited him, lilting ruminations of bowed melody and jangle of strums, the precision of plucking, the bodhrán's beating heart. It filled him, and he walked toward Marius' sword while searching his face. The Roman back-pedaled while Rokus approached unwavering in this non-attack.

Rokus was overcome by the thought of Veleda's embrace and more: her thighs around his own, her arms encompassing his neck, and her tracing fingertips across the landscape of his back. While Ulla's cry echoed, he heard Veleda's whisper and felt her breath on his cheek, and then came the scene of the children slaughtered at the river hamlet, and he was back.

Marius retreated to the horses, stepping away from the madman who seemed to invite death or at least the maiming strike, until his back brushed a legionnaire's horse.

The Batavians held everyone at bay during this showdown; somehow everyone knew there was a settling of accounts taking place, and, honor-bound, they would watch.

Marius' back pressed against a saddle.

"Stop," he shot at Rokus.

Rokus plowed into him. Then Rokus pulled a pilum from the saddle holster, hefted it, grabbed its ends, and broke it over his knee. Dropping the point, he took the wooden handle and advanced toward Marius.

The Roman raised his sword and then slashed down at Rokus' head. The Batavian jumped aside while deflecting the blade with the meat of his club. The blow jettisoned a chunk of yew into the air and the blade sank into the grain. Both of them shook club and sword free, loath as they were to be connected or disarmed.

Before Marius resumed his battle stance, Rokus clubbed him hard on the helmet. Marius teetered and then grasped at a saddle strap; not finding it, he dropped to a knee while the square stopped spinning.

Rokus lunged and swung at the same time, smashing Marius around his shoulders and head repeatedly until the helmet flew by and Marius lowered his protecting arms, sagged to one side, and toppled. Then Rokus stepped back, wound up a leg, and kicked Marius in the face. All heard the crunch and saw the splatter as Marius recoiled backward, rolled to his side, and smeared blood as his hands covered his face.

Rokus paused to evaluate him. Marius sat on his backside with his legs apart, panting, blood filling his mouth and pouring down his chin. He sought Rokus through the grotesque knobs covering his brow and cheeks.

Before he had located him, Rokus resumed, clubbing him five more times, far beyond any point of resistance and long after the blows thunked like a melon pulverized.

Thonkrik and Folkbern seized Rokus' arms as Labeo jumped in front of Marius.

"He's done," they said as Rokus broke their grip to seize Marius' hair. His fists hit him again, but a life of army privation had toughened Marius, and he only wavered under this last barrage.

"Enough!" Thonkrik exclaimed.

"Rokus!" Folkbern cried.

"It's all right, prince," Menfrid consoled.

"Stop!" Folkbern urged.

Now Menfrid and Liuppo had Rokus on one side opposite Folkbern and Thonkrik, and they pulled and dragged Rokus back.

"One sacrificial lamb left," Labeo asserted.

He motioned for Val and others to take Marius away. By now Rokus had eased and stood chest heaving in the grip of Menfrid and Thonkrik. Labeo swaggered up to him.

"You've given your spirit to murderers," Rokus panted while studying Labeo's face.

"Investing in the future," Labeo smirked.

"A pathetic lot." Rokus gestured with his head at the mounted force filling the square behind Labeo.

"You never understood how it works." Labeo leered.

"You never knew your kinsmen."

"No?"

"As a killer but not as blood." Rokus spat in disdain.

"Rokus, you've always let ideas seduce you."

"I'd rather a star guide me than an eagle."

"You never stop, do you?"

They glared at each other.

"Well, prefect Civilis, your cohort awaits you."

Another squadron of horse entered the square. Riders plied the crowd that had gathered, dispersing them back to their businesses. Nerva and Crassus gleamed in dress hauberks and greaves and red capes, plumed helmets, and gold and purple brocades; another officer, richly dressed, rode with them, his dour face set under the visor of his ornate helm. They put their horses to the Batavians and glared at them as if they were rabble. Menfrid and Thonkrik released Rokus.

"Julius Civilis?" Nerva demanded.

"That is my Roman name," Rokus declared, hands on hips.

"Fabius Valens, commander of the First Germanica," announced the officer from under his decorated visor.

"I remember Britannia. Hail, sir," Rokus responded as he pictured the man commanding troops and inventing creative strategies that brought victory.

"It is essential that you get to Castra Vetera," Valens reasoned.

"Orders await you there," Crassus interjected, impatience infusing his tone.

"Something about special camps?" Rokus asked as he shifted his weight onto one leg.

"Silence," Valens ordered.

"Get reacquainted with your auxiliary, then wait for us. Labeo, to the garrison," Nerva commanded.

When they left Colonia, Rokus had a new patch and a broken nose. Menfrid had fashioned the first from a scrap of leather and could only describe to Rokus the bruise at the bridge. He looked back at their train—Ulla on the bay gelding from Germania, then Thonkrik and Menfrid side-by-side, Folkbern and Gerulf, Bentet and Liuppo finishing the cakes and taking account of the river road and hills ahead, and Erenbrecht mounted on a mule. The old man looked dreamily at the landscape, then heeled his ride past the others to Rokus.

"That fight was a portent," he declared.

"It was stupid," Rokus asserted, touching the bridge of his nose.

"You were brilliant, lad," Erenbrecht enthused, swiping at Rokus' leg.

"I'm a fool."

"This is the foundation," Erenbrecht emphasized. "Of something big, something bold."

"I can't control myself, old fellow."

"No, you had a case and stated it."

"I got my nose broken."

"And you broke his from the looks of it."

The roan and donkey walked apace, and the men fell into silence. Erenbrecht looked down the distant track and back at Rokus several times.

"I just want to go home," Rokus confessed, weariness weighing his words.

"You will, prince, but now you have their attention."

"What do you mean?"

"You were audacious, intimidating." Erenbrecht fashioned the scene with his hands.

"Shit."

"Gerulf told me about the hamlet," Erenbrecht confided. "On the other side of the river."

"So?"

"You have declared to Rome that you will not abide the slaughter of innocents."

"I beat up an old friend."

"You exacted revenge for Roman infractions."

Ahead, three black vultures feasted on a carcass. Enormous and contemptuous of the approaching humans, the birds watched the men without moving. The riders were upon them when one vulture, flesh in beak, stepped to the side. But the other two did not move and the troop had to stop. The horses, intimidated by the vultures' scale, stopped and could not be kneed to continue.

"Erenbrecht, old man, friend, I want to go home to the island, I want to find a place for the girl, I want peace."

"And you shall have it, prince, but on your terms."

"Then let me be. You imply there is something else," Rokus explained. "But sometimes I believe something simple is best for me."

Erenbrecht reined his mule and withdrew to the rear. His eyes glistened in the morning light, and his mouth twisted in a grin.

Thonkrik dismounted. On the side of the track, he found several stones that he threw at the vultures in succession. Two found their mark, and the birds took off. The spectacle captivated man and beast as gigantic wings spread from one side of the track to the other. Fallen leaves stirred in whirlwinds, and they all felt the rush of air as the birds drew their masses off the ground and struggled at an angle to clear the treetops.

Rokus heeled the roan into a trot and then a canter, and so he led the train north into the hills that separated him from the lowlands.

At midday, he stopped to water the horses. Their flanks were wet and lathered, their nostrils flaring and mouths gasping. The train stretched almost a mile, some riders slowing during the day to walk their tired mounts, some to ease their saddle sore rumps. Ulla flagged and appeared as a speck on the road behind them.

Folkbern joined Rokus at the stream first. Dusty patches covered Rokus' face, and rings of mud had formed at his nostrils. His eyes seemed held in place by the dirty creases fanning out from them; his brow bent with concern.

"What or whom are we racing?" Folkbern asked, leaning over Rokus at the flowing water.

"Want to get back." Rokus cupped water and tossed it on his face.

"The horses can't keep up."

"They'll be fine. We can rest them soon enough," Rokus asserted, sipping from his hand.

"Ulla can't keep up."

"She can. She has great strength, even if you don't or won't see it."

Folkbern stroked his horse's neck and front legs as it drank. He looked askance at Rokus, stretched, and then sank to his knees at the stream. He plunged his face into it, massaging off the dirt, comforting the muscles that had squinted for three hours. "Your cohort has waited two years; they can wait one more day."

"I just have to get back."

Folkbern opened his saddlebag and extracted a cloth wrapping biscuit and jerky. He unlashed a leather bag of honey wine and flopped onto the grass. He ate and drank slowly as one by one the others entered the clearing.

In thirty minutes, they had gathered in a circle with Folkbern, passing einkorn cakes, pieces of smoked meat, dried fruit and the skin of wine. They ate in silence, holding items as if they were leaden things. A stranger coming upon them at that moment would have thought them forlorn refugees resigned to some dismal fate, when they were just feeling the will of Rokus. Now saddled, Rokus heeled the roan and was pulling away from the clearing.

Ulla saw him, went to her horse, mounted, and loped away from the Batavians.

"Rokus," she called, her voice a thin line cutting into the afternoon breeze.

He slowed, and she caught him, and they loped together around a lazy bend until he felt the child's frustration jump across the road and strike him on the side.

He drew up and walked the roan, and she the bay gelding. He looked at her. She formed a circle with her thumb and middle finger and linked that with another circle made with the thumb and middle finger of her other hand.

"Friends," she said.

He studied her sagacious eyes, her wispy hair, the worn tunic, the fur cloak that dwarfed her and made her look like the runt of some beast's litter.

"Friends," she repeated.

She had that look about her, as if she were being addressed from a source unseen and registering the words like a translation.

"Friends?"

She held up the interlocked rings she was making with her fingers. "Yes, like this."

She reined and sat her horse. Rokus continued a fair distance and then, not hearing her ride, stopped.

She was right, he thought, they were all friends, kin. There were things he did not understand but prayed to Donar for; there were things that were delivered, beyond words and explanation; there were things he possessed already. It was wise to embrace them when they arrived, acknowledge friends' willingness to be with him, and give thanks for gifts possessed and when they came. And so he saw himself on the road to Castra Vetera being admonished by a little girl. How she did this, he did not understand; but then, she, like Veleda, had been a gift from Germania, a place of many mysteries.

He reined the roan mare around and faced Ulla and held out his arms. She heeled her bay gelding, he the roan, and they met mid-road and clasped arms.

"There is time for everything, isn't there," he observed.

A spark of recognition shot from her eyes to his one, and they waited like that until the others joined them, and then they all became charged with the same purpose.

Reformed as a closely-knit organism making its way through the flatlands, they passed clusters of farmers baling the last fields of tall dried grasses, traveling merchants pulling creaky carts, single riders pushing toward distant destinations, and old men afoot, deranged or learned, shuffling in their manners. Advancing slowly and steadily, the train assumed almost militaristic precision hour after hour, and when the track turned on a sudden rise, Rokus drew up again, slid from his saddle, and waved them to come. He tied the roan in a stand of poplars and unhooked his haversack. Slinging it over his shoulder, he walked to the highest point and studied the fields stretching into the haze and the lone trees disappearing like milestones.

He pulled out a wine skin, swilled, and walked to the others with arm outstretched.

"At this pace, we'll be at Vetera by late afternoon," Folkbern stated.

"Maybe we should be easier on the horses—we have covered a great distance already today," Rokus announced, surveying the group and acknowledging his own intractability with slight dips of his head.

Folkbern and Thonkrik exchanged glances.

"Have a drink," Rokus proffered, his outstretched arm presenting the skin.

The wine bag went round the group, and all eased, smacked lips, and smiled.

"The sky welcomes us. Look!" Rokus exclaimed, pointing to the northwest.

A layer of swollen clouds broken in puffs spread before them. Rokus recognized the silver in the sky and the treasure of grays that dappled all aerial forms. The air was more humid, full of marsh and sea, and the chill and sunlight coexisted as the autumn turned in the cycle.

"Folkbern, have you more mead?" he asked.

First Folkbern's, then Gerulf's skins passed hands until both were emptied, and the group, now sitting in a circle, made merry.

Rokus walked to the road, a worn track that had connected settlements along the Rhenus since before memory. He studied the patterns of soles, bare feet and hooves—shod and unshod, cloven and equine—all pointing north or south, the past etched in dust.

His heart raced, and he was overcome with an unnameable compassion for these farmers, purveyors, messengers, and philosophers. The road seemed truly marked with the spirit of people and their reasons to travel. Heat rose from the strata of impressed dirt and was suspended as an aura imbued with mortals' lives. And into this he stepped, holding out his arms, absorbing its nourishment. And then he wished to toast to this past, but seeing mere traces of bygone days, he consecrated this moment and the countless ones to come.

"Liuppo, have you any more mead?" he called back to the group.

Liuppo extracted another wine skin from his haversack, and Bentet brought out his, and they popped stoppers and drank and passed them on.

When it was Rokus' turn, he held the leather bag aloft.

"I thank the god Donar for delivering us, and the Mother Earth and her handmaiden, Veleda, and I thank you all for your protection. I toast the forebears who have set the stage for us, but mostly, I toast our new lives in Betuwe, our island—because our lives will be renewed. These things I toast."

"Salute," they chimed.

Erenbrecht stepped to the center of them and held out his arms. "I propose we hold a special ceremony during the solstice feast. We shall eat and drink together, yes, but let us also crown Prince Rokus as our king. As Uulfnoth has joined his ancestors, Rokus is now the rightful heir. Hail, King Rokus."

"Hail," seconded Folkbern.

"Health."

"Here."

"Prosperity."

"Glory."

"Wisdom."

After constructing the edifice of hope and good cheer, they drank all the mead from the leather bags and soon stood swaying in the steely light.

"Labeo will shit," Folkbern announced as he studied Rokus erect and regal in his deerskins and tribal cape.

"Labeo is shit," Menfrid added, propping his elbow on Bentet's shoulder.

"A Batavian king must earn the rank, not just be born to it," Bentet proclaimed, waving his arm toward Rokus as if he were presenting him at some royal court.

"But Labeo is a cunning warrior," Rokus acknowledged.

"And so are you, Rokus," Folkbern asserted, grasping his hilt.

"Anyway, Labeo's turned Roman." Liuppo stated, his tone rife with insult.

"But I am called Gaius Julius Civilis, citizen of Rome," Rokus reminded the group.

"The better to defend the rights of Batavi." Erenbrecht shuffled to Rokus and clutched his arms while peering into his eye.

Bentet pushed Thonkrik to the side. "I remember once, a long time ago, years before my friend here arrived," he said patting his belly. "They conscripted me. Wasn't ready, just a pup. Got in with Labeo's century. He was called Liudger then. So Liudger decides to give me special training, make up for my inexperience. He could've just dumped me east of the Rhenus to see how I'd fare alone among our German neighbors, but, no, he had a plan."

"He fed you extra grain," Thonkrik smirked.

"Made you drink a century's ration of beer," Liuppo snapped.

"No, fools, we did the two–on-one. I wielded a sword like the fifteen year-old accountant-in-training I was."

"Should've thrown some numbers at him," cried Menfrid.

"Only if they were balanced," shot Folkbern.

"And sharply drawn," snapped Rokus, beaming.

"He brought in two Celts, strapping lads, veterans from Britannia, gave them staffs," Bentet continued, looking across his audience as he molded the story with his hands.

Bentet stooped over. It seemed as if he was acting out his defensive reaction to the two-staffed attack, but he wasn't. It was memory weighting him down, and he struggled out from under it.

"I got one good bash on each of them, but they were too much, the two entertaining themselves with me like that. They knocked me down."

"And then I introduced myself," Rokus remembered.

"Looked up, and what did I see? Rokus booted them, literally, kicked them off me. Liudger was furious. The Celtic lads saw they weren't wanted anymore and left. You told him, didn't you, Rokus? You told him, all right."

"I did, Bentet."

"Liudger yelled, oh my, did he shout. I could barely hear from the beating I took, ears ringing, but I saw him, and Labeo—Liudger, was out of his mind with anger. Rokus took my staff and sword, and then Labeo drew and set. Labeo brought his sword up in a wide stroke, one that would cleave a man, I'm sure. But Rokus thrust with the stick, knocked him back, and Labeo's stroke fanned the air. Rokus snapped the staff away, then clobbered the man on the side of the head. Labeo was stunned, but then Rokus repeated this on the other side of his head. Labeo wasn't in for any more, so he turned and stomped off, holding the sides of his head." Bentet acted Labeo's part, looking more a beaten dog than drill instructor.

"Hail, Rokus," Erenbrecht proclaimed.

Menfrid entered the circle and elbowed Bentet back in the line.

"It was in Britannia against the Silurians. I went down with an arrow." Menfrid lifted his tunic to show the scar crater in his thigh muscle. "And these Britons were coming for me. Off in the woods I was, but they saw me. They did their Silurian scream for my head and rushed in. I closed my eyes, awaiting my death, but instead heard swords and groans and men falling. I opened my eyes to see Rokus cut them all down. He was fast, furious, accurate; he just came from nowhere. Never saw the likes of that, ever."

"Hail, Rokus," Erenbrecht repeated.

Folkbern took Menfrid's place.

"We're in Britannia as well. There are more Britons than we'd ever seen. Fighting from ramparts and a timber wall. Romans aren't there yet to back us. Have to do something, right? Rokus sends a century of us into the teeth of their lines. We look at him like he's daft. 'Engage, then give ground steadily,' he says. No, my prince, a Batavian does not yield ground, gives no quarter. 'Trust me,' he says. Then he sends half a century to the left flank. 'Go deep into the forest. Come out behind them and attack when you hear the horn.' The other half goes to the right flank. 'When the Britons jump from their cover to take our center charge, attack from that flank,' he says. The last group he also orders to the left flank, only they are to attack the Britons from behind when the Britons leave their fort to support the charge. 'When the right flank attacks, you attack,' he says. He brings all the captains together to clasp hands and offer words to Donar. We feel the genius of the plan, but let me tell you, more than a few of us were sure we'd join the gods in the great banquet hall that day. But Rokus' plan was perfect. The center attack draws them out. The right and left flanks pinch them toward the middle. The horn blows long and loud. The rear attack hits them from behind and fills their fort with Batavians, so those who retreat are finished off. Then, this is brilliant, Rokus and several squadrons of horse crash into the melee. The Britons are surrounded, overwhelmed by a smaller opponent, soundly defeated, and the few remaining flee into the countryside. I can see it now as if it was yesterday. Brilliant, just brilliant, it was."

Erenbrecht took the center of the ring they'd formed. "It is clear we have our king. Let no pretender take the throne. Let us have our coronation on the solstice."

"Hail," they said in unison.

"Well, then, let's get there!" Rokus exclaimed, putting his arm around Ulla's shoulder and helping her on her horse.

The rest remounted, and they set off for Castra Vetera. As the light dimmed and the breaths of winter crossed the plain, Rokus embraced the full worth of the sky, unique to these northern flatlands, a vast universe of elements. It nourished every Batavian with its spectacle, an open theater of animated forces, sometimes a dazzling range of clouds, sometimes great mountains of vapor spilling overland, sometimes dense layers of sea-coated light bringing the celestial ceiling within reach.

They prodded the animals, crossing a vast plain that spread from the river and coursed into the winter mist.

Rokus wrapped his cloak around his shoulders and stuffed his free hand into his tunic pocket. Deep in the threads and grit there, he felt the shard. Pulling it out and examining it, his mind leaped with sentiment. A fragment of a vessel, a cup perhaps, it had glazing and a design, curves like waves or a woman's hair, and he placed himself in the memory that this relic aroused. It came from the farm despoiled by the Romans along the border of Lugdunensis and Helvetia. He had found it in the ashes.

He reined the roan and guided her to the side of the road. Dismounting, he walked somberly away into the brush and scratched a clear spot with his boot. He stooped to gouge a hole in the dirt and then held the shard out.

"That we do not continue these misadventures," he whispered.

He brushed lips to the ceramic then placed it in the hole, covered it, patted it down, and set a small stone directly on this simple grave for a memory.

Onward the train moved, and just before dark, the fort appeared in the distance.

As they approached the walled fort, flames erupted from within; and they heard mustering soldiers, the clank of metal and the stomp of boots, commands, creaking wheels.

"Batavians come in peace!" yelled Folkbern, prodding his horse toward the gate.

The furor inside the fort drowned his voice. They came to rest before the gate.

"Gaius Julius Civilis, proconsul of the Batavian Auxiliary!" Rokus shouted into the twilight.

Still, the fire and smoke and clamor of men called to arms rose over the stockade. Gerulf and Menfrid set their bows while Thonkrik, Bentet, and Folkbern drew swords. Gerulf pulled out of formation to gain an advantageous position. Rokus stopped him with a raised hand because there had been no musical warning, no singing bow, no palpitating bodhrán to high alert.

"Gaius Julius Civilis?" someone shouted from the rampart.

"It is I."

A loud thud emanated from the other side of the gate. Hinges creaked. The massive doors opened; firelight gushed out, blinding the night eyes of the Batavians.

At once, their orange faces expressed their wonder. Arrayed before them down the center of the square were rows of legionnaires at attention, banners flapping, standards held with precision, and burning torches everywhere. Splashes of firelight created phantasms of shadows; torches dotted the walls, the front of the principia, along the side streets of barracks and livery and workshops, the mess and the warehouse.

Roman legionnaires and Batavian Auxiliary saluted them as they entered. Drums beat, and trumpets sounded a fanfare. A figure emerged from the far end of the avenue of soldiers; he wore fine Batavian clothes: tunic over blue plaid breeches, a leather jacket and, instead of a fur cloak, a plaid cloak with fine bars of deep colors. His hair was combed back and his beard was full. He carried a gleaming sword in his outstretched hands, offering it higher as he approached. It was Renhard, the Praetorian Guardsman he'd last met on the bridge over the Tiber.

"At long last, Rokus."

"Indeed, friend."

They grasped forearms as the Batavians inside the fort burst with cheers, and the drums beat faster and the trumpets blasted.

"Welcome to Castra Vetera!" Renhard shouted.

He stepped aside to allow passage. Rokus dismounted and joined him, and they watched as the travelers entered the fort, beaming.

When Ulla passed, Rokus took her reins and drew the bay gelding to the side. Once the Batavians were in the fort, the big doors were shut and a huge beam was placed across, jamb to jamb.

"This is my young friend, Ulla. Ulla of Helvetia," Rokus spoke as if she were royalty.

"You could use some rest and a bath," Renhard consoled.

Ulla nodded, and Renhard led the group into the square between two bodies of soldiers each lined twenty rows deep. The trumpets sounded again. Pennants and banderoles wavered in the distance. They watched as mounted Batavi rode two abreast, turned, and came straight at them through the sea of men. As they approached, Rokus studied the sleek horses and finery of the men with their shots of red, yellow and green, blue plaid, and sumptuous furs. They carried spears. He realized they had retained few of the uniform elements of the Praetorian Guard. Now that they were home and no longer the Emperor's watchmen, they assumed the colors of the tribe. When ten paces in front of him, they divided, looped around the soldiers presenting arms, and formed new rows behind them, a formidable force in both numbers and regalia.

"I present you your Batavian Auxiliary and a new contingent of horse," Renhard announced.

"Salutes to you all," Rokus called out with his arms embracing the space between them.

"Scouts told us when you would arrive. Wanted to welcome you," Renhard said.

"A fine welcome, indeed, Renhard." Rokus placed his hand on his host's shoulder.

"Join me, all of you." Renhard signaled for their horses to be taken.

"Where are the legions?" Rokus asked, scanning the square.

"The legions? You've not heard? This way."

While the trumpets blasted and the drum corps beat their march, Rokus and the Batavians newly arrived followed Renhard into the principia. They went down a hall past the commandant's office and into a back room with a long table. There were pitchers of wine, platters of roasted fowl, sliced apples, flatbread and bowls of cranberries, chestnuts and walnuts. The travelers beamed, slapped each other for their good fortune, and turned to Renhard to shake his hand.

He bowed to the guests. His lieutenants entered, and they each recognized the others from previous campaigns and stations and layers of personal history stretching back to the island between the Rhenus and Vahalis Rivers. Jollity reined.

Renhard pulled Rokus to the side. Rokus nudged Ulla toward Folkbern, who took her hand.

"Most of the legions have gone to Rome." Renhard ushered Rokus into the hallway.

"To be the new Praetorian Guard? Senators' strong arms?"

"To represent the North."

Rokus looked back into the room and stepped further down the hall, gesturing for Renhard to follow.

"Whose interest?" Rokus asked, his voice subdued.

"Vitellius, of course."

"Rome could do better." Rokus thought of the man filling the chaise lounge and his mouth, the man's vainglory and appetites.

The Batavians reveling behind them roared with bellies full of glee. They clanked cups and gave the floor in turn as they re-created their histories with tales that were not easy to be believed. Ulla swayed and smiled as she watched them.

"Vitellius sends his generals?" Rokus asked.

"There's more. Old Galba adopted an heir, Calpurnius Piso Licianus, but the Guard, working for Otho, killed Galba. Opening the way…"

"Yes, and Otho is now Emperor," Rokus confirmed.

"The northern legions are a formidable force. Expect Vitellius to be your next emperor before too long." Renhard was matter-of-fact, as if he'd seen such things before.

"Ah, ambition, the Roman curse." Rokus shook his head.

"Blood will decide, as usual."

Renhard returned to the room and came back with two cups full of wine. Rokus took one and peered into it.

"I heard the legions have taken to Vitellius' style," Rokus stated.

"Wholeheartedly."

"And the auxiliary?" Rokus threw a hand toward the room of revelers.

"Same thing. But more than extra food and drink is that Vitellius sanctions forays into the villages and countryside where men pleasure themselves with the local maidens. He asks them to bring him girls."

"They don't see through him? Where's their training? Their virtue?"

"Given the choice, they would have gone south to battle for Vitellius, not stay here to defend the fort."

"And the Guard, your old Guard?"

Renhard stepped aside and offered the scene behind him with a sweep of his arm.

Bentet laughed deeply, and Thonkrik and Gerulf leaned against Liuppo for support. They faced Renhard's lieutenants who wielded the pitchers of wine like barmaids. Their hauberks were loosened, and their capes had been thrown over chairs. They grinned foolishly and bellowed with red-faced merriment.

"These men and others will sneak out tonight to visit the whores in the village, and those women will be waiting for them as usual. The guards will let them pass knowing their turn will come."

"You allow this?"

"As I said—Vitellius recommends it."

NINETEEN
To the Goddess on the River Lupia

They departed Castra Vetera at dawn on the second day. On the eastbound road, Rokus and Ulla led a line of riders that included Renhard and five more men. The winter mantel was down, laying a chill on everything, silencing crickets and morning doves, sending the crows aloft in search of food. The early light, dim and seemingly weak to rise, cast an eerie pallor on all things frosty white. Ulla pulled the fur cloak tighter, and Rokus, too, hitched the collar of his.

"We'll cross the river later. Your place is to the East. Down a small river that feeds the big one," Rokus explained.

"Don't want to go." Ulla's voice was full of resolve and curiosity.

"Veleda is like you. You are like Veleda." Rokus attempted to clarify the potential union of soothsayers.

"I don't want to go."

"You both have the gift of knowing."

She glared at him, and even in the dimness, he felt the cut.

"Don't know what will come to pass here in Germania. You'll be safe with Veleda," Rokus reasoned.

"She doesn't want me."

A chill climbed his back and flourished around his neck. He considered this possibility for the first time. Summoning his music, he waited, but it did not arrive; he pictured Veleda in her red-haired magnificence and listened for her rejection of this little girl.

"Betuwe is not a place for you. Conflict brews, safe places are few," he said.

"Want to be with you."

Rokus drew the roan closer to her bay so that he could reach her, touch her, comfort her.

"And I with you."

"Then let me."

"It's best for now."

By mid-morning, they came to the dock. The Romans had constructed a compound of buildings to service a small merchant operation that used the river to transport goods. Several long boats were roped to the quay; another arrived just as they did.

Brown slaves from Mauritania and white ones from Germania Magna worked the dock, using cranes and netting to lift the amphorae and crates from boat to dock, pushing wagons laden with containers, and loading bins of grain and dried beans onto carts.

Renhard heeled his horse to the fore and then loped over to the barge that nudged the riverbank like a sleeping giant. He dismounted, talked to a grizzled man in a dirty tunic and cloak, then returned.

"Says he can take us over now."

Ulla whimpered.

"Be strong; it's best," Rokus advised in a gentle voice.

The river barge accommodated three horses at a time. Rokus, Ulla and Renhard went first, followed a half hour later by the other Batavian guard. The remainder cared for the horses and caught up on their adventures.

At this section of the Rhenus, water flowed due west where it made the turn from its northward journey, and the banks drew closer and made a shorter passage across; but it was also deeper, with robust currents. Two massive cords were fixed to each side of the barge, extending in opposite directions. The starboard rope went to the eastern shore, the portside rope to the western shore. Each cord wrapped around a horizontal pulley and was fastened to a team of oxen that pulled the barge to the respective shore. The strong currents were thus neutralized by the control exerted by the taut lines and powerful beasts of burden, and the path taken by the barge was, generally, directly back and forth. Round trip was about twenty minutes.

They finally gathered on the German side and followed the track eastward along the River Lupia. An opaque layer of metallic sky burdened them, bringing the dimness of winter and its companion, cold. The wind started, and everyone sank lower in their saddles to offer less of themselves to it.

The Lupia didn't meander but flowed with conviction. The undulations of the German terrain determined its passage, and it poured overland and around the low rises so that it seemed to flow in all directions every mile. Its banks were still lush because the soil, thus provided, stayed moist and fostered a temperate air.

The track to Veleda's tower narrowed, twisted every hundred paces, and cut as a tunnel through trees with intertwined limbs.

At one turn, they saw the tower peeking over the treetops, a stone mass rising like some geological rarity generated by confluences of rock, magma and earthen spirit.

"There," Rokus gushed, and they pulled reins.

The path had stopped in a glade, and in the surrounding wood, they saw signs of men. Rough-hewn benches were ensconced in niches cut in the thicket, empty racks to hold weapons were lashed to the bigger trunks, and the floor all around was tamped down by hooves and boots. Covered with lichen and stain, a water trough rested at the edge and a wooden bucket sat on its side.

"They've taken their arms. No guards today?" Renhard considered out loud.

"Let me go first," Rokus stated, guiding Ulla to Renhard.

Rokus pressed on foot down a path. He walked slowly up the tower steps for the first time in two and a half years. He remembered the textures as he ran his hand across stone and slid his soles on the grit and limestone of the steps.

As he reached the landing, his heart pounded. A row of skulls lined the perimeter; the black eyes and cleft nose cavities seemed to dance across the wall, the many hollows leading to some Roman or Bructeri afterlife. He heard Veleda chanting, her Bructerian words invoking forces he couldn't identify but felt nonetheless.

He looked through a small window. With her back to the door, she sat on a cushion facing an altar. Flanking her were two candles set in an iron holder and several small bowls mounded with incense smoldering in curlicues.

Her fiery hair frizzed down to her waist so that her arms extended from the hair mass without visual support of a body.

Veleda drew a knife and offered it to the room. She held out her forearm and passed the blade across it, leaving a red line. Then she held out a palm of dirt and let the droplets of blood fall into it. She poured the mixture into a bowl, wrapped her arm with a cloth, and then stirred slowly the dirt and blood with her middle finger.

She chanted all the while, a low singsong that was devoid of rancor or zeal and sweet to hear. Rokus savored the lilt as one allows spring finches' chatter to live in the moment. She pulled her hands in so that he couldn't see them; after bowing, she was perfectly still.

Rokus thought to clear his throat, but then Veleda spoke.

"You can't see, but the little one does. How is that, Rokus?"

She turned to the window, stood, and held her arms out in an embrace.

"Come to me, Rokus."

He opened the door, a thick oak construction that creaked on huge iron hinges. They stood face to face. Veleda's tears shone in the light as she pressed into him. They enclasped to feel bodies underneath the winter layers and then buried their faces into the base of the other's neck.

Veleda's fragrance hadn't changed — pine and honey and something like fertile soil. He breathed her in, hugging tightly, as if to squeeze away desolation and replace it with the garden of her.

She pushed him back and lifted the patch.

While tracing the socket and brow with her fingertip, she moaned sympathy and seemed to summon the healing nature of her being to anoint him. And Rokus felt some infusion, then a lessening of pressure, as when a thorn has been extracted.

"And the girl?" she asked.

"How do you know?"

"These things were in the auguries of my sacrifices. I've been following you up the river these many days."

Fear stirred in him, erupting in a squall overwhelming his balance and peace of mind. He knew this feeling from the prelude to battles, the cessation of thought that allows animal awareness. Beginning in the stomach, it grows like a knot turning on itself until it unravels into the blood like poison causing hands to tremble and knees to shake uncontrollably. He tried to settle himself because fear and love could not possibly coexist, but there they were, the one welling up inside, the other ransacking his steady hands and solid knees.

She saw his wavering and leaned into him. He engulfed her with his arms and squeezed her to confirm his presence and to keep the fear at bay.

"You're home. Let it go," she said.

And he leaned into her, speechless, choking on sentiments that vainly sought words. He gasped as he fought for control.

"Here," she said, digging her hands under his jacket and rubbing his back.

This he felt like a prod, and then something shifted and he had no fight with it. He began to sob, free of judgment and expectation. And like the recoil of clanging swords that banishes fear from the battle day, her touch relieved him of his pride.

He convulsed in her arms, his silent war against fear and pain temporarily over. Many minutes passed while his sobbing settled, slowed, and stopped.

"I have something," she said.

She left him swaying. Near the hearth she took a lidded vase and spooned something from it into a small metal pot with a spout on the side. From a barrel spigot she drew water into the pot, before placing it on a grid over a bed of orange coals.

She returned to him.

"The others are at the guard post," she said, her answer to the unasked question.

"You'll like her," Rokus imparted.

"She has the sight, doesn't she?" Veleda said, more statement than question.

"Something," Rokus acknowledged.

"Rokus?" Veleda coaxed.

"She sees, yes," Rokus agreed.

Veleda took the pot of tea and a small ceramic mug.

"Drink this," she said as she poured.

"What is this?" he said, flinching.

"Tea."

"What's in it?"

"Secrets of the forest. Now drink it."

He struggled but drained it and wiped his beard.

"You will feel better." Veleda ran her hand across his cheek.

"No guards on duty today?" Rokus asked.

"I sent them for oil, wine, and grain."

"Is that safe?"

Veleda sat in a throne along the wall and Rokus took a chair nearby. They looked at each other, and Rokus forgot his question. Something popped in the hearth, a raven called outside; otherwise the room was silent, and each heard only their heartbeats. In spite of this, Rokus studied her face and grinned as Veleda searched his eyes, smiled extravagantly, and sighed.

She leaned back into the throne and rested her hands on its arms. A large stone seemed to shout from her finger; she saw him looking at it and held the ring up for him to better see. Rokus raised his hand with his own ring, the large bloodstone identical to hers.

"Look at that!" he exclaimed. "Coincidence?"

"No."

They sat, letting the winter birds in the breeze speak for them, the fabric of natural sounds, spirit music. The morning light entered tentatively, as if seeking permission from the hearth glow, and the two of them watched the dialogue of elements binding them. Finally, a single beam crossed the room, delivering the outside world with its shock of light.

"Rokus, I love you so."

Rokus smiled. "Your memory has kept me alive, Veleda."

He went to her, pulled her to him and held her tightly, feeling her supple strength, the unity of their forms. He stirred, and his dormant fervor awakened; warmth led to heat, then heat to fire. She leaned her head back to kiss.

Soldiers' commands and Ulla's scream shattered the mood. Horses in distress neighed, and the cling-clang of arms echoed up to the landing.

"The guard has returned," Veleda said, jumping up.

She ran to the door and pulled it open.

"They're very protective of me," she asserted, looking back to him before bounding down the steps.

Veleda and Rokus ran down the path to the clearing. The Bructeri guards had the Batavians at bay with spears and swords pressing them against the trees and down on the ground; one Bructerian had an axe raised and ready.

"Wait!" Veleda called in Bructeri. "These are friends, allies; do them no harm."

The sharp points drew away from their quarry.

"Where's the child?" Veleda demanded.

She stood in the middle, clear eyes shooting fire, her flowing tunic and shawl and long red hair commanding attention.

"Listen," she hushed.

She crossed the clearing and plunged into the underbrush. Without regard for the snarl of branches grabbing her clothes and hair, she found Ulla's refuge. Rokus came upon them in a cave formed in the network of twigs. Veleda held Ulla to her breast and stroked the back of her head.

"You are with Veleda now; men will not harm you."

In the clearing, Veleda took the girl in her arms. The two of them locked eyes like long lost kin.

"Peace now," she commanded, and the guards bowed to her and restored their weapons. The Batavians, ambushed and defeated in this bloodless battle, brushed themselves off as they watched Veleda take the girl into the tower.

Rokus studied the twelve Bructeri and savored the peace declared, because their formidable frames were square with muscle, their swords shiny and sharp, and their movement cat-like and dangerous.

"Wait for me," he told them.

"Shall I pasture the horses?" Renhard asked.

"No, Renhard, I'll not be long."

Veleda gave Ulla tea and stroked her hair. As Rokus crossed the threshold, she said, "Do you have something to give to her?"

"Like what?"

"Some token."

Rokus looked at himself and shrugged.

"A memory object with your force in it."

Rokus pulled off the bloodstone ring and gave it to her.

"Perfect," she breathed, slipping a leather strand through it. "She will wear this and think of you. She'll have you close to her."

Veleda placed the leather loop around Ulla's neck while Ulla watched Rokus watch Veleda. A sense of departure arose, and he searched for the words for his leave-taking.

Veleda came to him, hugged him strongly, and looked up at him. Rokus kissed her, squeezed her until he felt her bosom swell in a deep sigh.

"You have to go. Romans march," she said.

He kissed her again, then went to Ulla and touched her cheek.

"You are in good hands now, little one. Ulla, I will see you soon."

When Rokus entered the clearing again, he took the reins from Renhard but stopped in front of the Bructeri guards, raising his hand.

"Hail. They are precious to me, to us; I know you will protect them."

"Hail, Prince Rokus," said the leader. "But will you protect us?"

TWENTY

On the Road to Batavorum before the Longest Night

Rokus sat at the head of their table in the mess of Castra Vetera. His mind was really on the horses outside, the familiar road to the island of Betuwe, the settlement of Batavorum, and the Roman troops stationed there. The others picked at their food, some looking at soldiers sitting at tables, some staring at nothing, passing silence from hand to hand as if it were an odious concoction; the table vibrated with ruminations.

"Fabius Valens just declared Vitellius Emperor," Renhard announced taking a seat at the bench. He put down his tin plate and cup searching the men's faces for response.

"Northern troops are happy about that. They like his methods." Thonkrik stared vaguely across the table, as if some clear sign of the future would appear.

"Hail, the chief debaucher rules." Folkbern held up his cup in a false salute.

"Now they pack up for Rome," Gerulf reported. "Thrilled to fight for a man who softens them with poor discipline."

"To battle for his next banquet," Bentet snapped, looking left and right.

"The Auxiliary backs him, too. Heard Batavian troops are dancing in the streets of Colonia," Renhard added, shaking his head.

"And the old Praetorian Guard?" Menfrid toyed with his spoon.

Renhard shook his head. "They are for him, as well. I would hope ours might have held out for some ethical type."

"Gods, look at us—even they've lost their way." Menfrid's voice strained with anxiety.

"Who can stop them? Who wants to stop them?" Liuppo asked the room ambiguously.

"Strongmen without control," Folkbern pronounced. "Countrymen or not, I dismiss them for this breach."

"And Nerva and Crassus have gone south." Renhard stirred his food absently.

"Didn't like those two," Folkbern exclaimed. "Real cutthroats."

"Just Roman officers." Thonkrik sneered and looked at Bentet, who nodded.

"Men of the eagle." Menfrid's anxiety had turned to sarcasm, and he turned to look out the door.

"And Labeo," Folkbern continued. "He's thrown it in for the legions."

"Watch out; he's a clever one," Bentet warned, flexing his back and shoulder muscles in recollection.

"But he's blind to us." Menfrid's attention was back at the table, and he leaned forward to buttress his point. "He's blind."

"A blind fox." Renhard stated with emphasis.

"What becomes of the North?" Liuppo's plaintive voice seemed to end the discussion as no man had a plan of action.

Rokus placed his hands firmly on the table. "Let's just get to the solstice festival. That is our first order of business." He looked up and down at the men nodding one by one that they must move northward and stay fixed on their own affairs.

"And crown you king!" Erenbrecht exclaimed with his thin voice. "Men, we have a king here!"

Gerulf reached for nearby plates, stacked them with a metallic rattle, and carried them to the trough. They watched him. Rokus fidgeted; dissatisfaction crawled under his tunic and he couldn't relax.

"The season shifts and gods are active," he said. "On to the solstice feast."

"And the Batavi wait for their king," Erenbrecht reiterated.

"Let's ride, then," Thonkrik asserted, dropping his fist on the plank.

"To the sacred grove now, and deal with Rome and those Batavians who ride under the eagle," Renhard proclaimed.

Gray light enveloped them as they set off northward. They rode with the knowledge that this region of Germania, west of the Rhenus, was destined for change. Rokus had returned, Erenbrecht lobbied for a new order, and the Roman legions were pulling away.

"Labeo is a traitor," Renhard stated to Rokus and Folkbern riding abreast of him.

"Misguided fool," Folkbern agreed.

"Back when we were training, Labeo's family and mine," Rokus shook his head, "such a rivalry. And we were the sons. Then this," he said, pulling back his hair to expose the long scar that crept over the side of his head and disappeared under his cinched up cloak, "made it personal."

"The Batavian Auxiliaries are devoted to him." Renhard spoke while holding his carriage straight and true, and when he finished, he turned to each of them looking for an opinion.

Menfrid heeled his horse into their midst.

"With the legions leaving, Labeo will be Vitellius' second, not Valens' second. Labeo has the Auxiliaries, both horse and foot," Menfrid pointed out, and they considered this prospect.

"Friends, let's just get to our family fires and the grove. We will see clearly from there." Rokus kneed the roan to a trot.

The air became steely gray, and they cinched cloaks to their chins and spread the fur over their legs. Heavy moisture swirled in the breeze, and all looked to the sky for flurries.

They rode in silence several miles when they came to a tributary. Rokus didn't remember this impasse on the north-south road.

"Shit," Menfrid cried out. "The river's moved again."

The riders in the back heard him and spurred up to the front. They sat their horses side-by-side facing the water.

"Every other year, seems," Thonkrik mused as he scanned the terrain for a ford.

"I don't want to swim in this!" Bentet exclaimed observing the depth, the chill, and the rapid flow.

"Not that inviting," Liuppo agreed.

"Look for a crossing of some kind," Rokus instructed the men.

The group turned west along the water, shifting into different pairs.

"This land is full of surprises," Rokus offered.

"Don't want to be a frozen priest at the solstice," Erenbrecht remarked.

"Or a late one."

"This afternoon?"

"If you say so."

Rokus inched the roan into the muddy shoreline to test the depth and flow. Her hooves sank deeply, and she pulled back with great slurping sounds. Splashing and prancing, she reeled away from the water.

"Erenbrecht," Rokus called.

Erenbrecht heeled his big mule to Rokus' side.

"The Batavi should not have a king."

The old man stroked his beard and studied Rokus' face for irony.

Rokus looked at him. "Should have a council, a set of magistrates. Balance of views."

"But, prince, king, people want a strong ruler," Erenbrecht insisted.

"They want confidence in their leaders."

"And power should go to that man," Erenbrecht argued.

"Men."

"We've decided to crown you at the solstice," Erenbrecht reminded.

"I would be a chief magistrate, not a king." Rokus looked straight across the tributary to the flat expanse before them.

"Not king?"

"The Batavi deserve better than a king. They can all be kings," Rokus pronounced. A new satisfaction came over him having mouthed the words. Now he saw the Batavian future, and the music that had vanished returned. He heard the beat of the bodhrán and the jangle of strings in rhythm and a melody that sounded like a lover calling. It gained tempo, then he heard pipes and the trill of notes tumbling in a line across time. 'I love you, Rokus,' Veleda had said, and he inhaled again her fragrance of pine and the honey and earth of her hair. He watched Erenbrecht sitting his mule and knew now to keep him at arm's length with his talk of kings. "Let's go, old man."

As they walked their animals along the marshy shore, the land talked to him in a dialect of greens and grays. The sky, a metal sheet dense with foreboding, blotted out the sun; but that, too, was full of conversation and reminded him of his childhood—his first lover, the training, fires in the hearths that nurtured through the night—because that selfsame sky had seen those things. They walked farther, and the tributary became narrower with the promise of crossing. But then the music in Rokus' ear grew dark. Pipes disappeared, the jangle disjointed; the melody ceased gliding by but now cut saw-like into his heart.

The music was not about Betuwe, and he sat up straight to scan the horizon.

The ground quavered, and he heard the rumble of hooves. Raising his hand, he studied the landscape, the vastness, the mist that dulled the horizon far away.

"What is it?" Renhard asked reining beside him.

"Somebody rides." Rokus held up his hand.

"Don't see anything." Renhard studied the horizon.

"Neither do I."

After another mile along the tributary, they came to a ford. Rokus still studied the terrain and the fugitive force that assailed his senses.

The roan crossed the shallows with care as the men negotiated the water in pairs and slurried muddy water and slopped the banks with their march.

Rokus looked behind them, to the east, ahead. The flat land extended forever, the plain unbroken. The immensity consoled him, and he pulled the cloak to his chin and the fur hat to his brow.

Gradually the plain rose like a great plate tipped, and they rode to its edge that stopped fifty feet above the plain below. At the base ran a stream, the trace of eons of water flow and its eroding force, and it snaked below them along the escarpment until it disappeared in the distance.

"This way," Rokus directed, heeling the roan to the west.

They followed him and ventured along the edge until it declined into a set of hills that had been concealed by a fog rising like earth's breath. Boney outcroppings scarred the site, forming a spine of rock that ran westward before it became lost in turf.

They approached gnarled trees standing dormant and black. The sound he heard now tightened his neck muscles, and he remembered the aedile's push in his back at the Esquiline Gate, the young man's soft face and brown eyes, his posture that spoke of his entitlements. A flash of hatred blushed Rokus' face, then he blinked his good eye to slough off such wasteful thoughts so he could focus on the mist ahead. The music was now a fretful drone, some tortured chords repeating with the dull thumping of the drum.

The mist burst with a flock of black birds whistling into the sky. The Batavians looked toward the racket and saw the cloud of arrows coming their way; black needles whose trajectory was dangerously clear drove them off their saddles; they rolled as one, integrated parts of an organism, hiding behind the bulks of animals as arrows struck the ground—*thwit-thwit-thwit*—all around.

One horse screamed. Rokus and the others drew swords while Gerulf and Folkbern loaded their bows and waited for targets to appear.

"Save the horses!" yelled Rokus, slapping the roan, Erenbrecht's mule, and another horse. The Batavian mounts, nostrils flaring, back legs kicking with the fear that gripped them all, jumped away, while the men scrambled behind rocks.

Another great swoosh sounded and another cloud of deadly missiles rained on them. Rokus studied the trees and mist and the corporeal shapes that appeared in between the tangle of trunks. Gerulf ran to the side, taking cover behind a rock. All was still.

Then he stood and shot an arrow. Rokus saw a fog-shrouded shape jerk backward and slump to the ground. Folkbern rose to a knee, aimed, and unleashed his arrow, and another shadow recoiled and vanished. Then all was still, as if the fog was gorging itself on sound, growing stronger with the diet, consuming the ledge, cliff, trees, rocks, and all who might be there.

Rokus couldn't see, and the only sound he heard was his heart pumping. After sheathing his sword, he rolled away from his rock, slid over the edge of the escarpment, and clung to the top. He clambered, spider-like, across the face, grabbing for rocks, dirt, clumps of grass, digging his boots where he could for toeholds. After ten minutes of scuttling, he peeped over the top.

He flanked the ambushers and saw men in silhouette; archers crouched behind the wall of rock, and legionnaires poised for battle. They outnumbered the Batavians two to one.

Lowering his head, he returned to his starting point far in the murk from these men, then crawled to his own and called them together.

"Romans. Twice our number. Split up, flank them. Put helmets on the rocks to keep their attention. Stay here, old man. Lie low," Rokus directed.

Rokus reviewed the men. "Where's Menfrid?"

They looked about, all clumps of grass and rocks resembled supine men, and they skulked into the fog searching.

"Here," Gerulf whispered.

When Rokus got to Menfrid, he assessed the leathery face; it already had the final smile, and his eyes carried resignation in the colors between hazel and green. Menfrid's fist clutched the arrow shaft that protruded from the lake of blood across his chest. He spewed red juice and grimaced.

"Got it this time, didn't I?" He struggled to speak.

"You did, old friend," Rokus uttered.

"Didn't even get to see the whoreson who shot me," Menfrid groaned.

"We'll get him," Gerulf promised.

Menfrid choked, looked at something far way, then returned again.

"Look, Rokus," he said, squeezing the arrow.

"Dare not pull it out now."

"No, look."

Rokus studied his face quizzically. Menfrid stroked the vane of the arrow.

"Batavian arrow," Menfrid gurgled. "We're killing each other."

Rokus steadied Menfrid's head. "Menfrid. Menfrid," he whispered.

"Been a long road, heh."

"Long road."

"Good road."

"Great road."

"Sight thickens, friends."

"Easy," Gerulf whispered.

"Oh, it's my time; Donar's coming, and I'm going."

"Menfrid," Gerulf whispered again.

"Rokus?"

"I'm here."

"Can't see you."

"Here." Rokus slid his hand under Menfrid's head.

"Know what I regret?" Menfrid moaned.

"What's that, friend?"

"I'll miss what's next." Menfrid coughed, and a stream of blood overflowed the corner of his mouth.

Rokus brushed hair off his sweaty forehead.

"You're home now, Rokus." Menfrid struggled. "Good time for Betuwe. For Batavi. Those Romans," he whispered. "Don't belong here. This is Batavi country, right?"

"That's right. Batavi." Rokus looked into his eyes, now fading.

"Getting dark. Can't feel anything. This, Batavi country."

Menfrid's eyes bore into Rokus' one, but there was no man behind them. Menfrid drifted away in a quiet swoon, the eyes holding neither personality nor contact with them.

Rokus ran his hand down Menfrid's face and paused.

"Donar, take this fine Batavian man," Rokus prayed.

He looked up at his somber comrades.

"We must act. Flank them, wait for my whistle. Arrows first."

The Batavians set to. They disappeared into the mist, four scrambling over the edge of the cliff, three along the base of the hill. They stalked the ambushers, quick to the rigor of the approach and the silence-keeping. Rokus led Thonkrik and Liuppo to the place he'd been before; he peered over the top again.

Labeo crouched among the archers who were, as Menfrid said, Batavians. Marius stood behind a tree talking to young Val.

"Should have known. Labeo and Marius," Rokus whispered.

Liuppo and Thonkrik loaded arrows and inched to the lip of the cliff face. They drew partially, then nodded to Rokus.

"Wait. They want me, not the group. Hold." Rokus stood on the steep embankment, holding up his sword. "Marius, Labeo, I am here. To avoid battle if I can."

"Throw down your weapons and come up," Marius called.

"I don't trust you," Rokus called, holding his arms wide.

"I've come for you, Rokus," Marius proclaimed.

"Told you, I'm not starting those training camps."

"We'll proceed without you."

"Right. You've got your Batavians under yoke, use them," Rokus scoffed.

"I will."

Below the edge, Rokus motioned for Renhard, Thonkrik and Liuppo to keep moving down the escarpment. They crawled away from him to a place behind the Roman-Batavian force.

"Why've you come for me?" Rokus stalled.

"You're under arrest," Marius called through the mist.

"Already been arrested. I didn't like it," Rokus sneered.

"You can come peacefully or I will take you," Marius called with finality.

"I'm going home, Roman, an idea you wouldn't understand."

"I have my orders."

"You and your orders! Can you stand up without them?" Rokus mocked.

As they yelled back and forth, Rokus stepped over the lip onto the hillside; his hands were open and arms out. Folkbern, Gerulf and Bentet emerged from the fog opposite aiming arrows at the archers. The Auxiliary archers turned to aim at them.

"A standoff. How many have to die?" Rokus shouted.

He faced Marius, approached him carefully, studied his eyes. Marius, holding a spear and net, returned Rokus' stare.

"Orders to cage me like an animal?" Rokus jeered.

"To bring you in." Marius hefted his weapons, preparing for battle.

"I was sent to my men; did you forget?"

"Things are different now."

"Right. You've murdered children since I left Lazio." Rokus' disdain soaked his words.

Labeo stepped forward. He surveyed his kinsman and Marius, the Auxiliary archers, and Rokus' three Batavian archers beyond them.

"Countryman, we need to talk in private," he said to Rokus.

"This is as private as I get," Rokus stated with certitude.

"Batavian, be reasonable."

"You son of a whore. You useless thing. The two of you are vermin, scabs on the face of the earth," Rokus spat. "Murderers. I am a Batavian, and I live for Betuwe, the island of my people."

Marius signaled to Labeo. Labeo signaled to the Batavian archers and legionnaires. The soldiers formed a square three rows deep, overlapping shields in the front row, while the second and third made a shell of shields over all of them.

"Advance," Marius commanded.

Rokus looked over to Folkbern, Gerulf and Bentet. He made a fist, a gesture to hold fast, but they drew back their bowstrings more.

The legionnaires came at them, a slow march of a machine, armored, confident.

The archers under Labeo's command maintained their aim at Folkbern and his men while the armored beast machine marched.

Then Rokus put fingers to lips and sounded the call of a mourning dove.

They heard the *thwang* of bowstrings released and the *shoosh* of arrows flying. Three legionnaires in the back row grabbed the backs of their legs or reached in vain for the points that struck them between shoulder blades. Labeo and Marius spun round, but then another volley of arrows cut into the machine, now in disarray. Three more legionnaires fell punctured by arrows that sank deep.

"Shoot!" Labeo cried out.

But his Batavian archers lowered their bows.

"Shoot, fools!" he shouted.

Rokus rushed into him. Marius cast the net and it billowed and engulfed Rokus as he lunged. He seized handfuls of netting and rolled, and as he did, he tucked his frame while pushing it over his head. He rolled twice, sprang to his feet, and freed himself of the trap. Marius had been pulled along and prevented from spearing. Now he faced Rokus; in the split second when Marius sized him up, Rokus rushed again, grasping the shaft of the spear, directing it away.

Marius released it, drawing his sword. Rokus threw the weapon over the edge and slid his sword from its sheath; now they were matched in blades.

"Shield," Labeo called.

A legionnaire threw his shield that slid to the Roman's feet. Marius stooped for it, fixing it on his forearm.

"A fine end of the road," Rokus announced.

"And an end it will be," Marius growled, charging.

He slashed into Rokus, who raised his blade and sidestepped, deflecting the attack in a clang of steel.

"You've acquired bad habits, Marius, using the barbarian swing instead of the Roman jab."

They circled each other, brandishing blades, studying angles and openings, anticipating, feigning.

Marius' face bore witness to the beating he'd received. Purple blotches lingered on cheekbones and brow, and his lips were encrusted with patches of scab. His nose was much wider than before and leaned to the side like a mistake.

Labeo approached with his sword held out.

"Far enough, Labeo," Folkbern called.

Folkbern and Gerulf rose with arrowheads directed on Labeo, bowstrings pulled three quarters back.

Marius advanced toward Rokus, then stopped just feet away.

"I'll kill you now," Marius snarled. "You've ruined me."

"No favors from senators since I got away?" Rokus goaded.

"This will end it."

"We can stop."

"Never."

Marius thrust with his sword. The point shot at Rokus' middle. Rokus swung backhandedly, directing the point up and to the side. In a continuous motion, he brought his blade fiercely down and pinwheeled it around in a great slice across Marius' arm.

The Roman recoiled, pulling the stump back as he watched his hand and forearm fall to the ground. Blood pumped from the remnant, spurting across the grass like some appalling fountain gone amok.

Rokus was still in the follow through as a thought revealed itself: make a merciful end of this soldier.

He spun around as Marius dropped to his knees. They looked at each other, their eyes flashing in code, their understanding lodged in years of battle and killing and knowing gruesome aftermaths, both living and dead.

Marius held the stump to his chest as if so touching it would restore the arm. He glistened with his redness. Rokus stood by him as Marius surrendered to this circumstance and welcomed the escape from such dismal prospects. He opened, offering his chest unobstructed and nodding to Rokus. Instantly Rokus plunged his sword deep into Marius' chest, and the Roman toppled dead.

Rokus stood over the man's body, studying the scars that marked his limbs, shiny, raised tissue zigzagging across muscles, evidence of previous endgames. He pulled at his sword, but it wouldn't give. Placing his boot on the chest, he yanked the weapon, and it came, and he held it away from him as if it were tainted.

Then the moment seized him, and he instantly considered the tyranny of power that played on this low shelf near the island of Betuwe. The core of it was allegiance misplaced, a denial of land spirit and its wellspring of wholeness for the sake of authority and power, fleeting and false. His own blood now raced with rage, and he would not deny it.

"You're next, Labeo."

"Wait."

"You put him up to this."

"He wanted revenge for the whipping."

"You wanted your own revenge. From years ago. Now come and get it," Rokus taunted as he turned to him.

Wielding his sword as if it had a preordained target in Labeo, Rokus strode toward him, and Labeo backed up the hill to the legionnaires and archers. He saw he'd given much ground to his rival and stopped.

"Fight me, Labeo," Rokus demanded.

Both Batavians, in the raiment of their loyalty—Labeo, in the Roman tunic and mail, bracae and helmet; Rokus, in his leathers, fur hat and German boots—studied each other, weighing benefits and dangers.

"We're kinsmen," Labeo reasoned.

"Then why side with Rome?" Rokus questioned.

"The future."

"And what do you get?"

"I won't pad around the marshes gazing at the clouds, that is certain," Labeo explained.

"Rome gives you purpose, then?" Rokus challenged.

"And position."

Rokus explored Labeo's face, discovering boy and man, tribesman and Roman, the rival to hate and the fox to admire. He remembered the training grounds outside Batavorum—wide fields with horse pens and an armory full of wooden weapons—and the elders who'd survived their army service training them to jab with conviction, to counter blows swiftly, and to ride as an extension of the horse's power, not as its master.

As Labeo stood squarely facing him, the excellence of the man blossomed from the memories of their training. But there was the scar on Rokus' own head and neck evoking the point of rift—a distant battle when Labeo killed tribesmen for Rome and Rokus had struck him to prevent more of it—and now he swallowed deeply as the picture came to him.

Then he heard the bowed melody and the thumping of a drum and questions rose: how can it be like this? Do we just kill each other? And he reconsidered Labeo.

"We must bury these men and be gone."

TWENTY-ONE
Arriving at the Island of the Batavi
for the Solstice Festival

"Rokus is back, Rokus returns!" Ansgar shouted, running through the streets.

Heads popped out of doorways, women and men stopped their work. They put their implements down or leaned them against walls, and they gathered in the square to greet the Batavian travelers riding through the Batavorum gate. Children ran among them, daredevil boys darted under the horses, girls pulled at the furs and straps of the riders' tack.

Rokus looked back at his riders and the amalgam of solemnity and delight that dusted their faces. Beyond them were the Roman earthworks around the garrison, a seventy-year-old post that had not yet been converted to stone. Just as he remembered, Roman legionnaires strutted along the parapets observing the Batavi below, and the citizens of Batavorum looked over their shoulders at the fort while working the markets, shops, looms, forges, tanneries, and potteries.

Suspended over all was the cloud of suspicion, a seething vapor that Batavian and Roman breathed, fortifying one's dissension and the other's authority. It had always been like this.

Rokus observed the townsfolk and raised his arms.

"Hail, Rokus!" an old woman cried.

"Hail, Prince Rokus!" an old man bawled.

Erenbrecht heeled his donkey to a position next to Rokus; he waved to them as if he were the prince. "Look, Rokus, they prepare for the solstice," he said, pointing.

Down a side street a group of women bundled twigs. Behind them men loaded firewood onto a cart. Farther still, girls strung lanterns on a line and added these to flags and pennons, bins, platters, bowls and goblets on another cart.

Rokus nodded. Then he turned the roan to his riders.

"Been a long road. Let's go to our families, rest these horses, rest ourselves, and prepare for the festival. Thank Donar we're here. May Menfrid live in our memories."

"Thank Donar," Folkbern offered.

"Thank Donar," the others chimed with reverence.

Then Rokus scanned the cheering crowd and raised his hand again.

"Friends, I've come from Rome, a long journey. The road was full of dire conditions, much evidence of Rome's power, Rome's cruelty, and Germania's discontent. These circumstances are ever present. But we are in Batavorum now, safe and grateful, and we embrace you all—kinsmen."

They erupted with cheering, and some threw hats in the air.

"Pulling us on was our bond to you all and to the solstice festival, a momentous time, a time of hope as the days get shorter—a time for awakening. Seeds of the earth begin stirring; they struggle through the winter to emerge in the spring. We are like those seeds. We endure the cold and wind and rain and snow, but we will emerge in four months, whole and strong. We acknowledge this three nights hence. Let us, good Batavians, rejoice and give thanks to Donar and the earth goddess for strength and growth, protection and sustenance at this time of renewal."

"Hail, Donar!" someone yelled.

"Hail, the spirits that help us!" another yelled.

"Hail, Rokus!"

"Hail, Veleda!" shouted a third.

Rokus sought that speaker in the crowd, an elder man, and studied his bearing. His frame declared hardships and many campaigns of battle, and his face, a shriveled landscape of deep thought, examined Rokus, devoured him even; and then Rokus recognized him as Fretherik, the wise man he'd revered long ago.

Rokus raised both hands acknowledging their praise and thanks and passed an arm across the sky.

"Kind Batavians, time to rest these bones, eat good Batavian food, sleep. Great to be home."

The crowd cheered, nodding, throwing fists to sky, clapping.

The riders clasped each other's wrists in goodbyes and turned their horses to their homes. Rokus dismounted, handed the reins to the liveryman and walked through the crowd, allowing hands to touch his fur cloak.

"Treat you well in prison?" called out the baker.

"What was Rome like?" asked the midwife.

"Did you see a chariot race?" cried a young boy, whose voice had the crackle of early adolescence.

"Have you heard about the new conscriptions?" asked one of the town widows.

He came to Fretherik and embraced him. "What's this about Veleda, wise one?"

"Oh, Rokus, 'tis so good to see you, my boy. You're well?" he inquired, holding a shriveled hand to Rokus' brow.

"Veleda?" Rokus asked. "You referred to Veleda. How do you come by knowledge of her, wise one?"

"Great prophetess and haruspex." Fretherik held his open hands, palms facing Rokus.

"Yes. How do you know of her?"

"From Bructerian traders." Fretherik's eyes flashed left and right. "Rokus, we must talk later. I will call on you tomorrow."

"Tomorrow then."

"I'll bring mead. You must have worked up a thirst during your travels."

"I will drink your mead," Rokus grinned.

The crowd pushed Rokus into Ansgar, now barely recognizable with his first beard, thicker chest, and another foot of height.

"Ansgar, you are well?" Rokus asked, clasping wrists, then hugging him and slapping his back.

"Good, Rokus," the youth answered with a grin and the aspect of wholesomeness.

Rokus regarded him at arms' length but quickly pulled him near again. "Can you get word to Veleda right away?"

"I have a new horse."

"Perhaps a friend to go with you?"

"Three."

"And they've horses?"

"Fast ones like mine."

"Excellent, man. Go to Veleda. Tell her to come to the festival three days hence—with Ulla."

"Ulla?" Ansgar asked with a tilt of his head.

"A girl. Tell Veleda that Rokus wishes her company. Understand? Go."

"No poem this time, Rokus?" Ansgar asked.

"I will deliver it myself upon your return," Rokus smiled.

Rokus slipped down a side street while the townsfolk celebrated both his return and the coming festival. He found Menfrid's house on a track near the training field. It sank in on itself like a comfortable chair and seemed to gain some kind of grace in its weathered roof and crooked shutters, graying posts, and wattle and daub resembling an ancient's skin. He knocked. Menfrid's wife answered and looked at him with a face creased and leathery and with blue eyes that cast flickering light where hard work had lodged. She carried a vase full of wilted flowers and sheers.

"Rokus. You the cause of all this commotion?"

He bowed his head and rested one hand on his hilt and dangled the other, not sure of what to do with it. She looked him up and down, then stepped aside and pulled his sleeve into the house.

"He's not with you. Didn't return, did he?"

"Gita, he took a Roman arrow yesterday," Rokus explained, the words seeming feeble and inappropriate. "A brave, kind man, loved by all of us. A fine man."

The woman sank onto a bench as she digested this news and stared at her future somewhere in the shadows across the room. Rokus went to her side and put his hand on her shoulder, but she waved him off. He stood in the cloud of her grief for several minutes, then she gestured him out of the house. And as he backed away from her, her fingertips traced her wrinkles and tried to dam her tears. He stepped toward her to offer solace, but again she whisked him away.

He walked back toward the town center. He came to his family's house, two stories of posts and beams, planking and plaster surmounted with Roman tiles. It sat on a large lot near a green at an intersection and had one of the few stands of trees inside the town walls. A light shone through a window; smoke curled from the chimney.

He thought it must be the housekeeper, Hedy, and tried the door. It creaked open, and his familiar place was before him: the hearth and kitchen, the great room, the passages to the back rooms, the staircase. The firelight washed across the table and pots, the shelves of things. It smelled of ham and peat.

He stood in the doorway imbibing the place of his birth and youth. The harvest of memories shocked him with their remoteness, and only when he saw the figurine on the mantel did he feel it was his home. He went to it, a wooden carving of a man crudely proportioned and grossly featured, and studied its sardonic grin as if it knew something profound about the land where Rokus had unearthed it. His talisman as he grew up, the carving carried in it the spirit of Betuwe, or that essence he bestowed on it, and he clutched it many times as he grew older.

"Who's there?" Hedy called.

"It is Rokus," he answered. "Hedy?"

"They took Rokus away. To Rome."

"Back now, Hedy."

The old slip of a woman entered the great room, a shriveled vestige of the crone he once knew. She shuffled, leaning on a cane and dragging a shawl.

"Rokus, you say?"

"Let me see you, Hedy."

Rokus went to her and held her frailness as if she were dried clay.

"I've returned now, and I'm weary," he replied softly.

"Were they decent to you? In that prison." Hedy examined him with what sight remained.

"It was political. I wasn't an enemy. Treated fine."

"If they'd hurt you…" Her voice trailed off as she thumped the cane on the floor. "Sit."

"Where's Wulf?" Rokus looked around the room.

"They took the boy. Britannia, I think."

Rokus flopped in a chair covered with a blanket. The seat wobbled and creaked; one broken slat dug him in the back.

"I'll call for water, stoke the flame here. Have a bath, how is that?" she cackled.

When she returned, Rokus' head was back and he was sleeping.

The next day he walked through the west gate and in the neighboring field saw the offering structure, a mesh of branches and twigs looming in the mist. He followed the track over flat fields for half a mile where the terrain dipped and the track turned north, rose for another half mile, then dropped into a glen sheltered by a crop of ancient trees that stood like stout guardians of the clearing. There was a rise in the center, and on this they had erected a long table of planks. The sacred grove had seen initiations, celebrations, funerals, and ceremonies when men and women were compelled to reach out for the spirits in the wind, in the land, or within themselves.

Rokus stood before the altar at the end of the space. In the middle sat a skull, rubbed smooth, blotched with soot. Its empty eye sockets held the infinity people placed in them. Off to the side, there was a stone figure much like the talisman he found as a boy. Flowers wilted and fresh leaned out of clay vases all around, and candleholders lined the back.

Closing his eyes, he summoned the last three years and any logic it possessed. He waited. The sea breeze rattled branches, and crows glided high and low, filling the air with their cawing. Seagulls coughed and glided and dove onto the path for insects. He stilled himself, breathed the heavy air reverently, absorbing fugitive spirits that he divined.

It wasn't enough. He withdrew his knife from its sheath, held out his hand, and ran the blade across it. He watched the line fill; blood gathered at the end. He dripped this in front of the skull, then slid the skull over it as a bone house for his vitality.

As he listened to the crows and gulls, the wind picked up, and the temperature dropped. He stood straight, letting the cold air slap his neck and face, and soon he sensed a dialogue with his ancestors and the story of Betuwe. He closed his eye and watched through the red patterns of darkness, and the images rolled into his awareness as if he were there.

They crossed their meadows and entered the German forest, ten thousand walking and riding in an exodus from the Chatti tribe, their source people. They came to the great river and swam across. Men, women and children pulled at the current and hung on to ropes from their beasts. At one point, a crow would have seen an endless line of people flowing from the eastern forest, into the river, across the alluvial plain, and entering the thin wood of the northwest Rhenus lands, finally crossing into the marsh. On the island, they thrived—until the Romans came.

He stood there, letting the story fill his bloodstream and render his muscles a new supple life. There was Uulfnoth, his father, returning from battle wearing the Roman officer's battle dress; except for his beard, he was practically Roman. There was his grandfather and great-grandfather, both Uulfnoths, who used their new Roman names but declined to wear the Roman dress, preferring the advantages of Roman citizenship and the refinement of Batavian clothing. Then there was Labeo, throwing a spear that struck Rokus' own, and Rokus' arrow bisecting Labeo's at center target. There were his brothers and the young men of the settlement leaving for Britannia; there was the metamorphosis of the settlement from village to town, Batavorum, and the myriad villages throughout the island, all connected by blood.

The blur of Britannia erupted in his mind, more sounds than images, the experience digging into his consciousness like the blade across his hand. He bled for Britannia, as he now bled for Betuwe, as he bled for Donar and the fellow spirits; and he bled for Veleda, because now he felt her in his presence.

"You better pray for good luck." Labeo's voice broke the spell.

Rokus spun around, and there was his rival in Batavian clothes. Labeo aimed a spear at him and smirked from under the winged helmet.

"You've come for the festival?" Rokus asked.

"For you, you fool."

Labeo charged at him, spear point directed at Rokus' chest. Rokus braced himself and raised hands to intercept the spear, but Labeo whipped it aside just before contact and struck him on the temple with the butt of it.

The shaft smashed across his ear, jarred his head; his knees disappeared and he crumbled in place.

He stared into the gray sky, but it faded into the fields of Britannia. He heard the Catuvellauni's crazed yells as they charged and the rain of lead shot pummeling helmets and shields. A metal ball ricocheted off the helmet of the warrior at his side. Its conic shape was ruined and blood gushed down the man's face; his eyes fluttered, and he fell. Another cloud of lead fell on them, a deaf-ening storm of thuds, clanks and screams, and then something cracked, lightning and thunder, and his world turned black. He floated across Britannia for a lifetime; when gradually the dawn sky arrived, shapes became defined, and he heard the breath of the day. Lighter, louder it grew, and then he saw Labeo watching him.

"Get up."

Rokus rolled to an elbow and struggled to his feet.

"Not here, Labeo, not in the grove," Rokus implored.

"Your convention disgusts me."

Labeo came at him quickly and swung the spear club-like, and it struck the other side of Rokus' head. Again he dropped. Face down, Rokus pushed his cheek off of the dirt; his fingers sank deep, and he smelled the bouquet of minerals. He pushed to his knees and felt the stream from his hair run along his jaw, watched the dark soil spotting, a growing constellation of him-self in Batavian dirt.

"No allegiances, heh?" Rokus taunted.

"We buy and sell with different currencies, Rokus."

"But to give it all to Rome?"

"Get up. Let my spear kiss you again," Labeo jeered.

First one foot, then the other, Rokus straightened himself.

"I will never run from you again," Labeo declared.

"Your future may betray you, kinsman."

Labeo charged. Rokus raised his arm to protect his head when the spear came down. He staggered but caught himself and clutched the spear under his arm.

In a flush of instinct, he spun and stooped concurrently, and Labeo stumbled forward. Rokus wheeled around and seized Labeo's shoulders at the neck and drove him back, and back, and they tumbled together past the ring of ancient trees.

Rokus rolled on top of him, devoting himself to squeezing all life from his limbs. With clutching hands and single eye glaring, he throttled this kinsman; strength and quickness melded as animalistic instinct, and it blinded him.

Labeo choked for air, and Rokus strangled. Labeo looked at him goggle-eyed, surprised at this turn, and Rokus pressed on. Labeo struck as a man does who senses the end, but Rokus didn't feel the punches to his back and across his face and kept choking until the blows ceased.

Labeo's color changed. Then Rokus heard the melody and thump of music that haunted him, and it trembled with the spirits, and he released Labeo. Rokus stood up and backed away, watching Labeo's color return as he gagged air back into his lungs.

"Now, you get up," Rokus demanded.

Labeo staggered, gasping and holding his neck. He stumbled around while Rokus backed away from him. Then Labeo saw the spear.

He snatched it, overcome with the fever of revenge, and he charged Rokus on wobbly steps.

Now Rokus pulled his knife, and as Labeo came on, he got set for him, dodged the spear so carelessly wielded, and thrust his blade under Labeo's arm. He felt the blade gain purchase and withdrew it.

Labeo stopped. His hand went to his side and came out red. "You've cut me."

"I have. Not seriously."

Labeo and Rokus stood face to face. One's tunic blossomed crimson; the other's head rang. Neither man stood firmly.

Labeo faltered, bent over and vomited, spat, coughed, and spat again. Righting himself, he sneered but swayed unsteadily. Glaring at Rokus, he backed up until his feet were stopped, and he sat on the downed trunk in his way. The spear lay there, and he reached for it.

Rokus went to him, took the spear from his hand, then swung it overhead and smashed it across the log. He handed the point to Labeo and walked back into the clearing.

"Rokus," Labeo called.

Rokus stopped and turned.

Labeo had gained his balance and stood, wavering. He pointed at Rokus as if missiles might fly from his fingertip. His curled lip returned, and he pointed the scolding finger while clutching his side. He picked up his winged helmet and placed it askew on his head. He entered the path to town, turned to point his warning finger again, and disappeared in the mist.

Rokus walked back to the altar and placed his hands on it, palms down. He had just followed his intuition, a notion born of these long days on the road through the fog of meanness encountered in forests and glens, a vague awareness of peaceful days that glowed, like light around a nimbus.

He adjusted his patch, then closed his good eye and pushed his boots into the dirt and pressed his palms down and breathed in deeply.

Later, the coming festival blew through the streets of Batavorum, swirling cheer and carrying men and women into the tasks at hand. The town's face and sacred grove received their ephemeral masks according to custom, as twine and lanterns, husks and bark, and clay and leaves adorned walls and doorframes, eaves and rooflines, and wells and windows with faces of the spirits and ancestors and lights sparkling into dusk.

Rokus walked among the people, smiling at these preparations. People's faces flashed joy, and as daylight diminished, they grew giddy with the prospects of the night's renewal and swilled the beer that was poured at street corners.

Fretherik motioned to him; they left the main square and walked down several blocks to Rokus' house. Hedy shuffled into the kitchen and prepared hot broth. The men sat by the fire; stroking his beard, Fretherik leaned into Rokus and pulled at his tunic.

"My sight isn't what it was, and I see yours isn't either."

"Yes, Rome took a lot more than two of my years."

"Ah. But it is great to have you back," Fretherik smiled.

"Been a long road," Rokus sighed.

Fretherik surveyed the room, then sat back staring into the dim light of old age.

"Veleda," Rokus reminded him.

"Veleda," Fretherik answered. "To me, the name brings peace."

The old man reached down blindly and pulled up a haversack and placed it on his lap. Untying the strands on the flap, he opened it and took the flagon of mead he'd promised. He offered it.

Rokus turned to the kitchen and bumped into Hedy, standing there with three mugs.

"A little for an old lady," she said.

"Marvelous, Hedy," wheezed Fretherik.

Rokus poured, and they clinked mugs and drank. Hedy held hers out for more and then retreated to the back room, humming.

Fretherik leaned back again, his mug nestled in his hands. His mouth moved to form words but managed only a garbled moan. Finally, he whispered, "Remarkable powers. Beyond this world. Never before has there been such a soothsayer. I think she's a goddess."

"Have you met her, Fretherik?"

"Never. Traders just bring her predictions, sometimes messengers riding through, spreading her word. Last summer she announced you'd come. We thought you were dead. And here you are."

"I've invited her for tomorrow's fire."

"Veleda? Here? Marvelous."

"Should arrive soon."

Fretherik leaned forward, focused his eyes on Rokus, and cleared his throat. "You know, she said the Romans will leave, and the tribes will rise up victoriously. She said another man claims the Roman throne, Vespasian. Messenger brought that last week."

"That makes four this past year. Have more mead, old man." Rokus lifted the flagon and poured into Fretherik's mug.

"So good to see you alive, boy." Fretherik spoke with his thin voice quavering as much as his hands. Mead spilled onto his tunic, making a dark patch.

"There is civil war in Rome now, and with this Vespasian, it is likely to last a while." Rokus shared and drank again.

So, will they leave us alone?" Fretherik asked, pulling the patch off his skin.

"I don't predict, Veleda does," Rokus asserted, and as he spoke a wave of passion hit him.

"You know about little Wulf?" Fretherik inquired.

"I do. Britannia?" Rokus looked into his mug and, with affection, at the old man.

"Yes. Full of spirit, that one. Wanted to go so badly." Fretherik began shaping a narrative in the space in front of him, his gnarled hands conjuring the British hills, the army's tent rows, the parapets, and the young soldiers' faces.

"To be like his older brothers," Rokus helped.

"Ah, but Rokus, he is his own man." Fretherik lowered a hand down from his narrative and brought his mug up to his lips.

"To such a fate," Rokus finished, reaching for the flagon again.

"Rokus, my cup is empty," Fretherik announced.

Rokus filled their cups and went to Hedy's back room with the flagon. When he returned, Fretherik sat straight, staring into the shadows.

"When they go like that, some innate part of the tribe goes with them," Fretherik pronounced.

"It's youth," Rokus suggested.

"Tribe's promise," Fretherik clarified.

They finished the flagon and walked to the town square where Veleda and Ulla, the twelve Bructeri guards, and Ansgar and his three friends had just arrived.

Rokus brought Fretherik to Veleda, and he thanked her repeatedly for her visions, all the while his ancient head trembled and he pulled at his beard with twisted fingers.

Veleda touched his cheek. Then, smiling and nodding, he crossed the square among the people and disappeared. She took Rokus' arm and rested her head momentarily on his shoulder. She gathered Ulla under her other arm. Rokus held Veleda and hugged the girl gently.

Dusk dissolved the buildings and people's shapes until the liveryman and Ansgar went around with torches, lighting the strung lanterns and the stone lamps positioned throughout the square. Rokus knelt in front of Ulla. He'd never seen her face pink before. Her hair had changed, too, now thicker, flaxen. "You're well, I see," he observed.

"The tea," Ulla said. "And Veleda."

"Veleda can give you just what you need," he added.

She kissed his cheek and smiled, a beacon of joy in which he saw her relief. Finally, Ulla is burying brutality with Veleda's kindness, he thought.

A crackle and explosion filled the night air, and all the faces in the square became masks of fear lit by the torchlight. This eruption prompted some to seek refuge in the buildings, and with the roar that followed, some screamed impulsively. The firestorm they saw in the first field beyond the wall put them at rest, and they trickled out of their hiding and went to the gate to behold the bonfire celebrating the winter solstice.

Flames thundered up the offering structure, a forty-foot high inverted V made from tree trunks and limbs in a giant weave. Fire licked up the lengths, jumping from one to another and offering themselves to the greater holocaust. Smoke began to billow and roll far overhead, anointing the longest day with its scents of pine and willow and dogwood.

A giant came down the street. One of Ansgar's friends, dressed as a Batavian lord, waved awkwardly as he teetered on stilts ten feet high. His Batavian hat was something from their tales, his coat of a pattern long out of fashion. The children rushed to him, calling happy taunts and cheers, beckoning him to pull off his mossy beard so they could name him.

At the edge of the square, a man began juggling fire sticks. A crowd quickly surrounded him. He flipped three rods with flaming tips that tumbled end-over-end in the air; all the while, they rotated over his head in awe-inspiring spectacle. He did this as he walked, and the people followed him, their eyes riveted to the spinning flames.

Several wagons rolled into the square, drawn by men who joked with anyone nearby. Their wagons held large casks of beer, and they pulled the spigots to fill mugs and cups and handed these to anyone.

Rokus then heard the music; the haunting theme of these last thirty days had taken form in Batavorum. There in the square were the four musicians from Colonia, and they hunched over their instruments playing with a rhythm that throbbed with heart force. The people around them danced, and the people around them ogled to see these magicians of sound. That end of the square became a multi-headed, multi-legged organism bouncing in circles and throwing arms overhead euphorically.

Gradually the people in the square moved left and right forming some order out of the celebration of renewal and release. Gaps formed between clots of people, and soon a line twisted serpentine around the square and moved to the gate. There, several townsfolk handed out little clay oil lamps from a cart brimming with them. Down the line, several others held bigger lamps with tongues of flame glowing brightly, and they held these out to light the small lamps as all passed by.

Soon, Rokus, Veleda and Ulla held their own lamps and gazed momentarily into the mystery of fire before they became part of the procession into the countryside. Rokus looked over to the Roman fort, an ominous silhouette of might and the shapes of guards plying the parapets; but the music was too strong, and he laughed like everyone else.

The Bructeri guards, too, held their lamps and danced in the line of Batavi. This human force coursing into the longest night of the year now had five legendary Batavians depicted on stilts, and six more jugglers tossing fire; and the beer wagons followed them like pleasure stations, and the musicians now marched as well.

Then the procession turned back to the town, homing in on the bonfire that flourished just beyond its walls. The line of celebrants wrapped around the fire, gasping and crying out at each popping spark and upsurge of flame.

Men at the front of the line began a tribal song they all knew, and soon the chorus of the town rose thunderously into the sky with the sparks. It was noisy and heady and elating, and they drank more beer.

Some threw effigies of ancestors and lost babes made from husks and leaves, and some people, with creative flare, had fashioned wishes on pieces of bark or hide and threw them in as well. Saddles made from wood and leaves, bigger houses from bark and straw, and soldier sons of twigs and twine wearing leafy armor and bearing stick spears and whittled swords ignited as little bursts then disappeared as folding ash; and the young boys threw in their oil lamps to watch them explode.

After several tribal songs, a horn sounded over all—a resonant moan that vibrated into their hearts—and they left the bonfire to head down the path to the sacred grove.

Rokus took Veleda's hand in his right and Ulla's in his left, and they walked the path abreast as townsfolk skipped and danced by, wishing them all the best.

The sacred grove glowed like an unearthly vision. Strings of lanterns reached between trees casting an orange ring of light. Thick torches mounted on posts flared and quivered in the night breeze. Platters of apples and honeyed toasts covered the central table, lighted by many-wicked lamps that seemed to dance in time.

The procession entered the grove with reverence and revelry entwined; some were cloaked in solemnity, others inebriated with joy. All shared the recognition of the night and its many permutations, as if a cloud of ancestors looked at them from the ephemera of the past and the collective steel embodied in them held at bay the darkness and all its secrets.

A man stood on a stump and blew the horn again, and all fell silent, because horns within the grove were the voices of past and future and, they understood, they needed to hear these.

"Rokus!" he called after the third ceremonious blast.

The people turned to each other and into the crowd around them looking for Rokus. Fretherik, near the blower of the horn, raised his frail arms as if to hasten Rokus' discovery among them. Erenbrecht stood there, and he fulminated to some elders who stood by with half smiles clinging to their faces.

Rokus raised his arm, then the crowd parted for him, and he walked with Veleda and Ulla to the altar of the grove, to the very spot where he'd bled for his future and wished for a truce among men.

He faced the Batavians, who cheered and relished the moment of his return. He surveyed the grove choked with roisterers and lionizers and saw the fragility of his pledge.

His eye followed the crowd as it snaked out of the grove and into the night; he scanned the fort to the east and the land far to the west where he saw the columns of fire and smoke that can only rise from a legion's camp at war.

EPILOGUE

The flames of the solstice celebration illuminated the glee of the Batavians' red faces. Emboldened by their new king and the resilience he symbolized, they threw oaths into the night sky like so many swirling embers. The drummers beat their bodhráns and slapped and shook their tambourines. With syncopation and crescendo, they announced this night to the gods in the shadows and the people filling the grove. Thus, Rokus raised his sword, and the men raised theirs, and this extraordinary agreement was made.

Veleda returned to her tower a week later. When she left Rokus' house at dawn, Ulla and Ansgar and his friends, as well as Veleda's Bructeri guard, joined her, surrounding her horse as they trotted to the Batavian gate. She turned around to Rokus, who waved, and offered her raised hand as a blessing. The entourage disappeared into the morning fog.

Once in her tower on the River Lupia, the prophetess made sacrifices and offerings and forthwith issued proclamations. In concert with Rokus' speeches to reclaim Batavian hegemony, Veleda's predictions described battle after battle where Rokus' army triumphed over the Roman legions.

Her messengers rode hard across the plain of the northern lands and through the hills of Belgica and the river valleys of Gallia Lugdunensis. They repeated Veleda's predictions, and soon the rumors that had grown from this foretelling were supplanted by reliable accounts from traveling merchants and veteran warriors who knew such things.

In fact, one Roman fort after another did fall to Rokus' army. His amalgam of Batavians, Germans, Gauls and Belgae always seemed to be placed in the field at best advantage or to disappear only to flank or surprise from the rear. Stories of Rokus' winning strategies, as well as his keen insight into the Roman mind, spread from hamlet to village to town, and it became clear to all tribes and clans, to Romans and their sympathizers, that for the northern part of the Roman Empire, the rising son had a new glow.

GLOSSARY OF PLACES AND TERMS

Acumum — Montélimar, France

Aedile — an administrative position usually held by young men intending to advance to high political office

Aquitannia — Gallia Aquitania, a large region in southwest France

Arelate — Arles, France

Augusta Raurica — Augst, Switzerland

Avenio — Avignon, France

Aventicum — Avenche, Switzerland

Batavorum — Island of the Batavians, or Roman fort west of Leiden

Belenus — the Celtic sun god

Betuwe — Netherlands between Waal and Lower Rhine Rivers

Bodhrán — a Celtic framed drum, 14–18 inches wide and 3½–8 inches deep

Brigindo — the Celtic goddess of fire; her three aspects are (1) Fire of Inspiration as patroness of poetry, (2) Fire of the Hearth, as patroness of healing and fertility, and (3) Fire of the Forge, as patroness of smithcraft and martial arts. She is mother to the craftsmen.

Britannia — England

Bructeri — a Germanic tribe located during Roman imperial times in present-day North Rhein-Westphalia

Camulopdunum — Colchester, Essex, UK

Cananefates — a Germanic tribe living in the Rhine River delta

Castra Vetera — Xanten, Germany

Cohort — a military unit of the Roman army numbering 480 men

Colonia Agrippina — Cologne (Köln), Germany

Dacia — Romania

Dalmatia — Croatia

Donar — A Germanic counterpart to the Norse god, Thor; he is also associated with thunder and lightning, strength, protection, hallowing, and fertility

Einkorn — a hulled, domesticated version of wild wheat

Equestris — Nyon, Switzerland

Equite — a senior official in charge of administration and military affairs

Ernaginum — Tarascon, western Provence, France

Frisians or Frisii — a people who lived between the Lower Rhine and the Ems Rivers, experienced as sea traders and fishermen

Gladius — a short Roman sword designed for thrusting rather than swinging

Gallia Narbonensis — a Roman province including present-day Languedoc and Provence, France

Genava — Geneva, Switzerland

Hauberk — a shirt of chainmail

Helvetia — a Roman province, present-day Switzerland